Surge of Deception

by

Thomas Velsun

About the Author

Thomas Velsun lives with his wife in coastal Florida. He's a former Army officer and a veteran of the Vietnam War. After leaving the Military he spent forty years in business and retired from a large global technology company.

The knowledge gained from his three college degrees from three different major universities (a BS in Math and Accounting, an MS in Engineering, and an MBA) has contributed heavily to his success in business and to his grasp of the subject matter in his novels.

During his business career, he completed special projects with various government agencies in Washington DC, including the FBI,CIA,US Mint, and IRS. He has participated in special projects with RAND Corporation (a think tank formed after World War II to continue the activities of various experts accumulated during the war years). He has worked in many different areas in the United States and in foreign countries. He has researched many conspiracy theories and has included selected subject matter from some of them in his novels.

He's a former athlete and maintains fitness with daily workouts involving weightlifting. He also enjoys playing golf and tennis.

Chapter 1

On a Friday afternoon in June, Matt Baker, the top business analyst at Tustun Industries in Jacksonville, Florida, reached for his ringing phone. He saw on the display the call was from his boss, Ralph Gibson, President of Tustun.

Matt answered.

"Jack's dead," Ralph blurted out. "Elsie just found him slumped over his desk. She's already called Security and '911'. Get up here as fast as you can."

The wail of approaching sirens increased in volume.

Matt rose from his chair and sprinted down the hall to the stairs. He tried to keep his composure while many things flashed through his mind relating to Tustun's now deceased Chairman. After running up the stairs to the next floor he rushed into the large rectangular area that separated Ralph's office from Jack's.

Ralph, Elsie, and Maria Lopez (Ralph's secretary) stood in the middle of the area. Matt rushed toward them.

The noise from the sirens got louder for a few moments and then stopped.

Matt stopped close to Ralph. "What happened?"

"I don't know many details yet," Ralph said. "Elsie ran into my office screaming about Jack. As soon as she gave me the news, she turned and ran back toward Jack's office. Maria and I followed her just as Security arrived. I walked into Jack's office briefly and saw him slumped over his desk, not a pleasant sight. I moved back out here and joined Elsie and Maria. We're trying to stay out of the way."

Matt noted Brian Glascock and Harrell Johnson, the two members of the Tustun security team, were inside Jack's office. They were busy inspecting something.

At that moment, five men emerged from the hallway. Three were uniformed policemen and the other two were in civilian clothes. Matt immediately recognized one of the uniformed men as Justin Mason, the Jacksonville Police Chief. He figured the two in civilian clothes were police detectives.

The tall, slim, sandy-haired Police Chief walked over to Ralph.

"Due to the prominence of Jack Worthington, I decided to accompany our investigative team," Justin said.

Ralph gave a slight nod as he gestured toward Jack's office, "Two members of our security team are over there now."

"Stay in the area," Justin said. "I'll need to talk with you in a few minutes. He and the other four men walked over and started talking to the security team.

Shortly Brian and Harrell left the group of lawmen and walked toward Matt and Ralph.

"We found a suicide note on Jack's printer," Brian said. "We could read it without moving it and we left it in place."

Ralph narrowed his eyes. "Jack would never commit suicide." He glanced at Matt.

Matt nodded.

"What did the note say?" Ralph asked.

"Basically, that he didn't want to go on living so he decided to end things quickly," Brian said.

"Other than the note, did you find any clues about what occurred?" Ralph asked.

"Maybe," Brian said. "If it's okay with you, Harrell and I are going back downstairs to check some things. We'll plan to keep you updated."

Ralph gestured toward the hallway. "Okay, have at it."

Matt glanced at Elsie and Maria, they both still looked upset but each seemed to have recovered her composure.

"Are you going to be able to handle this?" Ralph asked, looking sympathetically at the two secretaries.

"It's quite a shock, and a sudden one at that," Elsie said, "but I'm adjusting. I think I'll be able to function."

"I'm good enough." Maria looked at Ralph. "What about you and Matt?"

Ralph glanced at Matt and then said, "This is a big shock for everyone, but, given a little time, we'll all get over it. We have a lot of work to do to keep this company running."

There was a brief silence.

Ralph leaned toward Elsie. "Do you feel like answering a few questions?"

"I can handle a few," Elsie said. "And then I need to get some rest. We all need some rest."

Ralph glanced at Maria. "Send out a message to everyone about Ralph's death and tell them I've approved everyone taking the rest of the day off."

Maria nodded and turned toward her desk positioned outside the doorway into Ralph's office.

Turning toward Elsie, Ralph asked, "What was going on before you found Jack slumped over his desk?"

"Jack was working on some new business ventures this morning and he emphasized he would be busy for a few hours," Elsie said. "He mentioned he would let me know when he needed help with correspondence and then he shut his door."

Ralph and Matt didn't comment as they waited for Elsie to continue.

"Around three o'clock I decided to check with him about the

correspondence and I knocked a couple of times, but he didn't answer." Elsie narrowed her eyes and pressed her lips together. "That wasn't like him, so I decided to open the door." She started to cry. "And here we are."

Ralph waited for a few moments and then asked, "Did he have any visitors after he shut his door?"

"One, Brian, he didn't stay long. I figured Jack had some kind of security issue he wanted checked."

Matt leaned forward. "Was Brian carrying anything?"

"I noticed he had a coffee cup. He had it with him when he went in and when he came out. I know he drinks a lot of coffee."

"We'll check with Brian later on the purpose of his visit," Ralph said. "We should see him again shortly."

Elsie gave a slight nod as she dabbed at her eyes with a handkerchief.

Matt saw Justin come out of Jack's office and walk toward them. He stopped in front of Ralph and mentioned they would bring in a special team immediately to remove the body and do a forensic inspection of Jack's office.

Ralph nodded.

After Justin turned and gave a signal to the policeman standing in the doorway of Jack's office he looked back at Ralph. "We might have some more questions. Is someone going to stay up here until we leave?"

"The four of us will stay up here," Ralph said. "And our two security people should return soon."

"Good." Justin kept his gaze fixed on Ralph. "Everyone needs to answer some brief questions."

Ralph continued to nod.

"We found a suicide note on Jack's printer," Justin said.

"Yeah, our security team told us about it, Ralph said, "The message was unlike Jack."

Matt leaned forward. "I agree."

"So, neither of you think it was a suicide?" Justin asked.

"That's exactly right," Ralph said.

Matt looked at Justin. "Do you have any opinion?"

"I don't want to speculate," Justin said. "I'll wait for the autopsy results and some more investigative information." You'll be hearing from somebody soon about the formal procedure we'll use."

After a little more discussion, Justin turned and left the area.

Matt watched more people come into the area with a lot of equipment.

The policemen were still busy in Jack's office as the other group approached. Four men were in the group: One carried a body bag. One carried a stretcher. Two other men carried some special equipment.

Matt had advanced degrees in mathematics, engineering, and finance and had maintained proficiency in all of them. An expert analyst, he knew Ralph was counting on him to develop some good ideas on what they could do to help solve Jack's murder.

Ralph leaned toward Matt. "So, what's your thinking?"

"We both know he was murdered. Whoever did this must be brought to justice."

"I hope you'll apply every ounce of your analytical skills." Ralph clinched his fists. "Jack wasn't just Tustun's chairman and my boss. He was also a close friend."

Matt started to reply when Justin returned accompanied by another man.

"Do you guys have time for a little more discussion?" Justin asked.

"Sure," Ralph answered as he stared at the other man who had dark hair, was heavyset, and about Justin's height.

With a quick gesture toward the man standing with him, Justin said, "This is Ben Fulton, the SAC (Special Agent in Charge) of our local FBI field office. After considering the information in some of Jack's files, I decided to get him involved immediately."

Ralph waved Matt and the other two men toward the round conference table in a corner of his office. He closed the door behind them.

Everyone settled into their chairs.

Justin leaned toward Ralph. "This isn't our standard procedure, but these are unusual circumstances. You and Matt have been thoroughly vetted and both of you can be a big help to us."

Ralph and Matt nodded and made no comment.

"We found a lot of files in Jack's office that might be relevant to Jack's death. We need to gain more insight into the business issues involved and that's a big reason we need your help," Justin said. "Several files contain information about upcoming meetings in Mexico with manufacturers of opium products. I saw where Tustun has some poppy fields down there and produces legal opium derivatives, such as morphine and codeine. Some of the names listed for the meetings are known cartel members who try to do some business in Florida on occasion. I'm sure they're more interested in the opium than the derivatives."

Ben nodded. "I agreed with Justin that we should trust the two of you and that the FBI should be involved. Since a lot of our investigation will involve Mexico, I'm guessing my boss will also get the CIA involved."

Ralph and Matt each nodded slowly.

"Our experts think the time of death was between two and three o'clock this afternoon," Justin said.

"Do you know the cause of death yet?" Ralph asked.

"No, but we'll know soon," Justin said. "Our medical team has already taken the body to the hospital for the autopsy."

Ben leaned forward. "I've met Jack a few times. If I remember correctly, his wife died four years ago, didn't she?"

"Right, no grieving widow," Ralph said. "There's a daughter, however, lives in Chicago. She and her husband are on their way down."

Ben turned toward Ralph. "Do you know much about what Jack has been working on?"

"Matt and I both do," Ralph said. "Jack was thinking about buying land here in Florida for future sugarcane crops. We've been growing all our sugarcane in Puerto Rico. He was also planning to buy more land for poppy fields and cocoa bean crops in Mexico and South America, Colombia in particular."

"What about you as you go forward?" Ben asked. "Will you continue the process to buy more land to produce sugarcane, poppies, and cocoa beans?"

"Not until Matt and I check into some things," Ralph said. "Last night, I received the latest sales figures from our foreign offices. They show we sold a million dollars of cocoa beans, a million dollars of poppies, and almost a million dollars of sugarcane in the past month. Those numbers seem far too high. Matt and I need to investigate. Jack's death has put a new light on all our business dealings."

Ben glanced at Justin. "Do you have any more questions for them at the moment?"

Justin shook his head. "I'm done for the time being."

Ben stood, "Same with me." He looked back at Ralph and Matt, who were also standing. "You guys look to be in great physical condition."

"Does that have any significance?" Matt asked.

"With your knowledge of Jack and of Tustun's business, Justin and I might need you to help us with some things that could be dangerous." Ben paused. "When Justin called me about the files, they found in Jack's office I knew this could get really complicated and dangerous quickly. I had my security people check both of you out, full background check. It was quick but thorough enough. We want you to be members of our broader team in investigating what I think will turn out to be a murder."

Justin nodded. "Ben and I both agree you can be a big help to us, and we agree conditions are going to get really dangerous quickly for anyone directly involved in the investigation."

"Being able to cope with dangerous circumstances in every way is extremely important," Ben said. "A casual observer on the street probably thinks you guys are professional athletes, not business executives. We think with a little special training you'll both be able to help us and stay alive."

"We both belong to the same fitness club," Ralph said. "That's how we originally met."

"We both were college athletes when we became weightlifting enthusiasts." Matt shrugged. "We've continued the weight workouts and we've both started playing tennis to sharpen our coordination."

Ralph gestured toward Matt. "He can bench press 340 pounds. He's a little ahead of me there but I can equal him on everything else."

"I hope you'll both fully participate with our investigative team," Justin said. "With some practice at our weapons training facilities I think you'll be able to protect yourselves at least as well as the other team members."

After a little more discussion, Ben walked to the closed door and opened it. After a departing gesture, he and Justin left.

Ralph and Matt walked out to check with Maria and Elsie who were standing together beside Elsie's desk.

Matt noted the yellow tape strung across the closed door to Jack's office.

"All the lawmen are gone," Elsie said. "They took a box full of Jack's files and I saw them snapping a lot of photos. They told me they didn't think they would need to return but to keep the door locked until further notice just in case they had to come back for some reason." She shrugged. "Then they put up the yellow tape and left."

"Since I'll be in charge of running the company now, I might need those files and I might need to get into Jack's office," Ralph said.

"They mentioned we should contact Justin if we had any issues with what they were doing," Elsie said.

"Okay, I'll talk to Justin and take care of that." Ralph glanced at Elsie. "Is Donald still on his trip?"

"Yes, but he's coming back tonight. I called him a few minutes ago to give him the news. I figured since he was our Executive Vice President he should know about Jack's death before he returns."

"Good," Ralph said. He gestured toward the two secretaries. "You two can go get some rest and start your weekend."

After Elsie and Maria left, Ralph glanced at Matt. "There's a lot more to discuss and we need a break to recover a bit more ourselves. Can you come back up here tomorrow morning?"

"Of course, given the circumstances," Matt said.

"We'll start early. Does eight o'clock work for you?"

Matt gave a thumbs-up as he turned to leave.

On his way home Matt vowed Jack's murder would be avenged. He knew Ralph had even stronger feelings since Jack was his immediate boss, but Ralph's analytical skills weren't on the level of his own.

Matt knew he would be expected to make some significant

contributions to the investigative effort and that Jack's death was probably connected to some issues they had failed to pay close attention to.

Maybe Jack was poisoned? And, if so, maybe someone used one of those undetectable poisons. There was a lot to check into.

Chapter 2

Early on Saturday Morning, Matt parked in his reserved parking space on one side of Tustun's modern four-story building in a business park south of downtown Jacksonville.

As he neared the front entrance, Donald Busby walked out.

"I'm surprised to see you here early on Saturday," Donald said. "What's the occasion?"

"Meeting with Ralph," Matt replied.

Donald raised an eyebrow. "About what happened to Jack?"

"It's mainly a general business discussion since Ralph is in charge of running the company now." Matt had formed the habit a long time ago of saying as little as necessary to Donald.

"I should have been invited."

Matt gave a slight shrug. "I think Ralph just wants to go over some statistics and, being the senior analyst, I'm the logical choice for that type of discussion."

Donald narrowed his eyes for a moment and then said, "I'm planning a meeting in my office at seven o'clock Monday morning. I expect you to come. I'll send Ralph an email and copy you."

"What's the topic?"

"Since Jack's no longer with us, we need to tie up some loose ends. I'll provide some more information in the email."

"If Ralph approves, I'll plan to be there."

Donald gave a slight wave and then continued toward his parked car.

A minute later when Matt arrived at his boss's office, Ralph waved him through the open doorway and gestured toward the coffee service. "Help yourself."

Matt poured a full cup of the hot liquid and eased into a chair across from Ralph at the round conference table. "Just ran into Donald at the front entrance, he was leaving. He mentioned he was scheduling a meeting Monday morning and he would send you an email. He mentioned he wants us to meet in his office early, seven o'clock."

"Did he give you the subject?"

"He mentioned he wanted to tie up some loose ends, no specifics. He told me more information would be in the email."

"I saw Donald's and Brian's cars out there when I pulled in. Guess they had some things to discuss and wanted an early start." He shrugged. "Well anyway we have some things to discuss too. Let's get started." Ralph leaned forward. "I learned one thing more after I got home, and it might be significant. Elsie called and told me she forgot to mention Jack had a meeting scheduled with Juan Medina this next Tuesday morning at ten o'clock."

"Who's he?"

"Big wheel in international oil from Miami, don't know much other than that except, according to Elsie, Donald was supposed to be in the meeting too."

"The meeting in Donald's office probably relates to something concerning the scheduled meeting with Juan Medina," Matt said.

Ralph stood, walked over to his office door, and closed it. "Best we talk in private, just in case someone happens by."

Matt waited for Ralph to return to his chair and then asked, "What dealings do we have with international oil?"

"None that I know of," Ralph said, "but Jack could have had something going on. Jack often bypassed me on certain issues he wanted to investigate first." He looked directly at Matt. "I take it you don't know of anything either?"

"That's correct." Matt studied Ralph for a moment. "Jack hadn't invited you to the meeting?"

"No."

"Since Donald apparently was on the agenda, he should know something," Matt said.

Ralph gave an acid grin. "He should, but he might not tell us."

Matt raised an eyebrow but didn't comment.

"I've never mentioned anything to you, but Donald and I don't get along. We haven't for a long time."

"So, you're telling me you don't think he'll share any secrets with us?" Matt gave a short laugh.

"Yep, that's exactly what I'm telling you."

"How long have you and Donald been at odds?"

After Ralph took a sip of coffee he said, "In a meeting a couple of years ago, Donald insisted on doing a lot more business in South America. I disagreed and we had quite an argument. Things haven't been right between us since then."

"Seems like I would have heard something about that?"

Ralph shrugged.

"That proposed business in South America could be significant to what happened to Jack." Matt stared over his coffee mug at Ralph.

"We'll keep that in mind in the meeting. You'll be there, you can form an opinion."

Matt gave a slow nod.

"Elsie didn't notice any sign of injury on Jack," Ralph said. "I asked her twice about that. Nothing showed. There were no scratches, no bruises, and no blood."

"A heart attack wouldn't leave any visible sign."

Ralph leaned slightly toward Matt. "It might have been some type of poison."

"If that's so, it should show up in the autopsy."

"Maybe, there are a lot of sophisticated ones being used now."

"How do you know that?"

Ralph gave a slight smile. "I read a lot of murder mysteries. Some poisons are undetectable according to many of the stories. Don't know if it's a fact or not. You're our best analyst. I want you to investigate that."

"When will we get results from the autopsy?"

"Justin told me he would come over Monday afternoon and give me a briefing on all the latest details. You should plan to attend, my office at one o'clock."

"I still think it's odd you weren't invited to the meeting Jack scheduled with the international oil guy, Juan Medina."

"It's consistent with what I mentioned earlier," Ralph said. "Jack often involved my subordinates in a lot of preliminary discussions; then, he would get me involved if they developed into anything."

Matt narrowed his eyes. "Does Elsie know anything about Medina?"

"No," Ralph said. "I asked her several times. She just recorded the meeting on Jack's schedule, at his request. I asked her if she tried to contact Medina about Jack's death and she told me she thought I would want to go ahead and meet with him."

"Be interesting to find out if Donald knew him earlier."

Ralph nodded. "Damn right." He narrowed his eyes and leaned forward. "I'm positive someone knocked Jack off and it might have something to do with this international oil business."

"Didn't Jack go on some trips to Mexico and Columbia earlier this year?" Matt asked.

"Yeah, and Elsie went with him on some of those trips. He was a bachelor again. There were no complications associated with taking his secretary. Jack needed someone to take good notes. He was no good at that."

"Elsie looks pretty good for someone 48 years old, got a few small streaks of gray in that jet black hair, but otherwise...."

"How do you know her age?"

"Don't forget I have access to all the company data."

Ralph grunted and didn't comment.

"Just a thought," Matt said with a slight shrug.

"I get your drift, but I never got the feeling Jack had any romantic inclinations in his later years. Business seemed his only interest. I don't think anything was going on. There would have been some indications."

"The name Elsie Farmer doesn't fit her looks. She looks more Latin. The files show that Jack hired Elsie twelve years ago. Her background check is in there, born in New York, American parents. Both parents were from Connecticut."

"Are you leading up to something?"

"Elsie looks every bit as Latin as Maria and we know for sure Maria's Hispanic. She was born in Monterrey, Mexico."

"I know Jack had complete trust in Elsie and she was valuable in many ways on his trips to Mexico and Columbia. She speaks fluent Spanish."

"So does Maria," Matt said, "she would also be valuable on trips to Spanish-speaking areas. I know she occasionally helps Elsie with Spanish translation, but I'm not aware of her ever being invited to make any trips with Jack."

"I get your point, but Jack never liked to overload his travel group, including his personal security detail."

Matt gave a slow nod. "That, of course, concerned Maria. She knows the territory down in Mexico well, and she still has family in Monterrey."

Ralph narrowed his eyes and didn't comment.

Matt clearly got the message that Ralph wasn't comfortable with the conversation concerning either of the executive secretaries. However, he knew Ralph understood they needed to be thorough in their investigation of the circumstances surrounding Jack's death. He figured Ralph would adjust.

••••

In his spacious mansion in Miami, Juan Medina sat in his desk chair in his luxurious office and glanced at his watch.

He had an important meeting in a few hours at his downtown office with his partner, Carmen Flores, but something was bothering him. He stood and paced the floor.

After a few minutes of pacing, he walked back to his desk and retrieved his favorite pipe, one with carved figures on the bowl of solid hickory.

Smoking calmed his nerves and helped him focus his thinking. It was an old habit of his. Maybe not healthy, but it worked. He stuffed the pipe with his cherry-blend tobacco and soon had it going to his satisfaction.

He savored a puff as he walked to the window. Sunshine bathed his manicured lawn, which occupied a full acre in the most affluent section of Miami. He had done well in business, at least so far, but there were some issues he needed to resolve.

Staring at the grove of palm trees in his view, he enjoyed a few more puffs from his pipe. He did have some advantages. He should be able to resolve the new issues with which he dealt. He vowed to take whatever measures were necessary.

He walked to his desk in the corner and fished some papers out of the top drawer. He spread the five pages of scrawled notes in front of him.

He had jotted down the most significant points when Carmen had briefed him after a recent meeting with the President of the World Bank. He ran his fingers through his pitch-black hair as he scanned the information.

What was bothering him?

Something Carmen had mentioned was gnawing at his subconscious. He just couldn't quite put his finger on it. As he read the notes again, nothing jumped out.

He now felt irritated.

A few more minutes of study and there it was: the new ship terminal in Jacksonville, Florida—the TraPac Container Terminal at JAXPORT.

Juan took a deep breath and leaned back in his chair. It was making sense now. Some old information was in the back of his mind. That information had triggered something at his subconscious level. Now he remembered what that old information was all about.

He stood and walked over to a hidden wall safe. After sliding the panel back, he turned the combination lock. A few manipulations produced the telltale click.

Juan opened the safe and shuffled through the contents for a moment before selecting a red folder. After walking back to his desk and settling into his chair, he placed the folder in front of him and removed some satellite photos of JAXPORT.

He opened a drawer and grabbed a magnifying glass. He scanned the area around the TraPac Container Terminal in the first photograph. Nothing caught his eye. He was getting irritated again; then, he noticed a small checkmark he had made at the bottom of the photo.

He studied the object just to the side of the checkmark and smiled. All the details of his brainstorming two years ago were returning. The trial run he had envisioned had been executed. He wasn't sure of the timing for the trial run because other people had overseen the details. They were supposed to coordinate with Carmen. Whether they had or not, Juan didn't know, but he would soon find out.

Juan continued to smile. This was going to be the key to a successful operation. This would provide the best solution for covering the trail of all his upcoming dealings with the World Bank. He shuffled through the stack of photographs and extracted all that had a picture of JAXPORT.

There were four more.

He trained his magnifying glass on each of them in turn.

The object was in two of them, the middle two. The photos were time sequenced.

After a few more minutes of study, Juan concluded the object was transported through the dock area at a rapid pace, in-keeping with his bold plan.

The test was successful. If not, there would have been some fallout by this time.

Juan stared at the ceiling for several moments. Things should be better now that Jack Worthington was out of the picture.

Knocking off Worthington hadn't been part of Juan's plan, but he was okay with it. There would now be one less American to negotiate with. Coordination should be simpler. That would be a good thing. The upcoming operation was complex.

As he pondered the overall situation, Juan knew it was going to be an interesting meeting with Carmen this morning. They would have to be careful as they moved forward, even if the Jacksonville Police didn't discover the alleged suicide was a murder.

....

At the Tustun offices, Matt mulled over a wide variety of thoughts. He took another sip of coffee. It was cooling off and he liked his hot. He stood and walked to the coffee pot.

"Jack might have discovered something he wasn't supposed to know," Matt said. After topping off his mug with the hot coffee, he settled back in his chair and glanced at Ralph. "Think Donald was involved in Jack's death?"

"Maybe, but I know he and Jack were big pals from many years back."

"I'm sure that made you nervous at times."

"At times," Ralph said. He hesitated for a moment and then stood and refreshed his coffee.

"Donald wants to do a lot more business in South America. That could be significant."

"Possibly," Ralph said as he returned to his chair. "We'll try to learn as much as we can in the meeting with him on Monday. He might have some connection to the oil business too."

Matt leaned forward. "There's one thing in particular I wanted to ask you about."

"What?"

"Have you read my recommendations on the best places to grow cocoa beans?"

"Scanned them."

"Meaning?"

Ralph gestured with his right hand. "Yes, I read your

recommendations."

"What did you think?"

"You sent the same recommendations to Jack, right?"

"Right."

"I'd rather wait and talk about that after we have some more information about Jack's death," Ralph said as he accessed his email. "Ah, here's the note from Donald." He stared at the computer monitor for a moment. "Seven o'clock, as advertised. He's a pompous ass, calling this meeting without checking with me first."

"At least he invited you."

"Yeah, and he mentioned the subject is an international oil opportunity," Ralph said, as he stood. "Let's continue our discussion after our meetings on Monday. We'll have a lot more information on the oil situation and we should have the autopsy results by then."

Matt nodded and rose to his feet.

••••

Later that afternoon, in his downtown Miami office, Juan looked across the top of his desk at Carmen Flores.

"I'm going to have some whisky" Juan said. "Guess you want more coffee?"

Carmen drummed his fingers on the arm of his leather chair. "Think I'll join you this time. I need something to calm the nerves."

"Nerves?"

"Playing the Tustun executives for fools can prove dangerous."

Juan walked to his elaborate wet bar in the corner and grabbed a decorative bottle with 'Jim Beam' on the label. "Three fingers of Bourbon okay?"

Carmen nodded.

Juan extracted a couple of clear glasses from a cabinet. After pouring the desired amount of bourbon, he walked over to Carmen and handed him one of the glasses.

Carmen raised his glass in a mock toast and took a sip.

Juan gestured a toast with his glass but waited to drink. He walked back to his desk and settled into his chair. After holding the glass to his nose and savoring the smell, he swilled the liquid around for a moment and then took a drink. He also needed to relax.

"Too bad about Jack Worthington," Juan said, "glad Donald told us."

"I was never certain Jack was fully onboard with our plan anyway. Donald will be more useful."

"He's not the chairman of Tustun, however. He's not even the President."

"We could have Gibson eliminated."

"Yeah, that wouldn't automatically leave Busby in charge," Juan said, "however, if we stick to our plan, we should wind up with a lot of power over the entire situation."

"Our old plan might not be sufficient now."

"We'll make a new one. Jack Worthington wasn't the only one with close association with Swiss bankers." Juan grinned. "We have some options we haven't utilized."

"Exactly what do you have in mind?"

"You want all the details or just the highlights?"

"Every detail you have," Carmen said. "I didn't invest my money in this venture for nothing. Omar has been waiting patiently in Saudi Arabia. He and I both expect to get a lot richer by pooling our oil resources and supporting your illegal drug trade."

Juan chuckled. "And both of you will, my friend."

"Only if we succeed in duping the Americans."

"Don't worry about it. We're setup properly here in Miami and I have everything under control."

"Give me the details and I'll form my own opinion."

Juan took his time and gave a detailed explanation.

"That might work," Carmen said.

"Do you have some concerns about the plan?"

"Agreeing to be part of the global energy components company Omar owns might be a good idea. You said the name is DUISONZ?"

Juan nodded. "I figured being part of it would come in handy in dealing with Busby. We need to get a handle on what he's going to do, and we need to move fast. Things are beginning to accelerate in Saudi Arabia."

"Omar is pressing you?" Carmen asked.

"Yes," Juan said. "Do you want all the details on that too?"

"Of course. I always want to know what's going on."

After giving the details, Juan leaned forward, "We'll increase our profits from oil and drugs and make the necessary payoffs to increase our influence with the United States Government. We'll stay aggressive."

"Some of your plan is still a bit vague to me," Carmen said.

"I've worked out all the necessary details."

"Let's hear more of them."

"To boost our drug trafficking, we can take advantage of the shipping procedures at the new container terminal in Jacksonville," Juan said. "It's near the TraPac terminal."

"Container terminal's new?"

Juan nodded.

"Don't you think we'll have some problems with their security?"

Juan laughed. "One of our companies will be handling the security. We were the low-cost bidder. It's costing us a bit, but we'll control the security system."

"How much are we losing on this job?"

"About a hundred thousand a month, but that's of no consequence. Our combined net revenue, counting Omar's portion, is now over two million U. S. dollars a day." Juan's dark eyes flashed. "That's why I didn't worry about losing a few million over the course of the security contract."

Carmen shrugged. "Still a significant amount."

"If it makes you feel any better, we're increasing our opium business."

"Legal or illegal?"

"Both. We're putting more poppy fields in Colombia, your homeland." Juan chuckled. "We'll soon be doing the same in Mexico. All the new production is registered as legal opium derivatives, such as morphine and codeine."

Carmen nodded and drained the last drop of bourbon from his glass.

"I don't want to throw too much at you too quickly," Juan said. "Some things are not fully worked out yet. I'm waiting on Busby to resolve some potential problems."

"Such as?"

"I'll keep you fully informed as things become more solidified. I don't want to confuse you with a lot of loose speculation, lot of things still need to come together."

"Are you worried I can't handle all the uncertainty?"

"Not at all," Juan said. "I just don't want to waste time on remote possibilities that may never happen."

Carmen remained silent and looked at his empty glass.

"More whisky?" Juan asked.

Carmen hesitated for a moment and then shook his head.

There was a brief silence.

"As soon as Busby does his research and some things get resolved, I'll let you know immediately," Juan said. "As we merge our oil enterprises with our expanding drug trafficking, we can operate like we're part of the regular legal business of the World Bank."

Carmen pursed his lips and gave a slight nod.

Juan leaned forward. "As things develop, I'm sure Ralph Gibson will suffer the same fate as Jack Worthington."

Chapter 3

Monday morning at seven o'clock at Tustun, Matt, Ralph, and Brian Glascock sat with Donald Busby at the round conference table in Donald's spacious office.

"There's a lot we need to cover," Donald said. "That was too bad about Jack." Donald focused his gaze directly on Ralph. "I hope you don't mind my calling this meeting."

"We'll see how it works out," Ralph said.

Donald nodded slowly and then put on his reading glasses. He looked at a sheet of paper in front of him.

"Last week, I was asked by Jack to meet with an important international executive concerning access to oil supplies," Donald said. "The international oil executive is Juan Medina. That meeting was going to be tomorrow, but—"

"When did Jack become interested in oil?" Ralph asked, leaning forward.

Donald stared over his glasses at Ralph. "He's always been interested in energy. Oil is a big factor in that regard."

"Did Jack tell you his reasoning?" Ralph asked.

"He mentioned he was concerned about our long-term security in this unstable world we live in." Donald gestured to Brian.

"I know Jack was concerned oil prices would get out of control," Brian said. "He wanted more leverage against high energy costs."

Ralph raised an eyebrow.

"A year ago, Jack asked me to keep an eye on some things for him," Brian said. "He was concerned about unstable oil prices and the proper management of all of our transportation assets."

"Funny he didn't mention anything to me." Ralph turned toward Matt. "You know anything about this?"

"No," Matt said.

Ralph looked back at Donald. "It seems the President of the company and the top analyst would have been part of the discussions."

Donald shrugged. "Maybe Jack wanted Brian to take a quiet look at things." He studied Ralph for a moment. "You know Jack didn't like to call too much attention to potential problem situations. He was always worried about something or the other, but he never wanted to panic everyone."

Ralph didn't comment.

"Jack didn't like to stir things up unless he found out his concerns were warranted," Donald said. He stared at Ralph. "You're aware Jack preferred to stay ahead of things. He always wanted to be working on a solution before he called attention to a problem."

Ralph turned toward Brian. "Were you investigating any specific concerns Jack had about getting involved with Juan Medina?"

"He hadn't mentioned any," Brian said.

Donald nodded. "I think Jack just wanted to move forward with looking into a possible deal."

Ralph pressed his lips together and made no comment.

Donald looked back at the sheet of paper in front of him. "Anyway, I wanted to call this meeting to review what Jack had in mind." He started explaining and his voice gradually rose in intensity. After a few minutes of scanning his notes and talking, he flashed a big smile and looked directly at Ralph. "That's about it. Jack wanted to make sure he didn't pass up a good opportunity."

"So even with Jack gone, you still want to meet with Juan Medina?" Ralph asked.

"Seems like the smart thing to do for Tustun," Donald said. "We wouldn't want to ignore a great deal."

"Do you see investing in the oil industry as being a hedge against higher oil prices?" Matt asked.

"We might have to pay outrageous prices for fuel in the near future." Donald looked at Ralph. "Why not be in on the profits? Why not get something back if the fuel price is high?"

"How much investment?" Ralph asked.

"I recommend three hundred million to start," Donald said.

Ralph looked directly at Donald. "Jack recommended that?"

"Sort of," Donald said. He sat back and took his glasses off. "Jack wanted to invest more. I talked him down to three hundred million."

"How much more?" Ralph asked.

"He wanted to start with a billion and a half."

Ralph shook his head slowly. "No way Jack would recommend that amount." He glanced at Matt. "Your opinion?"

"I agree with you," Matt said. "I can't see Jack wanting to invest that amount."

"I heard Jack say that." Brian leaned slightly toward Ralph and Matt.

Ralph and Matt remained silent.

Donald looked at Ralph and flashed a respectable smile. "I assume you want to come to the meeting with Juan, right?"

Ralph's eyes narrowed as he gave an acid grin. "There might not be a meeting. Last time I checked, I was still President of this company."

"I was just trying to carry through on what Jack recommended and see if you were interested in participating." Donald stared at Ralph. "Of course you can cancel this. That's why I wanted you to attend this preliminary discussion."

Brian looked directly at Ralph and gestured with open palms. "We wanted to make sure we kept you well informed."

Ralph glanced at Matt. "It shouldn't hurt anything to hear what Juan has to say."

"I think that makes sense," Matt said.

Donald brightened. "I'll call Juan right away. I contacted him last Friday night to tell him about Jack, and I told him you would have to approve any agreement."

"Go ahead and confirm the meeting," Ralph said with a slight shrug. "Keep me informed."

Donald continued smiling. "Yes sir."

Ralph checked his watch and stood.

Matt also stood.

"There's one more thing." Ralph fixed his gaze on Brian. "I heard you went to Jack's office just before he died."

"Elsie must have mentioned that," Brian said.

Ralph nodded.

"I hope she told you why."

Ralph shook his head. "She didn't seem to know."

Brian shrugged. "Jack wanted me to check on some imports from South America. I thought Elsie would have been aware of that. Jack always kept her well informed."

"Not this time, I guess." Ralph cocked his head to one side and waited.

"Jack was concerned about some shipments of cocoa beans," Brian said. "He didn't give me any details. He just instructed me to ensure the quantities coming in were being counted properly."

Ralph frowned. "That's not your job."

"I know," Brian said. "But when the Chairman asks you to do something, it's not good to question him." He gave another shrug.

"And he didn't give you any specific reason for his concern?" Ralph asked.

Brian shook his head. "He mumbled something about wanting more oversight. He told me he would explain later. He seemed to be in a hurry. I didn't argue. I agreed to check the next shipment and then I left his office right away."

"Have you checked any of the incoming quantities?"

"Not sure I will now. Don't know of any problems in that regard," Brian said. "I was going to do it just to humor Jack."

Ralph narrowed his eyes and seemed to be thinking.

"You think I should still do it?" Brian asked.

"Shouldn't hurt anything," Ralph said. "You might find something interesting."

Brian nodded.

Ralph turned and walked toward the door. He glanced back at Donald. "Thanks for the invite. Don't forget to keep me posted."

"Will do," Donald said, displaying a pleasant smile.

Matt gave a slight wave to the two men at the table and followed Ralph into the hall. He caught up with Ralph and whispered, "Interesting, huh?"

"You could say that."

"Do you want me to check anything?"

"Not at the moment," Ralph said. "I'll see you at our one o'clock meeting."

Matt gave a thumbs-up and headed back to his office. He had some analysis to do. Something smelled about this whole business with South America, including the international oil bit.

••••

At one o'clock, after receiving a prompt from Maria Lopez, Ralph and Matt watched Justin Mason walk through the doorway. Ralph waved him toward the round solid-mahogany conference table in the corner with seating for six.

The three men settled into the leather chairs.

Maria, her black hair flowing to her shoulders, walked into the office. "Coffee for anyone?" she asked, "Or something else to drink?"

"Coffee's fine with me," Justin said, "black."

After Ralph and Matt gestured they would have the same, Maria turned and quickly disappeared.

Justin cleared his throat and frowned. "Something strange is going on. Nothing adds up. The medical examiner doesn't think it was suicide, and he told me it wasn't a heart attack."

Maria, her dark eyes glowing, came in with a tray of three steaming mugs of coffee. She placed one in front of each man at the table and left, carrying the empty tray. She closed the door behind her.

Justin reached for his mug. "The medical examiner reported there were traces of a strange substance in Jack's system." Justin took a slow sip and stared at the two other men. "He hasn't yet identified the stuff, but he guesses it's some type of poison."

"So, he thinks Jack was poisoned?" Ralph asked.

Justin nodded.

Matt leaned forward. "How well do you know the medical examiner?"

"He's been our primary one for twelve years," Justin said. "He's an expert on poisons, in particular those that are almost untraceable."

"But he can't identify this one?" Ralph asked.

"Not yet," Justin said.

"Does he think this substance is one of those untraceable poisons?" Matt asked.

"Yes," Justin said, "different than any he's seen before."

Ralph narrowed his eyes. "So, Jack was murdered."

"That seems to be the case," Justin said.

"Can you tell us the exact wording of the alleged suicide note?" Matt asked.

"Two simple sentences," Justin said. "I have a copy." He removed a piece of paper from his pocket and unfolded it. He placed it on the table in front of Ralph.

Ralph read from the note, "I can no longer go on. I'm ending it now."

A brief silence ensued.

"Too vague," Ralph said, "not like Jack at all."

"Any fingerprints on the original note?" Matt asked.

"Only Jack's," Justin said.

Ralph rubbed his chin. "That wouldn't be hard to pull off. Someone wearing gloves could press Jack's fingers down on the note."

Justin nodded. "In this case, they were smart and made sure his prints were on both sides and in the right places. I'm initiating a murder investigation."

Matt gave Justin a thoughtful look. "Any opinion on who?"

"Still not enough facts yet," Justin said. "It wouldn't be professional for me to speculate at this time."

Ralph studied Justin for a moment. "We really need your thoughts. Matt and I will be looking into this too. Off the record, what do you think?"

Justin hesitated, taking a long sip of coffee.

"Any speculation you give us could be a big help," Ralph said. "Matt and I need all the ideas we can get. Remember, Matt's a top-notch analyst."

Justin narrowed his eyes and looked at Ralph. "You and Jack were pretty close, right?"

Ralph nodded.

"Okay, off the record," Justin said.

Ralph and Matt leaned forward.

"There was a folder in Jack's office with a lot of maps of Mexico," Justin said. "Each map had an area circled, different area on each map. There were two money amounts written by each circle."

Ralph shrugged. "They might be 'best case' and 'worst case' numbers. We're planning for additional business in Mexico, more fields of poppies and cocoa beans."

"But this is a little different," Justin said.

"In what way?" Matt asked.

"One number beside each circle is astronomical, hundreds of billions of dollars. The other number by each circle is only a few million dollars."

"Hundreds of billions does seem a bit high for our business," Ralph said. "But the numbers could still be what I was thinking." He glanced at Matt.

Matt nodded. "Jack might have been looking at what we could get if all aspects of the new business were perfect, and the lower number might represent what we could count on for sure. Like Ralph mentioned: 'best case' and 'worse case' planning."

"You don't think the high figures are way over the top?" Justin asked. "One of the numbers was five hundred billion."

"Jack was a visionary. Sometimes he could be a bit of a dreamer," Ralph said.

"The 'best case' for Jack was sometimes off the charts." Matt looked at Justin. "Was there anything else written on the maps, like products and such?"

Justin shook his head but then pursed his lips.

"You still have something to tell us, don't you?" Ralph asked.

Justin nodded. "There were similar numbers on several maps of South America, Colombia in particular."

"We're starting to do more business down there now," Ralph said. "The same things we just discussed could apply."

"Ben did a thorough investigation of Jack's finances; thought he might have had some money problems." Justin narrowed his eyes. "Just the opposite: he was getting richer every day."

Ralph raised an eyebrow.

"In every case, the smaller number by each of the circles matched recent deposits into various personal accounts Jack had."

Ralph and Matt exchanged glances.

"The plot thickens," Ralph said.

Matt looked at Justin. "Do you think Jack was getting paid off?"

"Seems that way," Justin said. He stared at the other two men for a moment. "Now I have a question for you, any idea why?"

Ralph glanced at Matt. Both men shook their heads.

"Well gentlemen, it seems we have a real mystery on our hands." Justin furrowed his brow. "And we need to solve it."

"I recommended to Jack that Tustun produce more products in Mexico," Matt said. "But increased revenue from that won't be significant for a long time."

"There's something else that could be relevant." Ralph looked directly at Justin. "Matt and I were informed this morning Jack had some interest in international oil. It's all a bit vague right now, but that could somehow be involved in what's going on."

"What do you know?" Justin asked.

Ralph explained what was discussed in the meeting in Donald's office.

Justin leaned back in his chair. "You and Matt will be in the meeting with this Juan Medina?"

Ralph nodded.

"How well do you know Brian Glascock?" Justin asked.

Ralph leaned forward. "He's been with us for twelve years, in charge of security for four years. As far as we know he's okay."

"You mentioned he was the last person to see Jack?" Justin asked.

"That's according to Elsie," Ralph said, "and Elsie has always been reliable."

Justin gave a slow nod as he stood. "We'll talk more soon." He made a farewell gesture as he left.

Matt looked at Ralph. "Think its Brian, or Donald, or both?"

"I'm guessing at least one of them."

••••

In his downtown office in Miami, Juan stared across the top of his desk at Carmen.

"Lot of variables, we need to solidify our strategy." Juan reached for his pipe and stuffed it with cherry-blend tobacco. "We should try to wrap up the latest details by noon." He lit his pipe and then leaned toward Carmen.

Carmen remained silent.

"You appear to still have concerns," Juan said.

"We obviously have some more issues to resolve, and I always want to know all the details on what you're planning. I put enough money into this operation to be an equal partner."

Juan started to comment just as his secure satellite phone rang. He glanced at the caller ID and said, "Busby." He reached for the phone and answered.

"When are you and Carmen going to arrive in Jacksonville?" Donald asked.

"Before the meeting of course but we haven't set a definite time yet. Do you want to get together and discuss things before the meeting?"

"Yeah, how soon can you fly up?"

Juan hesitated, thinking. "We can come up later this afternoon." He took a puff on his pipe and glanced at Carmen.

Carmen signaled a thumbs-up.

"Do you like seafood?" Donald asked.

"What does that have to do with things?"

"I know a great spot to have our meeting, and we can have dinner at the same time."

"Everybody I know loves seafood."

"Brian and I will pick you up at the airport. What time do you plan to arrive?"

"Around four."

"See you then," Donald said, before he disconnected.

"Are we going to mention anything about our legal drug business in our meeting tomorrow with Ralph Gibson?" Carmen asked.

"I don't think so. I'm planning on just discussing the oil business."

Carmen gave Juan a concerned look. "Are you going to mention anything to Busby tonight about that million or so per year being thrown away on the port security?"

"What about it?"

"Earlier you mentioned we'd more than make up the costs of the security by increasing our drug profits," Carmen said.

Juan took a long puff on his pipe and then spread some papers across the top of his desk. "I don't think we need to mention anything about that to Busby." He studied his notes for a few moments and then gave some details.

"What do you think?" Juan asked.

"I'm willing to move forward and I'm sure Omar will be too."

"We'll depend on Busby and Glascock to do their part."

"How much do you trust them?" Carmen asked.

"I think they're reliable enough." Juan shrugged. "I just don't know how well they'll perform. We must remain patient. Some things will take time. It's good we're both going to Jacksonville. We'll evaluate how reliable we think Busby and Glascock will be."

"We might not get that fully resolved in the next few days."

Juan nodded slowly. "We'll see how it goes."

"Do you think we'll be discovered laundering illegal drug money through the World Bank?"

"I don't think so. My planning might not always be perfect, but I'm always very careful."

"How did you ever think of shipping the illegal drugs in a container shaped like a horse?"

"We needed something the idiots on the docks would never overlook or get confused with another crate."

"So, our contact at the World Bank receives the shipment of illegal drugs and pays us for them?"

"Yes, and it should work like a charm, the invoice indicates they're receiving legal drugs for humanitarian purposes in third world countries. The horse design symbolizes galloping to the rescue."

Carmen leaned forward. "We're going to need a lot of luck. I hope your plan isn't too ambitious."

Juan laughed and said, "Let's discuss a few more items now and then take a break. We can prepare our strategy for the meeting with Busby and Glascock on our plane flight up there. Having a private jet does have its advantages."

....

Around four o'clock that afternoon, Donald and Brian met their visitors from Miami at Jacksonville International Airport (JIA) and the four men promptly got into Donald's SUV.

As Donald started the engine he said, "We have dinner reservations at five at Clark's Fish Camp. I think you'll like it."

In a little over thirty minutes, they arrived at Clark's and went inside. The smell of fried seafood permeated the air as a lady escorted the four men toward an outside table in the deck area alongside Julington Creek, a body of water that connected with the St. Johns River a few miles northwest of their location.

Donald noticed Juan and Carmen were scanning the vast array of stuffed wild animals as they followed the lady through the main part of the restaurant, which resembled a museum of big game hunter trophies.

After the men were escorted to a heavy wooden table and settled into their chairs, the lady handed out the menus and said, "Your waiter will be with you in a moment." She smiled and walked away.

"Unlike any other fish camps I've ever seen," Juan said, looking at the two Tustun executives.

Donald gave a knowing smile. "Most people seeing it for the first time have the same reaction." He glanced at his watch. "We ought to have some privacy for another hour or so. Place doesn't start filling up until well after six o'clock, and most people like to sit inside anyway."

A heavyset male waiter strolled up to their table. "May I get you gentlemen something to drink?"

"Beer, Corona," Juan said.

Everyone else ordered the same.

The waiter jotted something on his notepad and glanced at Donald. "Appetizers?"

Donald gestured to Juan.

Juan shook his head, and the waiter hurried away, coming back with four bottles of Corona beer, which he distributed. "Care to order, or should I give you a few minutes?"

Donald glanced at his guests. They were studying the menus but giving the impression they were about ready to order. Donald decided to get the process started while the others deliberated. He looked at the waiter.

"The combo with popcorn shrimp and deviled crabs," Donald said. He glanced at the sides on the menu. "Baked potato with butter and sour crème looks good. I'll also have the house salad with honey mustard dressing."

The waiter made an entry on his notepad and accepted the menu from Donald. He looked at the other three men.

Within a couple of minutes, all the questions were answered and the orders placed. The waiter hurried away.

After a few minutes of friendly chatting, Donald looked directly at Juan. "The deal is still the same as you discussed with Jack?"

Juan nodded. "Since you'll be listed as one of our partners, we'll ship fertilizers from refined oil derivatives to you for your crops at no charge if you want them. Just for agreeing to be on our list of partners, you'll you have an extra bottom-line profit of one million American dollars per month."

The waiter arrived and distributed the food.

"Will there be anything else?" The waiter asked.

Donald glanced at his three cohorts then looked back at the waiter. "We're fine." He watched the waiter nod and hurry off.

After devouring a couple of shrimp Donald looked at Juan. "There are some things I don't fully understand. Again, what's in this arrangement for you?"

"Other than selling you fertilizer, we just want to list Tustun as a company with which DUISONZ does business, a partner company, so to speak," Juan said. "We think it will help us have more of a presence in the United States."

"Who came up with that name? Donald asked.

"Our Arab partner Omar Karam." Juan shrugged. "I think the company had been in the family a long time. I didn't question it. It will work well enough for us."

Donald glanced at Brian.

Brian showed no expression.

"Does it bother you as to why we would want to make a deal like this?" Juan asked.

"To some extent," Donald said.

"We're courting some lucrative business with certain parties in Saudi Arabia." Keeping a steady gaze on Donald, Juan took a sip of beer.

"Having another United States component will be helpful in that regard. We expect to receive a lot more money than the million a month you'll be getting."

"That's why you made the offer to Jack?" Brian asked.

Juan nodded. "It's that simple." He gave a slight shrug. "We need to add Tustun to our list and we're willing to pay for it. DUISONZ is an odd name, and we want people in the United States to become familiar with it."

"And we do nothing but collect our million a month?" Donald asked.

"We would appreciate it if you would keep us informed on what's going on within your business," Juan said. "We're mainly paying you just to be listed as one of our partners, but some extra intelligence could be valuable."

Donald smiled. "I'm sure we'll have plenty of discussions."

"So, we have a firm deal?" Juan asked.

"We have a deal as far as I'm concerned," Donald said. "We still have to get Ralph Gibson's approval tomorrow."

Juan looked directly at Donald. "But it's a go as far as you can tell?"

"I don't think anyone will turn down an extra profit of twelve million dollars per year for being on your list of partner companies in your dealings with Saudi Arabia." Donald gave another big smile. "After all, they're one of our allies."

"That they are." Juan nodded. "That they are."

Donald gave Juan a thoughtful look. "In the meeting, you won't give Ralph the whole story, will you?"

"About our wanting the extra intelligence?"

Donald nodded.

"Of course not," Juan said. He gave a sly grin. "Leave the explanation to me. I know what to tell him."

Brian leaned forward. "Having been in the security end of things for a long time, I've done an extensive investigation." He stared at Juan. "We know you're involved in some illegal drug trafficking."

"Just rumors, not true," Juan said. "I've been aware of them for quite some time. We should ignore them.”

Donald took a sip of beer and kept his gaze on both Juan and Carmen. “This is a subject we need to discuss a bit and get any concerns out in the open.” He glanced around. No one else was nearby.

“We produce a lot of medical products,” Juan said, “all opium derivatives, morphine, codeine, and the like. It’s all legal.” He stared at Brian for a moment then shifted his gaze to Donald. “Since we grow a lot of poppies, you can see how rumors might get started. Nothing we can do about rumors.”

“On your shipments to us, are you going to load any of your medical products on the same ships carrying the fertilizer from refined oil derivatives?” Donald asked.

“Sometimes,” Juan said.

“What if we have delays with port security wanting to do a close inspection of everything coming in?” Brian asked.

Juan shrugged. “One of our companies runs the security at JAXPORT.”

“I think you’ve just taken care of that concern,” Donald said, smiling.

Brian stared at Juan. “We don’t want to be implicated in any, uh, unwanted situation. We have a reputation to uphold, you know.”

“Of course,” Juan said. “Don’t worry, you’ll have no trouble.” His glance took in both Donald and Brian. “You don’t have to worry about your reputation. DUISONZ is a respected company and has been in business for fifty years.”

“What if Ralph and that smartass, Matt Baker, bring up any of these topics tomorrow?” Brian asked.

“I’ll inform them that producing legal drugs is a legitimate part of our business.” Juan leaned toward Donald and flashed a big smile. “Our company is respected around the world and all my answers tomorrow will be good ones.”

Donald scanned the area, then flagged the waiter and told him they were ready for the check.

After Donald took care of the bill, the four men strolled out of the fish camp and toward the parked SUV.

"We'll drop you off at the Marriott," Donald said. "We'll pick you up in the morning at 9:30 and bring you to our office building."

Juan nodded. "Remember to let me handle things with your boss."

"You'll have the stage," Donald said. "But I think we'll need a little bit of luck. Ralph's a tough cookie to deal with."

Juan chuckled. "So am I."

••••

Elsewhere in town that evening, Matt settled into a comfortable chair in his den. He was by himself since he wasn't married and had no pets. He had some girlfriends, but he hadn't yet tied the knot with one of them. He knew Ralph had the same situation, he had girlfriends, but he wasn't married. The way things were going he figured their personal situations weren't going to change anytime soon.

Matt glanced at his watch (6:30 p.m.) and reviewed the events of the day in his mind.

International oil, what in the hell was Jack thinking? Matt shook his head slowly. Jack was a smart guy, but there were other ways to address energy costs. Many efficiency measures available to Tustun weren't being used. He contemplated the myriad of information that had emerged after Jack's death. There was a lot to consider.

Matt's beeping cell phone imposed an abrupt interruption to his thoughts. He glanced at the caller ID and saw it was Ralph.

"What's up?" Matt asked.

"I've been doing some more thinking, couple of things too sensitive to talk about over the phone. Are you available for dinner?"

"You buying?"

Ralph chuckled. "Of course, it's a business meal, a steak at Outback okay with you?"

"How soon?"

"I'm pulling up in your driveway right now."

"Care for a drink before we go? My house is more private than Outback."

"Yeah, sounds fine."

Matt walked to the front door and opened it. A dark green JAG sat in his driveway.

"Haven't had a coke in a long time," Ralph said. "I know you love them. That will work for me."

Matt grabbed a couple of cold bottles from the fridge and handed one to Ralph. They settled into a couple of chairs in the den.

Ralph removed the bottle cap. "This bit about Jack wanting to get into the international oil business sounds fishy to me."

"I'm thinking the same thing."

"Donald's and Brian's explanation might not be correct. You have any idea what Jack had in mind?"

"Nope."

Ralph took a long slow sip and then said, "If we go forward with this, we're going to be dealing with some dangerous people. Justin called me an hour ago. He had checked out this Juan Medina character, got some information from the CIA via the local FBI office. Medina is originally from Venezuela and he's a suspected drug lord."

"Though he ran an oil cartel?"

"He does that too."

Matt hesitated, collecting his thoughts. "Donald and Brian should have checked him out."

"Bit strange, huh?"

"Are you going to say anything to Donald?"

"Maybe," Ralph said, "maybe not."

"What does that mean?"

"It means I don't trust Donald as far as I can spit, and I'll decide on the best course of action as we go along."

"Think Brian is in cahoots with Donald?"

"Sure seems that way, doesn't it?" Ralph stared at Matt. "Harrell Johnson is the only guy I trust in corporate security."

"Do you think we should have a chat with Harrell before we spend more time on this?"

"Of course," Ralph said. "I'm guessing Donald, Brian, and Juan

Medina are all in cahoots."

"We might have a big problem. Seems like Jack would have known what he was getting into?"

"Yeah, it's a strange situation."

"So, what do you recommend?"

"We'll go along with Donald for now, play this thing out for a while. Donald and Brian might be lying. The oil thing might not have been Jack's idea after all."

"We'd better stay on our toes."

Ralph chuckled. "No shit."

Matt shrugged. "Okay, so I'm stating the obvious."

"How good are you with a pistol?"

Matt gestured with open palms. "I've used one before, hit the targets on a firing range. If necessary, I can defend myself. Do you think I need to start carrying a concealed weapon?"

"I think that will be a good idea for both of us," Ralph said. "Justin suggested it when he called, safety valve, just in case."

Matt set his jaw. "I'm in." His eyes narrowed. "I want to get the bastards who killed Jack."

"Good, I bought a couple of Glock 26 pistols. Justin told me he'll get our licenses to carry. We'll need to sign a few papers back at the office. I brought a pistol over for you. It's in the car."

"How do I carry it?"

"I got holsters with belt loops," Ralph said, "for concealed carry we'll each wear it toward the back of the right hip under a sports coat."

"I'll need some practice to be good at using it."

Ralph chuckled. "Justin has that already arranged." He glanced at his watch. "Let's go get a big steak. We need one."

"First, tell me some more about this training you mentioned."

"Justin pulled a few strings with the FBI," Ralph said. "We'll get special training at one of their facilities and some additional help from the CIA. The international aspects of this situation are about to get really complicated. We'll worry about those details later. Let's go enjoy those steaks."

Chapter 4

At eight o'clock Tuesday morning in McLean, Virginia, CIA agent Kevin Brown walked into his office in the CIA headquarters building and made a call to Gary Stennis, head of a special investigations unit for domestic threats at the FBI. He worked with Gary on a special taskforce dealing with domestic threats, the drug problem especially.

Having just reviewed the latest statistics on the drug problem in the United States, Kevin knew it wasn't a pretty picture.

Gary answered on the second ring.

"Seen the latest statistics on illegal drugs?" Kevin asked.

"Which ones?"

"The ones pertaining to the amount of usage in the United States."

"Yeah, situation's worse than ever."

"Any plans to do anything about it?"

Gary gave a tired laugh. "You lose your memory or something? Of course we have plans. They aren't working too well, but...."

"I meant any new plans."

"Why are you asking?"

"Just reviewed the latest report from the DEA."

"Haven't read it yet. You sound concerned."

"The new stats scare the hell out of me. You game for a brainstorming session?"

"Yeah, some new things going on in Florida could be related to this. Ben Fulton, SAC in Jacksonville, asked for help. Dan Maxwell is going down; you interested in tagging along?"

"When's Dan leaving?"

"This afternoon. He'll call you," Gary said. "I'm setting up a command center to monitor the activity down there, just in case."

"You worried about JAXPORT?"

"We're concerned about all our ports, but this one is in the spotlight right now."

"I think you know a lot more than you're telling me," Kevin said. "Want to enlighten me a bit?"

"The new information needs to be checked out before I start passing it around. Also, it's a long story. I'll fill you in later. I think the new problems down there will accelerate fast."

"Is that why you're suggesting I go down to Jacksonville?"

"On this one, the CIA should be involved from the start," Gary said, "lot of foreign elements mixed up in the situation. I'll make sure your participation with us gets full approval."

••••

In Jacksonville, Matt pored over the contents of several files in his computer.

Ralph had requested a report on the status of international oil (countries, production, revenues) from Washington sources via Justin's office. Justin, using his FBI and CIA contacts, had received the data from RAND's Washington DC office.

Matt knew RAND was founded in 1948 to help the U.S. Air Force prepare for World War III. The think-tank had evolved into an organization that today tackled many intricate societal problems in addition to those assigned to it by the government and the military. However, it maintained a strong focus on acquiring and analyzing information pertaining to national security.

The information in the files indicated some of the gigantic revenue from international oil was being funneled into drug trafficking by shadow cartels operating in Mexico and South America.

Matt sorted through the files again and selected one that contained data about the application of vast amounts of oil money to illegal drug trafficking. He looked up as Ralph rushed into his office and settled into a chair in front of his desk.

"Have you scanned the information Justin sent us?" Ralph asked.

Matt nodded. "It looks like a large amount of international oil money supplements the drug trafficking in Mexico and South America."

"But how the finances are handled is a mystery. None of the normal methods are involved." Ralph stared at Matt for a moment. "You're a big proponent of game theory. Maybe you can figure out some parts of the puzzle."

"You have any opinion?" Matt asked.

Ralph chuckled. "That's why I sent it all to you. You're a good mathematician and the best financial analyst I know. I thought you might come up with an idea or two as to how the bad guys are laundering money.

"I noticed RAND is starting a joint project with the CIA and FBI to analyze different methods of money laundering."

"Saw that," Ralph said. "Both organizations are supplying their best financial experts, but we need to come up with answers, even if they don't." He leaned forward, intent. "We might find some clues as to what happened to Jack."

"Are you considering expanding our business in South America and Mexico?"

"We'll see," Ralph said. "Jack's alleged interest in international oil is also a factor to be explored further." He glanced at his watch. "We should learn some more in the upcoming meeting with Juan Medina."

Matt studied Ralph for a moment. He could see resolution in his eyes, a grim resolution. He could even feel it.

"We both have a strong urge to avenge Jack's death," Ralph said. "We need to make some progress as soon as possible. Maybe some of the data RAND collected for the FBI and CIA will help."

"Speaking of the CIA, do you know where their headquarters are located?"

Ralph wrinkled his brow. "McLean, Virginia. Why?"

"Some people say McLean and other people say Langley."

"So?"

"Do you know which is right?"

"I've never thought about it." Ralph looked directly at Matt. "I'm sure you want to make a point. What is it?"

"In 1719, Thomas Lee purchased the tract of land the CIA occupies, named it Langley after his ancestral home in England." Matt said. "The town of McLean was founded in 1910 and included Langley. The Langley name still lingers. Either label is correct."

Ralph gave a half smile and shrugged. "Nice to know, I guess."

"That's why CIA headquarters is associated with either name. It used to bother me. I decided to find out what the facts were."

Ralph chuckled. "Spoken like a true analyst."

Matt leaned back in his chair. "Do you want me to keep working on this money laundering thing for a while?"

"I suggest you make it your top priority. I'll see what I can do to get you involved with the joint Rand/CIA/FBI analysis."

After a brief hesitation, Matt asked, "Think any aspects about this could come up in the meeting with Juan Medina?"

"Maybe, but let's not even give a hint about what we're working on. I don't want Donald and Brian to know either. For our own protection, it's critical we keep this whole thing as secret as possible."

"Got it."

Chapter 5

At ten o'clock, sunshine filtered through partially closed blinds as six men mingled around an elaborate coffee service in the Tustun boardroom.

Donald made introductions and waited for everyone to fill their mugs with hot coffee before they sat at the large conference table.

Matt settled into his chair and took a sip of coffee. He didn't plan to say anything, just observe. He studied the men around the table. Juan was slim with dark piercing eyes. He had a light brown complexion. Carmen was a little chubby and had the same skin color as Juan. They both wore polite smiles and seemed to be waiting for Donald to open the discussion.

Donald looked at Juan. "Will you elaborate on that offer you made to Jack the first of last month?"

Juan turned toward Ralph. "Carmen and I have been anxious for your decision, but we understand the delay."

"I only heard about this after Jack's death," Ralph said, "and I know nothing about it. I'm interested in hearing the details."

Juan smiled. "Of course." He took a sip of coffee and then cleared his throat. "Jack had approached us several months ago about getting into the oil business." He shrugged and stared at Ralph for a moment. "Based on Jack's reputation, we, of course, listened to what he had to say."

Carmen leaned forward. "We thought about Jack's request for several days before we did any detailed calculations. We soon arrived at the conclusion that this could be a profitable venture for all of us."

Juan nodded. "We immediately got back to Jack and made our offer."

Ralph fixed his gaze on Juan. "What was the offer?"

"For Tustun to be a partner in our international energy company," Juan said. "You grow a lot of crops, and we'll ship fertilizers from refined oil derivatives to you via JAXPORT at a reduced cost. You'll also be paid one million American Dollars a month for being on our list of partners."

"And your company is?" Ralph asked.

"DUISONZ," Juan said. "We're mostly a global energy components company. We produce some legal drugs such as Morphine and Codeine as a side business."

"I'm not familiar with them." Ralph pursed his lips and glanced at Matt.

"I've heard of them," Matt said, "but I've never checked any details."

Juan flashed a big smile, showing a lot of white teeth. "You must check us out. I think you'll like what you see. Carmen and I have calculated that Tustun will have increased profits of around twenty million dollars a year on this deal. We gave that number to Jack last week."

"How much will you make?" Ralph asked.

"About the same," Juan said. He took a long slow sip of coffee. "Carmen and I think it would make a good partnership." He again smiled at Ralph. "You'll be listed as our fertilizer distributor for the southeastern United States, but you won't need to do anything except answer any public-relations questions that come up."

"How solid is that twelve million a year?" Donald asked.

"Very solid," Juan said. He turned fully toward Donald. "You're guaranteed one million per month. It could be more, depending on the benefits we get from including your name in our advertising. We need some well-known companies headquartered in the United States that we can list as partners."

Donald looked at Juan and smiled. "I just wanted to double check the amount Tustun is getting. I'm sure Ralph doesn't want to make a foolish decision here."

Juan's dark piercing eyes shifted to Ralph. "We need to expand our business here in the United States. That will be much easier with some top American companies listed as partners."

"How many other American companies have you listed as partners," Ralph asked.

"You're the first one we're dealing with and that's why we're willing to make an offer like this," Juan said.

Donald turned toward Ralph and jerked his thumb toward Juan and Carmen. "Their offer is attractive. An extra twelve million a year for doing nothing sounds good to me."

"How much do we need to invest?" Ralph asked.

"Nothing," Juan said. "We'll send you all the fertilizer you want at a reduced cost, and a million dollars each month just for being listed as our partner."

Ralph rubbed his chin. "I'll see what our board thinks about it."

"Are you calling a special meeting?" Donald asked.

"Maybe," Ralph said. He stared at Juan. "If the board approves, how soon will we receive the first payment?"

"The first day, of course," Juan said. "We're ready now." He glanced at Carmen, who nodded.

Juan looked back at Ralph. "We're already shipping other products into JAXPORT. Adding shipments of fertilizer won't be difficult."

"What are you shipping now?" Ralph asked.

"Legal opium derivatives like codeine and morphine," Juan said. "Jacksonville has a lot of medical facilities who need them."

Ralph glanced at Matt. "You have any questions for our guests?"

Matt studied Juan for several seconds. "How big is your business with opium derivatives?"

"Five billion a year in the United States," Juan said. "We want to grow our fertilizer business here to at least the same level."

"What fertilizers do you produce now from oil derivatives? Matt asked.

"Ammonium nitrate, super phosphate, and potassium sulfate," Juan said. "And we plan to produce more types real soon."

Matt stared at Juan. "We need all the facts on your total business for DUISONZ."

Juan nodded. "I'll send you our annual report when Carmen and I return to Miami."

"Already have it." Matt looked down at his laptop computer. "There are a lot of footnotes that leave questions." He continued to stare at Juan. "We need to answer those questions."

Juan focused on Ralph. "I don't have any problem revealing some of our competitive secrets to the four of you. The information should be confidential, though."

"We need to study all the facts before we partner with anyone." Ralph gestured toward Matt. "He's our main business analyst and financial expert."

"I see." Juan smiled and glanced at Carmen.

Donald's gaze took in both Ralph and Matt. "Well, how long will you need?"

"You're the Executive Vice President around here and part of the equation on how long it will take," Ralph said.

Donald flashed a big grin toward Ralph. "I have the distinct impression that Matt needs to give you some numbers to look at first, right?"

Ralph gave a slight shrug. "I know you want to move ahead quickly, but I won't accept any analysis from Matt any sooner than Saturday."

Matt could see determination in Ralph's eyes. It was clear what his boss was up to. The old fox, Matt thought.

"Twelve million a year extra, we don't have to do anything, just agree," Donald stammered. "We can use that money."

"It'll come in real handy for increasing our security," Brian said. "We have some new problem areas I think you've become well aware of recently."

"Matt needs to check everything thoroughly," Ralph said. "I don't want to rush him."

"We'll be ready when you decide to proceed." Juan took a long slow sip of coffee.

Carmen kept his head down and seemed to be studying the tabletop.

"There's a legal business with opium derivatives," Ralph said, "and there's an illegal one." He stared at Juan. "If we become partners, I want to be sure we're only involved in the former."

"But of course," Juan said. He shrugged. "We don't want to incur any big risks."

Ralph looked at Matt, but didn't say anything.

Seeing Ralph raise his eyebrows, Matt figured Ralph wanted him to say something, but what?

Matt looked at Juan. "Send all the necessary data to me." He jerked a thumb toward Ralph. "I'll complete my analysis as soon as I can answer all of his questions."

Juan nodded, but didn't comment.

Ralph stood and scanned the faces around the table. "I'll give my answer on Saturday." He turned and walked toward the door. Matt followed.

••••

At the FBI field office in Jacksonville, Ben Fulton shook hands with Dan Maxwell from the Washington headquarters and Kevin Brown from the CIA headquarters in McLean. He waved them toward some chairs around the large table in the main conference room.

"Glad you guys could come down." Ben turned toward Kevin. "So, the CIA has an active interest in what's going on down here?"

"A big interest," Kevin said.

"What's the main reason for concern?"

"Port security."

Ben cocked his head and leaned forward. "Must be a little more than that, fill me in."

"It looks like JAXPORT is an entry point for illegal drugs from

South America." Kevin looked directly at Ben. "We're following several trails that originate down here."

"Gary likes the FBI working in partnership with the CIA," Dan said. "He thinks it will take both agencies to track everything down, huge combination of domestic and international issues."

"I'm not complaining. I asked for help, and I got it." Ben smiled and looked at Kevin. "What's the latest on JAXPORT?"

"It's likely the company running port security is directly involved in shipping illegal drugs," Kevin said.

"You're referring to DUISONZ?"

"Right."

Ben leaned forward. "We've picked up bits and pieces of information that indicate these drugs come in special packaging on the container ships."

"Yeah, odd containers," Kevin said, "with a distinctive horse design. All those containers are being shipped to offices connected to the World Bank; offices established to fight world hunger."

"The night shift security chief at JAXPORT mentioned the World Bank the other night. He told me those special containers had priority clearance." Ben narrowed his eyes. "What information do you have that throws suspicion their way?"

Kevin explained.

"The sequence of events the other night at JAXPORT fits the pattern you mentioned," Ben said. "The horse-containers moved through the port quickly. We were told some advisory board for fighting world hunger came up with the design. It represents galloping to the rescue."

"We need to intercept the next container with that design," Dan said.

"Did you bring the device?" Ben asked.

"Yeah," Dan said. "We'll get the suckers this time. We'll also have a talk with the new JAXPORT security about their special treatment for the containers with the horse design."

Kevin glanced at his Wenger Swiss Military watch. "We have some agents that should be taking care of that right now."

"You have CIA agents at the port?" Ben asked.

"They're working there." Kevin stared at the two FBI agents. "We received the proper congressional approval and I'm here to coordinate with you. Gary set up a command center in Washington to monitor activity at all major ports around the nation and facilitate the necessary coordination among the involved agencies."

"Okay then," Ben said. "Let's be prepared to kick this thing off tonight. The ship we're expecting is coming in at ten o'clock."

....

At Tustun, Matt eased into a chair in front of Ralph's desk.

Ralph had indicated he wanted more discussion. Matt figured it was something other than what they had discussed earlier in the boardroom.

Ralph drummed his fingers on his desk and looked at the person who sat to Matt's right, Elsie Farmer.

"Did Jack ever give you any hints about what he had in mind with this oil situation?" Ralph asked.

"He got very secretive a few weeks ago," Elsie said. "He seemed to be someone with a dark secret. I had never seen him act that way before."

Ralph's eyes narrowed and he asked, "So Jack changed?"

Elsie hesitated. Her expression grew more serious.

Ralph and Matt both remained silent.

Elsie rolled her eyes. "Yeah, hard to explain."

"Try," Ralph said. "It's important."

"He talked on the phone a lot more."

Ralph gave Elsie a curious look. "What's strange about that?"

Elsie looked directly at Ralph. "He started talking on the phone for hours at a time, all through the day." She paused. "Before, he always had me make his phone calls and deliver messages. He was seldom interested in talking to our clients on the phone, only special ones on certain occasions. He always had me set up meetings...."

"I know he always preferred to be up close and personal when he talked serious business," Ralph said.

Elsie nodded. "That changed. He had no face-to-face meetings on this new oil business, or whatever it was." She rolled her eyes again. "He acted strange in other ways too." She hesitated. "That's the best way to describe his behavior, just strange."

Matt turned toward Elsie. "The men he apparently was dealing with about the oil business were in Miami, that's pretty convenient."

"I think they were all trying to coordinate things with some people in South America. Jack was most interested in Columbia, the cities of Cartagena and Bogota in particular." Elsie gave a slight shrug. "Like I mentioned, it was all strange."

Ralph leaned toward Elsie. "Do you have anything else to say about Jack's strange behavior?"

"He mentioned a lot of things, but it was all so general. He kept saying we could make a lot more money if we would just take a few more risks." Elsie glanced at the wall and gave a tired laugh. "I hate to even think about this. It's all so frustrating. Nothing was specific." She shrugged. "Jack often mumbled about a lot of things in Columbia. Nothing tied together."

"Maybe Matt and I should go down there and look around," Ralph said. He smiled at Elsie. "I guess we've taken enough of your time."

Elsie stood and quickly turned toward the door.

Ralph had no expression. He seemed content to wait for her to leave.

Elsie got almost to the door and turned back toward Ralph. "There is something else I should probably mention. I overheard a few things when I took some stuff into Jack's office while he was on the phone. He mentioned JAXPORT a lot of times."

"In what context?" Ralph asked.

Elsie shrugged. "I wasn't paying that much attention, but I heard him mention imports from Columbia." She narrowed her eyes. "It just occurred to me that could end up being significant."

"Thanks," Ralph said.

"Oh, and there's another thing." Elsie brightened. "I remember now; he also mentioned a bank a lot." She pulled on her left ear. "Universal Consolidated Bank, I believe." She stared at Ralph. "Yes, that was it: UCB, the big one."

"Any chance you remember the context?" Ralph asked.

Elsie shook her head. "Just remember the name."

"Okay, thanks. If you remember anything else of significance, let me know." Ralph gave her a friendly dismissal-like wave.

Elsie smiled. "I'll do that." She turned and walked through the doorway.

"We have a lot to do in a short period of time," Ralph said.

"You want me to rush my analysis?"

"I think your weapons training comes first. You need to get up to the FBI Academy right away. Your appointment is at four o'clock tomorrow afternoon. Elsie has already booked your travel and hotel reservations."

"What about the analysis you wanted?"

"That was just a bluff. I think I already know what the answer is."

Matt gave Ralph a quizzical stare.

"Your priority right now is to develop efficiency with your Glock 26. I'm sure things are going to get dangerous. We need to be ready to defend ourselves," Ralph said. "I'm a little ahead of you. I've spent a lot of time at my local gun club, special instruction and all."

"So, you think we're about to run into a lot of danger?"

"Yeah," Ralph said, "especially if we go to Columbia. You still game?"

"Of course."

Ralph studied Matt for a few moments. "Are you wearing your Glock?"

"Not yet."

"Start right away." Ralph narrowed his eyes. "Here at work too, you're licensed." He fished a card that looked like a driver's license out of his coat pocket and handed it to Matt. "Put this in your billfold."

"Do you think the bastards who killed Jack might come after us?"

Ralph nodded. "When you get back from Quantico, we'll spend some time together at a local firing range where we now have a corporate membership. He gave Matt a wave of dismissal. "We'll both damn well need a lot of weapons training. We want to find out who killed Jack, and we want to be able to contend with all the related issues."

Matt nodded as he stood and turned toward the doorway. He knew the upcoming training would get his best efforts. On the analysis side, there were still a myriad of details to piece together. He had to continue looking for all the clues and all the things that matched.

The two business executives from Miami were Hispanic. Was Ralph's executive secretary, Maria Lopez, involved in this in some way?

Chapter 6

At four o'clock the next afternoon, Matt arrived at the FBI Academy in Quantico, Virginia. He wore casual slacks with a sports coat. His Glock 26 was in a holster attached to his belt and positioned toward the back of his right hip.

He stood in a large building that served as a hi-tech firing range.

The instructor studied his new student. "You look to be in good physical condition."

"I'm a former athlete and I've continued my exercises," Matt said. "I think I'm well prepared for physical activity."

"Good." The instructor continued to study Matt. "I understand you need a lot of basic instruction. I'm told you need to especially work on being able to execute a fast draw."

Matt nodded.

The instructor continued with a lot of basic instruction during the next hour while Matt practiced shooting the Glock 26.

Matt felt like he performed okay. He hit all the stationary targets.

"Not bad for a start," the instructor said. "Now, you'll need to be able to execute a fast draw from that holster on your hip. No one can foresee every possible situation. You must be proficient in getting your pistol into action quickly." He gestured toward a wide hallway. "Lot of obstructions down this hall, obstructions you'll need to contend with."

Matt didn't comment. He waited for the instructor to continue.

"Bad guys could pop up anywhere." The instructor held up his stopwatch. "You need to shoot them as fast as you can, computer will time you. I'll check some of the times."

"What kind of bad guys?"

"In this case, images on popup cardboard targets," the instructor said. "They won't all be bad guys. You'll have to judge." He jutted out his jaw. "Don't shoot the wrong ones."

Matt scanned the area. He noted a lot of stacked boxes. There were a lot of filing cabinets too. He glanced at the instructor. "I'm not a professional. Isn't this a little much for right now?"

"If you want to be a great swimmer, you have to get in rough water."

"Not when you're first learning to swim."

"Your boss wants you to become proficient as fast as possible. He told me it could save your life," the instructor said. "Along that line of thought, we try to make the conditions realistic. It's going to be hard to see the targets. You could be in a place that isn't well lighted,"

Giving a slow nod, Matt decided to put forth his best effort.

"Slap in a full magazine," the instructor said, "time to get started."

Matt inserted the 10-round magazine containing 9mm cartridges into his Glock 26. He pushed until he heard it click.

The instructor watched with no expression.

Leaving the safety on, Matt executed a few practice draws,

The instructor stared at his student. "You need to be a lot faster than that."

"Just trying to warm up a little, I plan to improve."

The instructor turned and ascended a small stairway to a raised platform. He looked down at Matt. "When I dim the lights, move forward and engage the targets. Do you have any final questions?"

Matt pushed off the safety and chambered a round. He figured he might as well get started and find out how bad he was. He had never been through this exact exercise before, and he didn't have any unrealistic expectations.

The lights dimmed. The training area was transformed by an eerie glow. Multiple faint shadows stretched across the long hallway, the end of it still discernable in the dim light.

Matt moved forward. There, to his right, in the shadows. He drew and aimed but held his fire; it was a 'good guy.' He holstered his Glock and moved forward. Another target, he drew and fired. Missed, but it was a 'bad guy' all right.

The instructor stayed on the platform and remained silent.

Matt missed target after target. He carried four extra full magazines, giving him fifty bullets. He knew that after every fifty shots there would be a break in the action, and he would receive five new magazines.

After several hours of effort, Matt started hitting most of the targets. He still had a lot of stamina, and he was getting better.

In a couple more hours, the instructor called a halt. Lights came on and he descended from the platform.

Matt holstered his Glock 26 and watched the instructor approach.

"We've got work to do." The instructor looked directly at his student. "At least you didn't shoot yourself." He shook his head and mumbled, "Had that happen before with novices like you."

"I got most of the targets there toward the end," Matt said.

"You did." The instructor gave a slight shrug. "But some were good guys."

"I've never expected to be an instant expert at this."

The instructor glared at his student. "And you're not. However, based on what your boss told me, you better damned well plan to be an expert very soon."

Matt could see checkmarks on a printed sheet the instructor carried. He waited for the instructor, who was still frowning, to continue.

The instructor studied the sheet for a few moments and then locked his gaze on Matt. "On the targets you hit, your average time was three seconds."

"Doesn't sound too bad," Matt said.

"An expert averages less than one second."

Matt didn't comment.

"Even some experts have been too slow in coping with skilled opponents," the instructor said. "Some of the men I've trained have been killed." He shook his head. "They never got fast enough."

Matt narrowed his eyes. "What are the timing details again?"

"Time starts when the target pops up. When the target goes down, elapsed time is recorded by the computer system." The instructor waved his stopwatch. "I always check a few to make sure the system is working right. Results are printed." He waved a sheet of paper. "I have all 600, right here." He stared at Matt. "At least you're in excellent physical condition and can keep going."

Matt nodded and remained silent.

"And you need to keep going a while," the instructor mumbled, "if you want to reach an acceptable skill level."

"I'll keep working on it."

"You didn't knock down a single target in less than 2.1 seconds." The instructor glared at his student. "It was a piss-poor performance. That's the most appropriate phrase I can think of." The instructor shook his head slowly.

Matt grinned inwardly. It had been a while, but he remembered it well. His college coaches had all gone through similar routines to motivate all the players. He knew he would continue to give his best effort, and he would get to the skill level he needed, maybe not as quickly as he wanted, but he would get there.

"How do you feel?" the instructor asked.

"I'm still ready to go full speed," Matt said. He gestured with open palms. "But remember I'm brand new at this. How quickly do you expect a beginning student to progress?"

The instructor gave a slight shrug and said, "I just know to survive in these types of situations when they're for real you'll need to be able to eliminate any target in around a half second."

Matt grunted.

The instructor handed Matt five more magazines. "You're still a second and a half too slow."

Matt put four of them in a coat pocket and then slapped the other one into the Glock. He wiggled his arms, which were getting a little stiff.

"You ready?" the instructor asked, after he had climbed back to the platform.

Matt gave a short laugh. "Ready as I can be."

The instructor glared at his student for several seconds. "I'm guessing you'll get your ass shot off as soon as you do this for real."

"I'll get better," Matt said.

The instructor glared at Matt. "Better do it fast. Your boss indicated you don't have much time."

Matt clinched his jaw and tried to concentrate. He was determined to improve, and fast.

The lights dimmed again.

Shadows stretched down the long hallway. Matt eased forward in the dim light past filing cabinets and stacked boxes, seemingly placed at random between open doorways.

Matt hit more of the targets as he worked his way slowly forward. When he expended his ammunition, bright light flooded the training area almost immediately.

The instructor rushed down from the platform and hurried over to where Matt was standing. "Still not fast enough."

Matt looked directly at the instructor. "I think I only shot the 'bad guys' this time."

The instructor nodded. "At least you got that part right."

Matt smiled. He knew he was improving fast, no matter what the instructor ranted about. And again, he thought about his college coaches. This instructor's training technique had no negative effect on him, he rather enjoyed it.

"You need to cut at least another half second off your time." The instructor studied his stopwatch for a moment. Then he nodded as if to verify his statement. He looked up and glared at his student. "I'm trying to keep you alive when you do this for real."

"No argument about that."

The instructor glared at Matt for a moment; then, turned and stormed back to the steps. He ran up to the platform and looked down at Matt. "It's time to get off your ass. Get faster, a lot faster."

Matt suppressed a grin. He knew the instructor was doing everything he could to motivate him. Matt figured he was probably an ex-Marine.

After returning his Glock to the holster located toward the back of his right hip, Matt shook his arms to improve the circulation. He adjusted his sports coat and faced the target area. He took a deep breath and nodded he was ready to continue.

The lights dimmed.

"Draw faster or get your ass shot off," the instructor yelled.

Matt reviewed the exercise in his head. He had to make quick decisions on which targets to shoot. If it was a 'bad guy,' he needed to take him out in less than a second.

He had to react fast but hold his fire if it wasn't the right target. He knew he would continue to improve. He scanned the area and moved forward.

There, to his left, in the shadows, a 'bad guy.' His right hand brushed back his coat and moved the pistol from the holster with a sliding motion. He executed a quick forward snap, aimed at his target, and pulled the trigger.

The target went down.

Matt returned the Glock to the holster and remained alert. He stayed in a semi-crouch and kept his balance on both feet while seeking more targets.

Time after time, he repeated the action with constantly better results. He was improving fast now.

Ralph was going to be surprised.

The lights came on and the instructor hurried down the stairs. Bright light flooded the hallway.

"Better," the instructor said. "You're getting closer to being able to stay alive."

Matt smiled.

The instructor held his hand out for the empty magazines. "You're done. I've got more students to attend to." He gave Matt a brief stare; then, turned and hurried to another part of the building.

Pleased with his performance, Matt holstered his Glock and fished his secure satellite phone out of a coat pocket.

After he punched a digit, Matt said, "I'm done for now."

"Yeah, I already have the report. You did okay for just starting out."

"I think the last part was better than okay."

"Maybe but don't get cocky. That could lead to some big mistakes."

"Roger."

"Since your flight from Reagan is at six, you should get home in plenty of time to get a good night's rest," Ralph said. "You'll need it. We have a lot we need to cover tomorrow. I'll give you a full briefing in the morning, best to not discuss things over the phone."

Chapter 7

At eight o'clock the next morning, Matt walked into Ralph's office as sunshine filtered through the blinds to his left. At least the atmosphere was cheerful.

"Justin called a few minutes ago with even more news," Ralph said. "A combined FBI, DEA, and CIA taskforce shut down JAXPORT for a while last night, confiscated a shipment of illegal drugs from South America. Opium and Cocaine were prevalent."

"How many containers?"

"Fifteen and they all had a horse-design."

"Do we know who's behind the shipment?"

"Not precisely but the containers were marked as hunger relief supplies sponsored by the World Bank. Justin told me there was some kind of center being set up here for that."

"By the World bank?"

"A facet of the World Bank," Ralph said. "Justin's in the process of getting more information from the FBI. It seems Jacksonville is now a strategic location for staging relief supplies going to certain disaster areas."

"World Bank denies any knowledge of the drugs, I assume?"

"Of course, and the origin of the containers can't yet be traced by law enforcement to any known source."

"Was Justin on the taskforce last night?"

Ralph shook his head. "It was run out of Washington, but the local FBI office was involved. Justin had another piece of interesting news. They now have a handheld device for detecting illegal drugs. It was used last night."

"How does it work?"

"Justin couldn't give me a full explanation, but he mentioned it picks up certain odors from the air and simulates what a drug-sniffing dog does." Ralph shrugged. "He told me it was like a volatile organic analyzer and has something to do with gaseous ions. It can work in open air at a range of up to 200 yards."

"I can see how a scientific explanation could be hard to understand."

"Yeah," Ralph said. "Anyway, it works, and the taskforce detected the drugs."

"Who owns the ship?"

"Some outfit in South America."

"Could our new friends from Miami be involved?"

Ralph gave a short laugh. "That was the first thing I checked. There was some other company name. The FBI arrested the ship's crew. We should find out more real soon."

"What's next for us?"

"You and I will get more training with the pistols. After that, we're going to Washington and then down to Colombia to check some things Jack was interested in when he died."

Matt raised an eyebrow. "Colombia might be dangerous."

"That's why we're getting more weapons training."

"Probably not enough for down there."

"We should be okay," Ralph said. "Justin pulled a few strings again."

Matt gestured with open palms. "Okay, quit playing this out like a suspense movie. What's going on?"

"We're going to get a lot of help from the FBI and the CIA. We have a meeting scheduled with some CIA agents in Washington DC before we go to Colombia. The meeting is tomorrow at the Hay-Adams Hotel. That's where a lot of the powerbrokers in Washington meet. They thought the hotel would be okay for a short meeting prior to the trip to Columbia and it would be more convenient for you and me."

"Know who we're meeting with?"

"Couple of CIA agents, one was in town last night."

"Involved in the situation at the port?"

Ralph nodded. "His name is Kevin Brown. We're meeting with him and a black-ops specialist, don't have his name yet."

Matt raised an eyebrow. "I guess the obvious question now is why do we need this meeting?"

"The CIA is going to work with us during the investigation. Jack's murder involves some issues they want solved," Ralph said. "Justin knows how strongly we're motivated, and he got this set up for our involvement. He sold it to law enforcement by emphasizing our inside knowledge of Jack's business dealings. We have some mutual interests with law enforcement as well as some common goals."

Matt leaned forward. "This is a big leap for us. We're businessmen not special agents."

"Working closely with the CIA is in our mutual interest in several ways," Ralph said. "The people who arranged Jack's murder are probably foreign. With Tustun being a global corporation and a big importer of goods through JAXPORT, we offer some advantages businesswise to the taskforce."

"The CIA should be a big help in finding the bastards who killed Jack. When are we leaving for Washington?"

"Tomorrow morning."

Matt studied Ralph for a moment. "Looks like you're putting everything on the line to avenge Jack's death."

"I don't want the bastards to get away with it," Ralph said. "I also want to protect Tustun."

"I'm guessing you suspect Juan and Carmen are involved in some way."

Ralph gave a harsh laugh. "You're right about that."

"What do you think about Donald and Brian?"

"It's likely they're also involved."

Matt stared at Ralph through squinted eyes. "I'm assuming our trip to Colombia will be under the guise of regular business?"

"Yes, and we'll deal with some legitimate Tustun business issues Jack was pursuing. We should develop better insight into the circumstances leading up to his murder." Ralph leaned back in his chair. "Justin told me Carmen Flores is from Colombia, Bogota to be specific."

Matt nodded. "That fits with my research and Juan Medina is from Caracas, Venezuela."

"It's likely they both have a lot of connections in Colombia," Ralph said. "Justin mentioned the FBI team killed an assassin at the port last night. They ran an ID check. He's from Bogota, Colombia, too many coincidences." He paused. "This is about to get really dangerous. You still game for this?"

"Is the CIA going with us to Colombia?"

"Kevin is for sure. Don't know about the black-ops guy."

"Either way, I'm in."

"We'll spend some time at a special firing range this afternoon, compliments of Justin," Ralph said. "The Jacksonville Police have one just for their use. It has updated equipment, including computer-controlled popup targets in different settings."

"Should be challenging enough."

"I'm concerned the bastards who knocked Jack off are coming after us next."

Matt gave a short laugh. "I think you've made that clear."

Ralph stared at Matt for a moment. "I'm a firm believer that the best defense, especially in this case, is a good offense."

Matt grinned. "So, we definitely need to become skilled gunslingers."

"Yep, and we have to assume we're going up against some tough bastards." Ralph checked his watch. "We need to be at the firing range at one o'clock. Justin wants us to stay alive and he's providing all the help he can."

••••

At the FBI field office in Jacksonville, Ben Fulton sat at the large table in the main conference room with Justin Mason, Kevin Brown, and Dan Maxwell.

"Do you think the circumstances surrounding Jack Worthington's death might be directly related to what went on at the port last night?" Ben asked.

"Lots of possibilities for a connection," Justin said, "but I've found no solid evidence of that yet."

Kevin looked at the other three men. "The CIA has uncovered a lot of related data, and we've shared it with you."

"Not much ties together yet," Dan said. "No matter how much analysis I do, I can't get a clear overall picture of what's going on."

"That's where Matt Baker can be a lot of help as we move forward." Justin scanned the faces around him. "He has a reputation for being an exceptional analyst on a wide scope of issues."

"You initiated the formal investigation into Jack's death this morning?" Ben asked.

Justin nodded. "Everything is now in motion."

"I think there's a connection between certain international oil activity and the drug cartels down in Columbia," Dan said. "The drug cartels in Mexico and Venezuela are also involved. I'm guessing the World Bank is involved in the money laundering aspects for all of them, but we must be able to prove it."

Ben looked at Kevin. "Does the CIA have any evidence of criminal activity at the World Bank?"

"Not yet, but we're still investigating," Kevin said. "Someone needs to handle the money from the drug trafficking. Some facets of the World Bank probably have a damned good way of doing it. They, of course, deny any connection to those containers we intercepted last night."

Ben nodded. "Yeah, we know."

"Look at the facts," Justin said. "We know for sure Jack was talking to those guys in Miami. It's interesting they have South American connections in Colombia and Venezuela." He looked at Ben. "Was there anything illegal on that ship last night besides opium and cocaine?"

"No, but they had a lot of legal drugs, morphine and codeine among them," Ben said.

"Those last two drugs you mentioned are made from poppy straw, aren't they?" Justin asked.

"Concentrate of poppy straw," Dan interjected. "It's referred to as CPS."

"Lot of that on board too," Ben said, "every bit legal, all going to American pharmaceutical companies."

"They put illegal drugs in the odd containers to make them stand out." Justin gave a slight shrug. "The head of port security acknowledged those containers got special handling per his instructions."

Kevin grunted. "Yea, all containers with a horse design were supposed to gallop through."

"Don't know much about the company running port security so far, but that's going to change," Ben said.

A brief silence ensued.

"Jack's daughter and son-in-law came down from Chicago for his funeral which is coming up in a few days," Justin said. "They're lawyers. I had a few questions for them."

Ben leaned forward. "Such as?"

"First of all, I asked if they were aware of Jack's interest in international oil," Justin said. "They told me they were, and they had already done some legal work for him in that regard."

"What's their last name?" Ben asked.

"Fisher," Justin said, "Brenda and Todd Fisher."

"Name's familiar," Dan said. He did a search on his phone.

"They both defended a food giant based in Chicago a few years ago." Dan studied the information for a moment. "The company was Ziggler Foods, and they were indicted on shipping illegal drugs along with their legal ones."

"Any connection to DUISONZ?" Justin asked.

Dan scanned the information he had received from his search. "No obvious connection." He read a little more. "Ziggler Foods doesn't exist anymore. It was a huge conglomerate, but the owners sold off all the individual companies."

Justin nodded. "I remember something about that. I think Tustun bought a piece of it."

"That's right," Ben said. "I remember the article in the Times Union. Tustun got quite a bit of publicity for that."

"Speaking of Tustun, another agent and I have a meeting with Ralph Gibson and Matt Baker in Washington tomorrow." Kevin turned toward Justin. "Heard you thought we could help each other."

"Should be synergistic, Ralph is following up on Jack's desire to expand Tustun's business in Colombia and he's also passionate about avenging Jack's death," Justin said. "You have resources already down there and you'll both be investigating an international connection to Jack's death."

Ben scanned the faces around the table. "Does anyone have any suspicion about Ralph or Matt being involved in Jack's murder in some way?"

Justin gave Ben a quizzical stare. "Some of your agents checked them out immediately after I called you."

"With Tustun buying part of Ziggler Foods and all," Ben said. He gestured with both palms out.

Justin studied Ben for a moment. "In my opinion, Ralph and Matt both seem beyond reproach."

"Good enough for me," Ben said. "I'm just turning over every stone and being careful, that's all."

"Actually, I was also wondering about them." Kevin gave a thumbs-up signal to Justin and Ben. "Since I'll be in Colombia with them, it's good to hear they're okay guys."

"You'll like both of them and you can trust them," Justin said.

Kevin nodded.

"Are the Columbian officials concerned about the drug problems in their own country?" Ben asked.

"Seem to be," Kevin said. "That's a big reason we cooperate with them."

Ben nodded and glanced at Dan. "Are you planning on joining them down in Columbia?"

Dan looked directly at Kevin. "If all of our bosses get things worked out, I plan to join you on every aspect of this, including activity in Columbia."

Kevin grinned. "Welcome aboard. We can use all the help we can get."

"Yeah, I've become aware of some scary things," Justin said, "and we've just begun our formal investigation into Jack's death."

"I think we're going to need a lot of close cooperation and some great intelligence information to cope with all the danger we'll probably encounter." Ben narrowed his eyes. "Especially since that danger is now likely to expand rapidly both inside and outside our borders."

••••

Afternoon sunshine illuminated the large expanse of grass a few miles north of downtown Jacksonville. Small trees and shrubs dotted the area. A soft wind blew from the direction of the Atlantic Ocean, providing a cooling effect.

Matt noticed the distinct smell of salt air as he and Ralph walked toward open slots at the firing range. They each wore cargo shorts and sandals. Hawaiian-style shirts completed their attire.

After inspecting his Glock 26, Matt reinserted it into the holster positioned toward the back of his right hip. His shirt concealed the presence of the holster. After his fast draw training at Quantico, he felt ready for action.

Ralph positioned his Glock in the same way and glanced at Matt. "Want to make it a contest? That could make things more interesting."

"I think you're ahead of me as far as skill goes. You've been doing this longer than I have."

"You might have more natural talent."

"Okay, you're on," Matt said. He stopped at the open slot he had been walking toward on the firing range. Ralph stopped in a practice slot next to him.

The instructor walked over and explained that this exercise was exclusively designed to practice the fast draw. He mentioned that targets would pop up in many places within the well-marked boundaries of each target area. Some targets would be covered in part by bushes or trees. The instructor emphasized that a computer would control everything and that each shooter would have the same degree of difficulty.

After pointing to a small red light at each ready post, the instructor said, "Gentlemen, when that light turns green, you start engaging the targets. When the light turns red, it's over, you stop. It's that simple." He looked at his two students. "Any questions?"

"How long in between targets?" Ralph asked.

"Ten seconds, plenty of time to re-holster your weapon." The instructor stared at them. "You're here to work on your reaction time in getting your pistol into action. This exercise is tailored for you to start over for each target."

"Is the speed of our fast draw the only criteria for grading?" Matt asked.

"You're also graded for marksmanship and judgment," the instructor said. "I'll give you the results after each session." He studied Ralph and Matt for a moment. "You gentlemen ready?"

Both Ralph and Matt nodded and faced their respective target areas.

"Game's on," the instructor said.

The lights for Ralph's and Matt's slots turned green.

Ralph and Matt each fired at a target; then, the lights turned red.

They repeated the process nine more times.

While studying a handheld device, the instructor shook his head. "Hope you don't run into any professionals." He looked at Matt. "You hit seven of ten targets. Your average fast draw time for the hits was 1.9 seconds." He shook his head again and looked at Ralph. "A little better, but not much, eight targets hit, 1.8 seconds average time."

Ralph grinned. "Not too bad for a first try. Some of those targets were almost behind a tree, and about fifty yards off too."

The instructor stared without expression at Ralph. "If the targets were top professionals, and you were in a gunfight, you'd be dead."

Ralph shrugged. "That's why we're here, we want to get better."

"Pop in a fresh magazine and we'll go again," the instructor said.

After a couple of hours of practice, with a few short breaks thrown in, Matt noted a lot of improvement for each of them.

The instructor checked his hand-held device. "Your best showings yet: each of you hit nine targets with an average elapsed time of 1.4 seconds. You've reached a good stopping point."

Ralph glanced at Matt. "We both made a lot of improvement. Let's call it a tie."

"Agreed," Matt said. "However, being outgunned by a skilled assassin is a sobering thought. I'd like to go longer and try to improve a little more."

Ralph shrugged and looked at Matt. "I have the same concern, but my right arm is sore after one hundred and fifty draws. You're younger, so be my guest." He walked over to a nearby bench.

The instructor supplied Matt with five more fully loaded magazines.

After inserting the two-pound weapon in his holster, Matt faced the target area and glanced at the light: it was still red. He took a deep breath and kept his gaze on the light; then, he was interrupted.

"Haven't seen you out here before?"

Matt turned and saw a muscular figure standing about five yards behind him. The brown-haired man looked to be a little over six feet tall. The athletic looking stranger smiled and kept his gaze fixed on Matt.

The instructor remained silent and displayed an amused look.

Ralph also remained silent and watched with obvious curiosity.

"My first time on this range," Matt said.

The stranger glanced over at Ralph and then looked back at Matt.

Matt shrugged. "Just visiting, trying to get in some needed practice."

Ralph stood and moved beside Matt. "Yeah, we're just trying to get in a little practice. Do you mind?"

"Nah, I don't mind."

Matt flashed a curious glance at the instructor, who still seemed slightly amused.

"You've been practicing fast draws?" the stranger asked.

Ralph glared at the man. "Yeah, as if that's any of your business."

The stranger gave a sly grin. "It could end up being some of my business." He fixed his gaze on Matt. "Care for a little demonstration?"

Matt studied the stranger for a few moments and then glanced at the instructor. The instructor was smiling big now.

Ralph walked back to the bench where he had been sitting.

Matt looked at the stranger and gave a slight shrug. "Okay, why not?"

The stranger glanced at the instructor. "This station has the advanced option?"

The instructor nodded.

"Let's do it," the stranger said. He gestured for Matt to step back; then, he strolled up to the ready position.

The light turned green, and five popup targets appeared at the same time.

Five shots happened so fast that it sounded like one long noise. All five pop-up targets went down. The stranger reinserted his Heckler & Koch USP in the holster. "Those 9mm slugs carry one hell of an impact." He grinned at Matt.

Another five targets appeared. The targets went down again. This time, Matt thought, it seemed even faster. He glanced at Ralph, who looked astonished.

The instructor walked up, checking his handheld device. "Not too bad, 1.2 seconds for the first five, 1.1 seconds for the next five."

"I usually do better," the stranger said as he slapped a fresh magazine into his Heckler & Koch USP. "But that wasn't too bad." He slid the pistol back into the holster toward the back of his right hip. He turned and grinned at Matt and Ralph.

"That's the kind of skill you might be facing." The instructor stared at Matt and Ralph.

Ralph shook his head. "Impressive."

"I think we need some more practice," Matt said.

"Keep working on it, don't give up." The stranger smiled as he turned. He disappeared as fast as he had appeared.

"Who was that guy?" Matt asked.

"Don't know his name," the instructor said. "I just know he's an agent with the CIA and he's cleared to use this practice facility."

"Does he use it often?" Ralph asked.

The instructor shrugged. "Periodically comes around on and off throughout the year. That's how I know how good he is. I was informed he was going to drop by."

"Someone wanted to show us what kind of talent we might come up against?" Ralph asked.

"That's what I was told." The instructor looked at Matt and Ralph. "I take it you now have a little perspective on the skill you could face."

"Damned right." Ralph moved his right arm in a circular motion, loosening it up.

"Going to practice a little more?" the instructor asked.

"Looks like I need to get better than I am now," Ralph said, "and that's for damned sure."

The instructor handed Ralph five more fully loaded magazines. "Practice as long as you want. I'll stay until you finish." He gave a slight shrug. "Justin and some very influential people in Washington want me to help you all I can."

Ralph studied the instructor for a moment. "I have to agree that demo worked."

"Definitely shows us how far behind the top-notch professionals we are," Matt said. "He got five targets in less time than we got one."

The instructor gave a slow nod as he narrowed his eyes and studied both Matt and Ralph for a few moments. "The demo you just saw was given by a guy who's head and shoulders better than any other agents I know." He smiled. "You guys aren't bad, don't lose your confidence. But you're not yet anywhere close to the best, so keep practicing. I think your having more awareness now could turn out being very useful."

The two men continued their practice for several more hours. A look of determination dominated both faces.

Matt knew they'd better make a lot of improvement if they wanted to remain alive.

••••

At Miami International Airport, a short chunky man deplaned from his private jet parked at a remote hangar.

Juan and Carmen stood beside a parked SUV.

Omar Karam took a deep breath of the air stirred by the prevailing sea breeze and exhaled slowly while he strolled toward them.

"Is this meeting in Miami really that necessary?" Omar asked as he approached the two men.

"More secure this way," Carmen said. "There are some highly sensitive issues we must handle real soon."

"If Ricardo does his job down in Columbia, our planning will be much simpler." Juan gave a sly grin. "Eliminating Gibson and Baker will pave the way for our closing the deal with Tustun."

Omar frowned as he surveyed the other two men. "I wouldn't be too sure about the benefits of getting rid of Gibson and Baker. I think we have some other problems."

"That's why we need to talk," Juan said, as the three of them climbed into the SUV. He glanced at Omar. "We spent a lot of money on a state-of-the-art office. We might as well use all the tools we have."

Within about thirty minutes, Juan parked in front of his new headquarters.

After entering a large lounge and conference area in his office suite, Juan gestured toward a mahogany conference table designed for twelve people. He glanced at Omar as they were settling into their chairs. "Good thing you were over in the western hemisphere at this time."

"I often check firsthand on my business interests," Omar said.

Juan cast a satisfied glance toward a long curving hallway that connected the lounge to the conference area they were in. The wide hallway was decorated with original oil paintings of jungle creatures in elaborate settings, some ready to pounce.

The paintings had a direct connection to his own situation, Juan thought. On several matters, he was ready to pounce.

Looking at Omar, Juan asked, "So how did you find things on your inspection of our facilities in Colombia?"

"Things were okay, but I thought Ricardo seemed a little too preoccupied with other matters." Omar stared at Juan. "Perhaps it was due to some of the things you had him working on."

"He has an important mission coming up," Juan said. "You spent a lot of time with him. What's your take on his state of mind?"

"He seemed okay."

Juan nodded as he stood and walked over to a section of the wall. He pushed an inconspicuous button. Part of the wall slid open, revealing an ornate steel safe. He opened the safe and extracted a stack of folders.

After walking back and placing the foot-high stack on the conference table, Juan settled into his chair.

"Here's all my analysis on current threats to our illegal drug business." Juan gestured toward the folders.

"You have all the latest technology," Omar said, "why all the paper?"

"Paper is safer," Juan said. "As you can see, I keep it well protected, and no one can hack into it."

Omar remained silent.

"Curious?" Juan asked. He gestured toward the folders again.

Omar shrugged. "I know you always do a careful study of everything. That's why I don't mind letting you invest in my company."

"There's a lot of new information here that we need to consider right away," Juan said. "We can't afford to let much more time go by before we make some necessary decisions." He leaned toward Omar. "I understand DUISONZ now has moles in all the intelligence agencies, including several in the CIA. Are we receiving any benefits?"

"I have the latest details about what certain people are planning to do in South America, Colombia in particular." You will no doubt consider much of the news to be explosive."

Juan and Carmen waited with no expression.

"The CIA is sending some of their top agents to Colombia along with Gibson and Baker," Omar said.

Juan frowned. "When did you find out about this?"

"Ten minutes before I got off the plane."

"Why didn't you mention this on our drive here?" Juan asked.

"I wanted to relax and enjoy the scenery for a few minutes before we got serious about things. We need our best concentration."

"We must alert Ricardo about the information you just mentioned," Juan said.

"Of course, I called him immediately after I got it."

"What did he say?" Juan asked.

"He told me he would be prepared," Omar said. "He didn't seem overly concerned. He mentioned Panther had already alerted him." He leaned toward Juan. "Do you know who Panther is?"

"Did you ask Ricardo if he knew?" Juan asked.

"Yes," Omar said. "He doesn't know, but he mentioned he's received communications from him before and they've always been accurate."

Juan nodded slowly. "I've heard of Panther. His identity is obviously a well-kept secret."

"So, you don't know who he is either?" Omar asked.

"No," Juan said without any expression. "Ricardo is adding another level of security to our illegal drug business down there and we need to discuss several issues relating to that right now."

Juan peeled off three folders from the top of the stack and slid two of them toward Omar and Carmen. "The CIA and FBI have discovered we run the security at JAXPORT."

Omar opened the folder in front of him and scanned the contents. "Is that going to be a big problem?"

"Maybe," Juan said. "But if Ricardo does his job, it will give the American intelligence agencies something new to think about." He leaned forward and explained.

Omar raised an eyebrow.

"In the meantime," Juan said, "I have some of the best lawyers money can buy working on our behalf regarding the port security. I've hired some of the best in Washington DC plus a couple in Chicago. They all have experience on this sort of thing."

"Do you think the United States government will threaten us on legal grounds?" Omar asked.

"Yes, but it will be an empty threat." Juan glanced at the ceiling. "They have no proof we've done anything wrong, and they won't get any."

Omar frowned. "The Americans might find something in Jack's files."

"We'll make sure they don't," Juan said. "The lawyers from Chicago are watching our back. They'll sanitize anything Jack left behind."

Carmen looked at Juan. "What if the Americans find something damaging against us when they're in Colombia?"

"Ricardo will prevent that from happening," Juan said.

"I hope he's good enough." Omar gave a slight shrug.

"He is," Juan said. "With his background experience and our new level of security, he won't fail. Ricardo is better than anyone the CIA has. His men are pretty good too. He'll get it done."

Omar leaned forward. "Tell me more about Ricardo."

"He's a killer, one of the best on the planet. He's been handling my dirty work for ten years. He's never failed me."

"Where did you find him?" Omar asked.

"Goes way back," Juan said. "Ricardo worked for the largest drug cartel in Mexico. I made him a better offer."

"How did he get so good?" Omar asked.

"A lot of natural talent for one thing," Juan said. He laughed. "He also got a lot of special training from the Mexican government."

Omar gave Juan a quizzical look.

"The Mexican government, not knowing he was already in a drug cartel, hired him to fight the cartels along the United States border," Juan said. "Some idiots in the United States government helped fund the training program. Ricardo has hurt them in many ways, and they don't even know it."

Omar nodded and flashed a big smile.

Juan peeled more folders off the stack and slid them toward his two cohorts.

"Satellite photos, how did you get these?" Omar asked.

"Moles come in handy," Juan said.

Omar studied the photographs. "What are we looking for?"

"Those are shots of JAXPORT. Notice anything unusual?" Juan asked.

"Some men, I suspect FBI agents, are hiding behind several stacks of crates," Omar said.

Juan nodded. "Notice anything else?"

"One of them is pointing some type of handheld device," Omar said.

"According to our moles, FBI agents can now detect containers of illegal drugs." Juan pursed his lips. "And they can do it from a considerable distance, up to several hundred yards."

"How can a device do that?" Carmen stared at Juan. "It seems impossible. Detecting radiation is understandable, but illegal drugs?"

"The moles don't know the details; they just know it works." Juan took a big puff on his pipe. "That's how the FBI detected the drugs the other night."

"So, what are we going to do about that?" Omar asked.

"Nothing right now," Juan said. "But knowing about it gives us some leverage."

"How?" Carmen asked

"We'll hold shipments until we find out how the device works." Juan looked thoughtful. "Then we'll find a better way to shield the drugs."

Omar nodded. "That shouldn't be too difficult. We have plenty of money to pay for our own scientific research."

"Yes," Juan said. "And I already have some men working on it."

"How soon will they know something?" Omar looked directly at Juan.

"I have no idea," Juan said. "Remember they just started and, first of all, we have to obtain one."

"Do you have a plan?" Carmen asked.

"Several moles are working on a way to get a device. One of them is in a high position," Juan said. "He's confident he'll be able to get one for 'further testing' as they say in the FBI."

Both Carmen and Omar grinned.

Juan studied the two men in front of him. "Do either of you want to take a more active role in what's going to happen in Colombia?"

Carmen and Omar exchanged glances. Both shrugged.

"What do you have in mind?" Carmen asked.

"One of you can go to Bogota and oversee what Ricardo is doing. You can set up a control center of sorts, a liaison between Ricardo and me."

Omar frowned. "Thought you were leaving all the decisions up to Ricardo on how he handled things down there?"

"Right," Carmen said. "And I thought you told us the moles were feeding Ricardo direct information."

Juan gave a sly grin. "I'm leaving the specific strategy and tactics up to Ricardo. It's true the moles are feeding him direct information, but I have sources of information other than the moles. Here's what I have in mind." He leaned forward and explained.

Carmen smiled. "I like it. I'm willing to oversee the activity down there." He glanced at Omar.

Omar gave a slight shrug. "It's fine with me for you to take care of that. I need to get back to Saudi Arabia. I have some operational issues that need my close attention. If we want to maintain all our funding, oil must keep flowing to the market."

Chapter 8

The next morning in Washington DC, Matt and Ralph walked into the lobby of the Hay-Adams Hotel.

"Having second thoughts?" Ralph asked.

"Why do you ask?"

Ralph gave a slight shrug. "Over the years, I've become an expert at reading people's feelings."

"And mine are?"

"Let's just say you're showing some concern."

"Concern yes, regret no," Matt said. "I've never worked closely with the FBI and CIA before, but I want to avenge Jack's death just as much as you do, and I want to get some answers about what's going on."

Ralph gave a thumbs-up and strolled over to a complimentary coffee service in a spacious lounge surea in the corner of the lobby. He filled his cup and walked toward a Victorian-style wingchair.

Following Ralph's lead, Matt, holding a cup of hot coffee, settled into an identical chair, both a dark shade of maroon. He looked toward the front doors, no one coming yet. That was okay. Relaxing for a few more minutes would be good.

Matt studied the various groups of people in the lobby. He knew this was one of the most popular places in the United States for Washington powerbrokers to hold their meetings. Everything looked routine now except for an approaching storm.

After a flash of lightning and a loud clap of thunder, Matt turned and looked at the rain pounding against the window to his right. He checked his watch (10:05 a.m.) and glanced back at Ralph.

"Relax," Ralph said. "They'll be here. Weather's not that bad."

Matt took a long sip of the hot coffee and savored the strong aroma of the Colombian blend.

The lightning flashed again.

Matt waited for the clap of thunder. There it was: loud and close. The windows shook. Was it an omen?

Almost instantly, two men in raincoats appeared in the lobby and walked toward them.

"Sorry we're late," one man said. He held out his hand. "I'm Craig Parker, head of terrorist threat investigation for the CIA."

Matt and Ralph shook hands with Craig.

Craig nodded toward the other man. "This is Kevin Brown. He works for me."

Kevin extended his hand and said, "Nasty weather."

Matt and Ralph both nodded and respectively shook the extended hand.

Craig scanned the area. "Just you two?"

"You were expecting more?" Ralph asked.

"He'll probably be along any moment," Craig said.

Matt and Ralph didn't comment.

"You picked a good spot." Craig studied the arrangement of chairs in a secluded part of the lobby, a short walk away from the coffee bar.

While Matt and Ralph were waiting for the CIA agents to occupy two of the empty chairs around them, Craig glanced at the coffee cups Ralph and Matt held in their hands. "Believe I'll try some of that myself." He walked over to the coffee service. Kevin followed.

After Craig and Kevin filled their cups and sat, a tall muscular man walked through the main doorway. He folded his umbrella and after looking around for a moment, came straight toward the foursome in the corner of the lounge.

Ralph and Matt both grinned in recognition as they watched the stranger approach.

"Butch Reilly," the stranger said, as he extended his hand to Ralph and Matt in turn.

"That was quite a display at the range in Jacksonville yesterday," Ralph said.

Butch smiled. "Thought it might give you a benchmark, there are plenty of villains out there with similar skills."

"Thanks for the demo," Matt said. "It gave us strong motivation to improve a lot."

Butch glanced at the coffee mugs held by the four men around him. "You have the right idea" He walked over to the coffee bar and poured a cup of the steaming hot liquid with the strong, but pleasant, aroma.

After Butch settled into a fifth chair in the corner of the lounge, Craig looked at Matt and Ralph. "It's unusual for us to include a couple of business guys in our operations, but it's synergistic to do so in this case. Your insights into a lot of relevant things will be necessary when we need to make quick decisions in the middle of the action we expect. The FBI and Jacksonville police are helping us to make sure you get the training you need to minimize your risks"

Ralph and Matt each gave a thumbs-up.

Craig explained his perspective on how the situation in Colombia should be handled.

After Craig finished, Ralph fixed his gaze on the tall lanky CIA department head. "Matt and I were going to do this anyway. I don't think we could ask for better support."

Craig looked straight into Ralph's eyes. "We're going to support your objectives, but we want full cooperation with our agents, no arguments about any of their decisions."

"Since we now have more insight into the bigger picture, you won't get any arguments from us." Ralph glanced at Matt.

Matt nodded.

"There are a lot of things going on that the public doesn't know about." Craig jerked a thumb toward Kevin and Butch. "These men are going to stay with you all the way." He studied Ralph and Matt for a moment. "Our best intelligence tells me you're going to be in big danger. No matter how much you've been improving your weapons skills, you're going to need our support."

Ralph leaned forward, intent. "Can you give us more details?"

"Some of the drug cartels in Columbia know you're coming," Craig said.

"How?" Ralph asked.

"We're not sure yet." Craig wrinkled his brow as he took a slow sip of coffee. "NSA picked up bits and pieces of phone conversations coming from down there into the United States. Assassins were mentioned, assassins to knock off the Americans who were coming to Columbia."

Matt knew the NSA (National Security Agency) was headquartered at Fort Meade, Maryland, about ten miles northeast of Washington DC. He knew their ECHELON system site at Sugar Grove, West Virginia, monitors international calls received in the eastern and central United States.

"I guess those Americans could be us," Matt said.

Craig gave a harsh laugh. "Yep, the names Gibson and Baker were both mentioned multiple times."

"NSA couldn't determine who they were and how they knew we were coming?" Ralph asked.

"Calls were encrypted, damned well too," Craig said. "NSA is still working on it. The name Panther was mentioned several times. We hope to learn more later."

"How can the bad guys have better technology than we do?" Ralph asked.

"They have a huge amount of money. They can afford advanced technology as well as expert help," Craig said. "We were fortunate to extract as much information as we did and at least be forewarned."

Ralph turned toward Butch. "Glad you're coming along."

Butch gestured toward Kevin. "He's not too shabby with a pistol either."

Kevin looked at Ralph at Matt. "I heard you guys have been practicing quite a bit."

"Matt and I were going to do this no matter what obstacles we would face, and we wanted to be able to handle trouble if we ran into it," Ralph said. "But we didn't know the full extent of what we're getting into until now."

Craig leaned forward. "We have a lot of agents in Columbia, and you have specific knowledge that can be a big help to us. We can be a big help to each other, and we can help keep you alive. We're supporting your mission for a specific reason: we think Jack Worthington's death had a connection to some things dealing with our national security and we want to get to the bottom of it."

"Wow, can you elaborate?" Ralph asked.

"The CIA gets a lot of data from NSA and NRO." Craig seemed to be organizing his thoughts.

Matt knew the NRO (National Reconnaissance Office) designed, built and operated the reconnaissance satellites of the United States government. He knew it was an agency in the Department of Defense that coordinated collection and analysis of information from both airplane and satellite reconnaissance by the military services and the CIA.

"After some careful study, we discovered your new South American friends now living in Miami are directly tied into the security setup at JAXPORT," Craig said.

Ralph raised an eyebrow. "Juan Medina and Carmen Flores?"

"A subsidiary of their global company runs port security," Craig said.

"That subsidiary is part of DUISONZ?" Ralph asked.

Craig nodded. "Our goals are tied together. What you're planning to do in South America fits right into our needs."

Ralph hesitated for a moment. "Matt and I were planning to spend some time checking our farming options down there. We want to retrace Jack's footsteps and learn more about additional crops we might need for producing a variety of Tustun products."

"That's good, it'll add to our cover." Craig studied Ralph for a moment. "There's something else: Omar Karam from Saudi Arabia just had a meeting with Juan Medina and Carmen Flores in Miami yesterday, and I got a notification on my way here that Flores is now in Bogota as we speak."

"Doing what?" Ralph asked.

"We're not sure yet," Craig said. "Our agents spotted him talking with the notorious Ricardo Garza, a former leader of a drug cartel in Mexico. We've recently discovered Garza is currently connected to a lethal group of organized assassins in Columbia."

"What about Karam?" Ralph asked.

"One of the richest men on the planet and he hates the United States." Craig gave an acid grin.

"Rich from oil?" Ralph asked.

Craig nodded. "He's part owner of DUISONZ."

"I understand Medina and Flores aren't too shabby themselves when it comes to wealth," Ralph said.

"DUISONZ is well funded." Craig took a sip of coffee. "Medina and Flores have added to their wealth by being partners in DUISONZ."

"In our meeting in Jacksonville with Medina and Flores, no mention was made of Karam or of any current Saudi Arabia connection," Matt said.

Craig narrowed his eyes. "They have reasons for not advertizing it." He went on to explain.

"That adds to the puzzle and complicates things even more," Ralph said.

Craig pursed his lips and gave a slow nod.

Butch's gaze took in both Ralph and Matt. "You should know that Ricardo Garza is a real bad dude. I've run into him once before. He's damned good with a pistol."

"How did you find that out?" Matt asked.

Butch grunted. "Let's just say I was in a firefight with him and some of his assassins."

"You obviously survived," Ralph said.

"I managed to knock off a few of them and then I got the hell out of there." Butch shrugged. "I was vastly outnumbered."

Ralph looked at Matt. "This thing is getting scarier and scarier, and we haven't even started."

"I think we're gaining on being able to hold our own," Matt said.

Ralph frowned. "You're a great analyst, but don't let your ego override your brain. We still need a lot of improvement."

"After all that training, I wouldn't miss this for the world," Matt said. He looked at Ralph. "We're both in great physical shape and we're becoming better fighters fast. There's no way I want to be left out of this."

Ralph didn't comment.

"Okay, back to business." Craig leaned forward and gave Ralph a thoughtful look. "We're working hand in hand with the FBI and we're working with the Jacksonville Police, namely your friend Justin Mason."

"It's good we're closely coordinated," Ralph said. "We have a mountain of trouble to contend with."

Craig kept his gaze fixed on Ralph. "We've also learned more about some of the circumstances surrounding Jack Worthington's death."

Ralph and Matt exchanged glances and waited for Craig to continue.

"Looks like he had a connection to trafficking illegal drugs," Craig said. "We should pick up more useful information by accompanying you to Colombia."

"Are you aware our good friends in Miami want to create a business partnership with Tustun?" Ralph asked with a slight grin.

Craig nodded. "Justin filled us in on all of that." He studied Ralph for a moment. "Do you think they murdered Jack?"

Ralph narrowed his eyes. "I think it's likely they were involved."

"So does Justin," Craig said.

"It's interesting this Omar Karam is a rich oil sheik." Ralph stared at Craig. "Jack wanted to invest in the global oil business. Now we have a third oilman involved."

Craig gave Ralph a knowing look.

"Oil and illegal drugs," Ralph said. "Not your usual combination."

"Greed, it's all about greed." Craig gave a slight shrug. "Using big money to produce more big money, any way they can."

"Tustun is still mainly in the food business, at least, last time I checked." Matt glanced at Ralph. "Up until now, that's been our major focus. This thing is getting stranger all the time."

"The global economy is fostering a lot of changes," Ralph said. He looked directly at the CIA agents. "Jack was concerned about staying competitive in the expanding global economy. That could have been why he was looking into the oil business."

"Ralph and I think Jack might have gotten in too deep with the leadership at DUISONZ and wanted to back away some," Matt said. "There's a possibility he double-crossed them."

Ralph gave a slow nod. "Jack was the kind of person who would have the guts to do that.

There was a brief silence.

Craig glanced at Ralph. "We might as well get started right away on our joint venture. Can you be ready to leave for Columbia tomorrow afternoon?"

"Of course," Ralph said. "This is a necessary business trip Matt and I have already discussed. We're both sitting on ready."

"We'll take care of the travel arrangements, and I'll make sure you get all the latest details before you leave." Craig extended his hand. "Good luck on your trip."

Everyone stood and shook hands.

Kevin slapped Ralph on the shoulder. "Butch and I will be prepared for action. I know you and Matt will be too."

Matt smiled but fought back a shiver. He glanced at Ralph and noted he seemed fully aware of the enormity of the situation they were getting into. Matt knew they were both determined to move forward despite the risks. He was confident they would have a reasonable chance of survival when they encountered the adverse conditions that were sure to come.

••••

That evening back in Jacksonville, Matt contemplated the new rush of events in his life. He knew he wasn't yet a great warrior, but he was in great physical condition. He also knew he wasn't a great detective, but he was a good analyst, and he was a thinker.

He was also becoming very expert with his Glock 26. He had a strong feeling he could succeed in his new endeavor.

At least, he didn't lack confidence.

He mulled over the conversation with the CIA agents and, after seeing Butch's performance on the pistol range yesterday, he was glad to have him on the team in South America.

As he started replaying more of the recent events in his mind, a familiar sound interrupted his thoughts. He glanced at the caller-ID displayed on his secure satellite phone.

It was Ralph.

He answered.

They had stopped using their regular cell phones and had employed better security measures.

"Having any second thoughts?" Ralph asked.

"Not yet."

"You don't have to stick with this, you know. I'll be the first to admit our planned business trip to Colombia has taken a different twist."

"Like I mentioned before, I wouldn't miss this for the world."

Ralph was silent for a moment. "Okay then, glad to have you along. There's some new information I thought you might want to know about as soon as possible."

As he waited for Ralph to continue, Matt watched the last streaks of red fading behind the treetops.

"Justin called a short while ago. He's well into his investigation now," Ralph said. "He suspects Brenda Fisher and her husband might have played a larger role in Jack's life than we knew about."

"Oh?"

"Justin thinks some of Brenda's activity went far beyond the norm of what a daughter would do for her father."

"Referring to her legal work?"

"That's right," Ralph said. "She was also handling all of the preliminary legal work for Tustun to partner with DUISONZ."

"That's not so unusual, is it? I would guess Jack trusted his daughter more than any other lawyer."

"That's probably true, but there's something else."

Matt waited in silence.

"She and her husband did a lot of work on tariff issues for legal drugs for a food conglomerate a few years ago and they're now on the defense team for a certain party involved in the problems at JAXPORT the other night."

"DUISONZ?"

"Right."

"Are the Fisher's involved because DUISONZ runs the company in charge of the security at JAXPORT?"

"Right again."

Matt whistled.

"You're the expert analyst, any profound thoughts?"

Matt was silent for a few moments, thinking.

"Take your time. I want a well-thought-out opinion."

"After a few minutes, Matt said, "I think the Fishers have other connections to DUISONZ."

"My conclusion also and I think Jack's daughter might have introduced him to Juan. What do you think?"

"I would say that was a high probability."

"So where does that leave us?" Ralph asked.

"I think our trip to South America is more important than ever," Matt said. "If we're going to solve the mystery of who murdered Jack, we must broaden our scope. I'm convinced Colombia holds some answers."

"Speaking of the trip, a CIA plane will pick us up at JIA at nine o'clock tomorrow morning. Craig told me to pack for a week's stay and be sure to bring our Glocks and plenty of ammo. I'll pick you up at seven."

"I'll be ready," Matt said. "You're not going to trust Donald to run the company while we're gone, are you?"

"He'll be in charge of the daily stuff, but Elsie will keep a close eye on everything that goes on."

"You trust her that much?"

"Jack did," Ralph said. "Don't worry about it. I know Harrell doesn't trust Brian or Donald. He'll help her look after things. Get some sleep. I'll see you in the morning."

Matt heard Ralph disconnect. He took a deep breath and relaxed as much as he could.

After a few minutes, he glanced at his watch. It was time to get some dinner.

He would start packing after he ate.

While walking back into the house toward the kitchen, Matt continued to mull over what he and Ralph had discussed. Were the Fishers in cahoots with Donald and Brian?

Were they all plotting alongside Juan Medina and Carmen Flores? Were the six of them in this together? How much was Omar Karam involved in the details of what they were doing?

Chapter 9

At 8 o'clock the next morning at CIA headquarters in McLean, Craig Parker hurried into the spacious corner office of his boss, Joe Frank.

"I need an update on this new wave of foolishness you're up to," Joe said. He flashed a big grin as he stared over a mug of steaming hot coffee.

Craig knew the CIA Director used humor as a tool for relieving pressure. Being accustomed to Joe's approach to things, he returned the grin and said, "Kevin and Butch got off fine." Craig glanced at his watch. "They left Reagan in one of our private jets ten minutes ago."

"Good." Joe waved Craig to a chair. "They're still picking up Gibson and Baker in Jacksonville?"

"Yes sir." Craig reached over and grabbed the mug of coffee, placed there for him on the corner of Joe's desk. He savored a quick sip.

"Although I agreed to this, I have a bit of concern about them going along with us," Joe said. "We both know Gibson and Baker don't have the proper training for what they'll likely run into."

"They were already planning to go down there," Craig said. "Giving them some assistance fits well with our mission to check the international aspects of some suspicious activities and also support the FBI investigation into the murder of Jack Worthington."

"We could have encouraged them not to go."

"According to the FBI, there was no way to talk Gibson and Baker out of it. Besides, I think they can help us."

"How so?"

"They obviously have a much better understanding of their business than we do." Craig took a sip of coffee. "They'll have a better idea of what to look for that might have a connection to Jack Worthington's death."

"We have copies of Jack's notes."

"But we don't understand all the nuances," Craig said.

Joe gave a slow nod.

"There are a lot of subtleties tied to the Tustun business objectives," Craig said, "especially with a lot of the activity pertaining to the cocoa bean, poppy, and sugarcane production."

Joe pursed his lips and looked at Craig through squinted eyes. "Okay, I'll buy that."

"I also checked on how Gibson and Baker performed in their weapons training," Craig said. "The reports showed they're pretty damned good with their Glock 26 pistols."

"Glock 26 holds ten 9mm shells, right?"

Craig nodded.

"At least they'll have a little stopping power, but they don't have the necessary experience."

"Butch Reilly gave them a demo. They're aware of what kind of talent they might come up against. They'll be prepared."

"I hope Butch's better than anyone they'll encounter down there."

"That's likely the case, and Butch's demonstration should help keep them on their toes."

"Do you know specifically what Gibson and Baker will be looking for in Colombia?"

"Not in great detail, but I know they think it's necessary to get a close look at some of the business-related activities Jack was interested in, such as buying more land down there for producing their crops."

"Do you think Gibson and Baker understand how big of a chance they're taking?"

"I'm not sure, but they've been properly warned. Justin Mason gave them some advice about various crime aspects of the business operations they plan to check."

"He's the police chief in Jacksonville?"

Craig nodded. "I've chatted with Mason quite a bit. He came up through the ranks as a detective. He gave Gibson and Baker pointers on things to look for relating to illegal drugs."

"I thought Jack Worthington was interested in oil?"

"Jack wanted to expand their cocoa bean production in Colombia and partner with an international oil cartel. DUISONZ is heavily involved in both."

Joe hesitated a moment and then asked, "Anything else?"

"Gibson wants to explore Tustun expanding their cocoa bean production by partnering with some other growers in Colombia."

"Why Colombia?"

Craig shrugged. "I just know Jack Worthington made some trips there and Colombia is the third largest producer of cocoa beans in South America."

Joe took a sip of coffee. "Who's ahead of them?"

"I asked that same question: Brazil is by far the biggest. Ecuador is way behind Brazil, but they're a little ahead of Colombia."

Joe leaned forward. "So, what's the significance of all these facts you're giving me?"

"Even though DUISONZ is considered a legal grower of poppy and coca plants, it looks like some of their partners might have a side business in illegal drugs."

"What do you base that on?"

"It's the consensus of experts in the FBI and DEA who've been analyzing this."

"They've been collectively discussing this?"

"Right, they've concluded DUISONZ, in addition to producing legal drugs from the poppy, such as morphine and codeine, also produces opium and heroin."

"Colombia produces some oil, don't they?"

"Over half a million barrels a day, but they're only the fifth largest producer in South America," Craig said. "Venezuela was producing almost three million barrels a day before they had their problems. Brazil is close behind that number. Argentina and Ecuador come next."

"So where does all this leave us?"

"We should be able to gather new intelligence, and we should be able to confirm some of the intelligence we already have. Gibson and Baker are planning to ask a lot of questions to a lot of producers of various crops."

Joe took a sip of coffee and didn't comment.

Craig held both hands out with palms up. "Bottom line, we know we have a big puzzle to put together and we hope to find a few more pieces to it on this trip."

After a few moments, Joe smiled. "I think you've put together a reasonable plan. Good luck and keep me informed." He made a gesture of dismissal.

••••

In Bogota, Columbia, a modern two-engine jet landed at El Dorado International Airport. As the plane taxied to a private hangar, Carmen gazed out the window at a slim dark-complexioned man of medium height standing alongside a black Ford Victoria. He knew Ricardo Garza would be waiting for him.

When Carmen deplaned, Ricardo walked over and extended his hand. "Juan mentioned you need me to set up some kind of control center here."

Carmen smiled. "It doesn't need to be a real fancy control center. I just need some private accommodations with the right communications equipment."

Ricardo nodded and turned back toward the Ford Victoria. The driver was now out of the car and standing beside it with a door open to the back seat.

"Juan thought the control center of sorts would be a good idea. He wants to provide you with extra support." Carmen stared at Ricardo. "That's just in case you need it."

"Whatever the boss wants," Ricardo said. He looked at Carmen and grinned. "In fact, I have it already set up. Juan has supplied plenty of money for it."

After both men settled into the back seat and closed the door, the driver sped toward a secluded airport exit.

"Juan told me you maintain a security company as a legal front." Carmen glanced at Ricardo. "Where's your office located?"

"North of the city in the International Center, one of the most important financial areas," Ricardo said. "Being in that location gives my business an air of legitimacy."

"Is that where we're going?"

Ricardo nodded.

Carmen glanced at his watch. "How long to get there?"

"This time of day, maybe thirty minutes," Ricardo replied. "The new control center is in my headquarters. The equipment is there waiting for you, along with the technicians. Juan wants to get a head start."

As the driver sped east from the airport on *Av. El Dorado*, Carmen said, "I'll soon have additional sources of information available about the Americans. It could come in handy."

Ricardo made no comment.

Carmen watched the driver turn north and decided to hold any further comments until they reached their destination.

In a little less than thirty minutes, the driver slowed, and the car came to a stop alongside a modern six-story building.

The two men stepped out of the car and walked toward a set of glass doors.

Ricardo led the way past three armed guards. They walked through a spacious lobby to a bank of elevators.

One elevator was open and waiting. Both men walked inside. Ricardo pushed the button for floor six.

After the elevator door opened, they strolled down the hallway to a large office suite. Ricardo nodded to his staff, and waved Carmen to a plush lounge area adjoining his office.

Ricardo gestured toward a couple of large stuffed chairs and they each took a seat.

Carmen looked around. "Business must be booming."

Ricardo smiled. "Juan pays the bills."

"I pay a lot of the bills too," Carmen said. "And this is my homeland. Keep those things in mind." He looked directly at Ricardo. "Juan should have given me more details about your security business."

Ricardo shrugged and made a sweeping motion with one hand. "This was designed to impress the high-level clients, including the government officials."

Carmen stared at the luxurious surroundings.

Original paintings adorned the walls surrounding the floor of thick pile carpet. Tasteful marble statues, accompanied by tropical plants in expensive planters, occupied selected places in the décor.

Carmen studied Ricardo for a moment. "How well does this particular setup work for you?"

"Very well," Ricardo said. "Sometimes I'm observed in places I shouldn't normally be in." His dark brown eyes flashed. "Running a high-level security company gives me a lot of options for legitimate excuses. I now do a lot of work for the Columbian government."

Carmen nodded slowly and then looked around. "I'd like to get started. Where do I go?"

Ricardo gestured across the large room toward a hallway. "The secure area is down the hall ready for your use. The technicians are in place and all the equipment has been tested."

For a moment, Carmen studied the person sitting beside him. He felt Ricardo's eyes were like the tinted glass encompassing the building. They allowed Ricardo to see out, but no one could see in.

Ricardo stood and walked toward the hallway. He gestured for Carmen to follow.

Carmen figured Ricardo didn't have to be a warm personality. The important thing was for Ricardo to do his job. After giving a slight mental shrug, he followed Ricardo down the hall.

····

At Jacksonville International Airport, a sleek jet sat in front of a secluded private hangar.

Kevin and Butch stood beside it.

As he and Matt walked toward the two men standing in front of the jet, Ralph ran his fingers through his red hair and said, "Guess we're as ready as we'll ever be."

Matt nodded.

"Good to see you again." Kevin smiled and extended his hand. Ralph and Matt shook it in turn and followed the same process with Butch.

"We also have a private hangar at the El Dorado International Airport in Bogota," Kevin said as they boarded the plane. "We're going to use it as a control center to help us with our activities in Columbia."

Ralph nodded. "You've used it before, I assume?"

"We've had several missions over the last two years in Colombia," Kevin said. "We work with the Colombian government and get a lot of cooperation for what we're doing, mutual interests."

Ralph and Matt remained silent.

"Craig has been working with Gary Stennis, the head of an FBI special-investigations unit for domestic threats. Gary's office is in the J Edgar Hoover Building, and he's heavily involved in this whole matter." Kevin gave a slight shrug. "Anyway, due to the combined domestic and international aspects of this, a couple of FBI agents will help operate our control center in Bogota." He glanced at his watch. "They should already be there."

"Who are they?" Ralph asked.

"Ben Fulton, the SAC of the Jacksonville FBI office, and Dan Maxwell, a technology specialist who reports to Gary Stennis," Kevin said.

Ralph narrowed his eyes. "Good they'll be down there. I think we'll need all the help we can get."

Kevin nodded. "They'll be helpful in many ways, plus they'll furnish the required liaison with other necessary elements of the FBI. That will help cement our cooperation for this large-scale mission."

"The illegal drug problem is a big domestic issue," Butch said. "The FBI has been down there with us before, along with DEA agents."

"Is the DEA involved in our situation?" Ralph asked.

"Not this trip," Kevin said, "but we're staying in close touch with them."

"Is it true you have a fleet of Hummers down there?" Matt asked.

"How do you know that?" Butch asked.

"Extensive research," Matt said with a glint of humor showing in his eyes.

"We're well equipped for missions in Columbia," Kevin replied. "The illegal drug problem has been a thorn in our side for a long time. We've even done joint missions with the Colombian government."

"Are we kicking everything off immediately after we get there?" Ralph asked.

"Soon as you're ready," Kevin said. "We've built our mission around what you're going to do."

Ralph glanced at Matt. "I think we want to get started as soon as we can."

"That gets my vote," Matt said.

Kevin grinned. "No problem, we're sitting on ready."

"Who in Washington knows about this trip?" Ralph asked.

"Not many, just those with a need to know," Kevin said. "Why do you ask?"

"I'm always concerned about security." Ralph gave a slight shrug. "I kept it quiet around Tustun. Most think we're checking out the sugarcane crops in Louisiana."

"Under these circumstances, it's good you're not advertising your whereabouts," Kevin said, as they settled into their seats on the plane.

....

In Columbia, Ben Fulton and Dan Maxwell stared at a row of monitors in the hangar they occupied at Bogota's El Dorado International Airport. The control center was in full operation with an expert team of technicians, all CIA agents.

"A little better equipment than what we have back home, huh?" Ben flashed a big grin in Dan's direction.

"The CIA must have a hidden budget somewhere," Dan said.

Ben rolled his eyes, "That's the understatement of the year." He appeared thoughtful for a moment. "At least we're getting some benefit right now out of their shadow funding process." He jerked his thumb toward one of the monitors. "Look at that."

"Looks like a fortress of some kind." Dan walked over to a technician and pointed to the image on the monitor. "How're we getting that shot?"

The technician studied Dan for a moment; then, shifted his gaze to Ben who had walked up beside him. "It's classified, sir." The technician started to say something else, but before he could speak, his supervisor joined the group.

"It's okay," the supervisor said. "They have the proper clearance."

The technician looked back at Dan. "The image is sent by a Predator UAV, sir. We use a lot of them."

Dan turned toward the control center supervisor. "How many unmanned aerial vehicles have you deployed around here?"

"Five at the moment," the supervisor said, "they can fly over 100 miles per hour, and they have a range of around 450 miles."

Ben and Dan both nodded.

"Exactly what is that?" Ben gestured toward the image of the fortress again.

"Don't know," the supervisor said, "spotted it an hour ago. It's a hundred miles southwest of Bogota and we haven't seen any activity around it yet."

"It's in the jungle?" Dan gave the supervisor a quizzical look.

"Yes, a cleared spot right in the middle of some of the thickest foliage in Colombia."

"Any guesses as to what it's for?" Ben asked. He glanced again at the image and then back at the supervisor.

"I'm guessing it has something to do with drug trafficking," the supervisor said. "It's close to a spot where we've uncovered a lot of activity in the past."

"Why would anyone build a fortress?" Ben asked.

The supervisor gave a slight shrug. "Beats me, but we'll find out. We're going to keep monitoring it until we see some activity. I'll send fresh UAV's when needed. They all have infrared. We can observe at night any time we need to."

Ben and Dan thanked the supervisor and strolled around the hangar. They continued to scan the feedback from the UAVs on multiple wall monitors.

Dan glanced at Ben. "Do you still plan to double check the latest DEA reports?"

"Domestic problems are our business. And illegal drugs are one hell of a domestic problem."

"Kevin and his group should be arriving soon. How're we going to work this with Gibson and Baker?"

"We plan to use Tustun as cover to check on the illegal drug trafficking," Ben said. "I'm sure Kevin will have suggestions once he gets here." He studied Dan for a moment. "You're one of the FBI's top analysts. I think you're expected to stay in the hangar and get involved in the technology we're using. My understanding is that Kevin will set it up with his people when he arrives."

Dan looked around the hangar again. "This setup is impressive. Maybe we'll have some equipment like this stateside before too long."

"Hopefully our bosses have plans for that." Ben gave a slight shrug.

••••

Carmen scanned the files in the computer on the desk he occupied. He soon found one that sparked his interest.

While he studied the data, a soft beeping noise interrupted his thoughts.

Carmen picked up the phone connected to a secure private line and answered. He knew by the caller ID it was Juan.

"Everything set up to your satisfaction?" Juan asked.

"It should meet our needs."

"You'll be interested in some new information I just received," Juan said. "The United States Navy is lending a hand to the Americans."

"Yeah," Carmen replied. "We already know about the Hawkeye, and we know about some UAVs too."

"I assume you'll make any necessary adjustments."

"Right, I will."

"Good," Juan said, "got a little more intel too. CIA has a control center set up at the airport over there."

"El Dorado International?"

"Yeah, it looks like the Americans are kicking off a big operation," Juan said.

"Any suggestions?"

"Some, but I need to give you more information first."

"I'm listening."

"We have a new game plan. I altered some things for you a little bit. However, under the current circumstances, I don't think you and Ricardo will mind."

"What did you do?"

"I staged a meeting in Cartagena for Gibson's bunch. I think they took the bait," Juan said. "I've set up an ambush for them when they arrive for the meeting."

"Should I ask Ricardo to hold up?"

Juan hesitated for a moment. "I suggest Ricardo go ahead with his plans just in case."

"Are you going to tell him?"

"Yeah, but I thought I'd let you know first."

"Don't worry about calling Ricardo," Carmen said. "I'll give him the new information. However, you told me earlier you were leaving the assassination up to him. He might not like your interference."

"I don't think he'll mind. I prepared for Gibson not taking the bait. Now that he has, it could save Ricardo some trouble, but we'll let Ricardo make his own decision."

"Good luck on the ambush."

"I'll keep you posted. We'll need to stay closely coordinated."

"Roger," Carmen said. "I'll get back to you after I talk to Ricardo."
Juan disconnected.

Carmen didn't feel comfortable. Something was gnawing on him, something ominous. He couldn't quite put his finger on the concern, but it was there, deep inside.

••••

At the DUISONZ branch headquarters in Miami, Juan savored a puff of his cherry-blend tobacco while he mulled over his conversation with Carmen.

So, the Americans were using UAVs in addition to the Hawkeye. There were more things to consider now. He needed to tighten his coordination channels.

Juan savored a long puff from his pipe and decided to give Omar a call. He needed Omar's opinion on some more things. He punched a digit and heard Omar answer.

"What's up?" Omar asked.

"More news."

"Such as?"

"I had a conversation with Carmen. You need to come back over here, don't want to talk on the phone."

"Problems?"

"Just some potential complications, your opinion could be valuable," Juan said.

"I'll head back there as quickly as I can." Omar's voice had a hint of irritation.

"You're still in Miami, aren't you?"

"Right, but I'm doing some other things, important things."

"They probably aren't as important as the things we need to talk about."

"I'll get to a stopping point as soon as I can."

"Okay, see you when you get here." Juan gave a slight shrug and then disconnected. He didn't really care if Omar was irritated.

In less than an hour, Juan heard some familiar greetings in his outer office. He glanced up and saw Omar strolling past some of the secretaries.

When Omar walked into Juan's office, Juan motioned for him to close the door and then waved him to a chair at the round conference table with seating for four.

"Things have changed since we ended our last meeting," Juan said. "Gibson took the bait I tossed out. I got all the details from one of our most trusted contacts."

"Who?"

Juan told him and then said, "Gibson, Baker, and two CIA agents are flying down to Bogota." Juan glanced at his watch. "They should be arriving in a few more hours."

"So?"

"They'll leave Bogota later today and go to Cartagena for the meeting I set up. I'll have some men waiting for them."

"With Ricardo?"

"Maybe, maybe not."

Omar studied Juan for a moment. "I thought Ricardo was going to take care of Gibson and Baker. Won't this piss him off?"

"No, I don't think so. I don't think he has any personal attachment to knocking them off, besides, he's soon going to be taking out the CIA control center at the airport in Bogota."

Omar pulled on his left ear and didn't comment.

"You know Ricardo well," Juan said. "What's your opinion?"

"Knocking off the CIA control center is a big challenge. That should be sufficient to keep his attention focused."

"My thinking also," Juan said. "I don't think Ricardo has an equal on the planet. He needs a big challenge every now and then."

"I figured from the start that knocking off Gibson and Baker might be a bit too easy for him."

"Why didn't you say something?"

"Everyone must do some grunt work now and then. I figured, if he needed to, he would do it without complaining." Omar shrugged. "However, having some CIA agents in the group will make it more interesting."

Juan nodded. "And since I have some other men taking care of the grunt work in Cartagena, he doesn't need to get involved unless he chooses to."

"Either way, we should eliminate the Americans."

"Yes," Juan said with a twinkle in his eye. "I think they'll soon learn to quit interfering in our business down there."

Omar nodded.

"The American Navy has a Hawkeye in the airspace around Bogota," Juan said. "It came off a carrier out from Cartagena."

"A surveillance plane?"

"Yes," Juan said. "They also have some UAVs in the area."

Omar leaned toward Juan. "While I'm here, do you want my opinion on anything else?"

"Having an uninterrupted financial flow is even more important now." Juan looked directly at Omar. "Think we ought to keep using the World Bank for laundering money?"

"Yes, of course," Omar said. "Even if the American authorities get suspicious, they'll find it hard to prove anything. We have it all set up extremely well."

Juan narrowed his eyes. "Okay, I won't push for any changes on our money laundering scheme. As for Tustun, Gibson and Baker won't be around anymore to interfere. We'll only need to work with Donald Busby to control things."

"What about Brian Glascock?"

Juan shrugged. "I'm convinced he'll follow orders from Donald."

Omar nodded slowly and smiled. "I think we'll soon be able to finalize our partnership with Tustun."

Chapter 10

After slowing to 120 miles per hour and homing on one of the runways, a sleek private jet approached El Dorado International Airport in Bogota from the north.

An MH-60R Seahawk (Romeo) also approached the airport. It was a mile or so behind the jet.

Standing outside the CIA-owned hangar, Ben raised a pair of binoculars to his eyes. Late afternoon shadows stretched across the landing area, as he studied the scene. Both aircraft were silhouetted on the distant horizon.

Ben punched a digit on his secure satellite phone and had a short conversation. After disconnecting, he glanced at Dan, who had walked out to join him. "Kevin and his team are arriving along with the Navy officer we're expecting." Ben gestured toward the approaching aircraft.

"We're ready for kickoff," Dan said. "All the equipment is functioning at maximum efficiency."

The private jet touched down and taxied toward the private hangar. After the jet came to a complete stop, four men soon walked out to meet

Ben and Dan.

A minute later, the Romeo settled in an open area beside the hangar. A uniformed individual stepped down from the chopper and hurried toward the group.

Introductions were made all around.

"It's game time," Kevin said. "I hope we're all prepared for action."

Each man in the group gave a thumbs-up.

As they walked into the control center, Ben turned toward Kevin. "Bet you never figured you'd have an FBI agent running a CIA control center."

"You're the most qualified for this," Kevin said. "Besides, we're also dealing with a huge domestic threat. Illegal drug trafficking is killing us back home."

"Guess we have enough organizations involved in this operation." Ben glanced at the Navy officer. "I was informed you've been giving us some extra support."

"The USS Truman is a hundred miles from Cartagena, sitting out in the Caribbean." The Navy officer looked directly at Ben. "Right now, we have an E-2 Hawkeye overhead. Our captain though you could use the extra eyes."

Ben turned fully toward the Navy officer. "And your job is?"

"Just checking things," the officer said. "Making sure you're picking up the feed from the Hawkeye consistently." He studied the monitors for a moment. "Our captain always likes one of his direct reports to verify things firsthand."

Ben nodded and turned toward the large monitor displaying the feed from the Hawkeye. It showed a section of Cartagena in vivid detail—San Pedro Claver Square. On the wall beside the monitor were numerous close-up photos of the square. He glanced at Ralph and gestured toward the collection of images. "Is that where you're going tonight?"

"Correct," Ralph said. "We have a meeting with some high-powered cocoa bean growers. Long story short, Elsie Farmer is helping to run Tustun while I'm gone. She called when we first started our trip and informed me about some growers who had heard we were coming down here and were requesting a meeting."

After a short inspection of the control center, the Navy officer said, "Looks like you're up and running okay. Let us know if you have any problems with the Hawkeye or need more support."

Everyone nodded and after a little more conversation the Navy officer bid everyone farewell.

Ben looked at Ralph. "Exactly where is the meeting in San Pedro Claver Square?"

"Conference room at the art museum," Ralph said.

"I know the place. I've been there before." Kevin walked over to a large monitor and studied the display.

Ben glanced at Ralph. "Anything about the meeting strike you as suspicious?"

"Elsie told me the invitation came through normal business channels," Ralph said. "Before I left Tustun, I put out feelers to major growers that we wanted to discuss some potential new business."

Ben shrugged. "It's your show."

"We'll be prepared for anything," Matt said, "and we have some great security with us." He gestured toward Kevin and Butch.

"Speaking of being prepared," Kevin waved everyone going to the meeting toward a table with a large map spread across the top. The four men huddled over it and checked their routing for the meeting.

Kevin glanced at his watch. "We'll grab a bite to eat and then take the jet into Rafael Nunez International Airport in Cartagena. We'll come back here after the meeting."

"For tomorrow, are you okay having talks with more cocoa bean growers?" Ralph asked.

Kevin nodded. "We need to add to our knowledge base on who's growing the cocoa plants. We might find new leads that help us devise a way to stop the drug trafficking."

Ben looked at Matt and Ralph. "Are you carrying your usual weapons?"

"Yes," Matt said. "Glock 26, holster toward the back of my right hip."

"Same for me." Ralph turned slightly toward Ben.

Ben extended a Glock 19 with two extra magazines toward each of them. "These will give you more firepower, 15 rounds per magazine instead of 10, still 9 mm, and still fits your holster."

Ralph and Matt reached for the pistols and magazines.

"Best to stay with concealed carry," Dan said. "You guys don't want to be conspicuous on the streets anymore than you'll already be, *Gringos.*" He grinned.

Ralph and Matt each returned the grin.

Ben looked at Kevin and Butch. "What're you guys carrying?"

"Glock 17 for me," Kevin said. He jerked a thumb toward Butch. "He still uses the Heckler & Koch USP."

Ben chuckled. "Each of those pistols will have enough stopping power."

Dan narrowed his eyes and focused on Ralph. "Something bothers me about this bit in Cartagena."

"What?" Ralph asked.

"Not sure, just a general gut feeling," Dan said. "We'll keep a close eye on that area from here."

Kevin slapped Dan on the shoulder. "That's what you're here for. We'll take all the help we can get."

Dan gave Kevin a quick smile and then gestured toward the monitor showing San Pedro Claver Square. He used a laser pointer and positioned a red dot on the art museum. "I suggest you get more familiar with the area before you leave."

Everyone studied the monitor for a few minutes.

"We'll let you know right away if we see anything suspicious," Ben said. "We need to prevent any surprises."

Ralph nodded. "Good."

Dan gestured toward another monitor. "The map and all the photographs are in the system." He pressed a button, and a map appeared on the monitor. San Pedro Claver Square was in the center of the map.

"I suggest we all have a seat," Ben said. He motioned toward a large table.

After everyone was seated, Dan showed several more scenes on the monitor.

Ben studied the faces around the table. "No tall buildings. I would be concerned about the rooftops."

"We'll take all the precautions we can," Ralph said, "even back home. Elsie told me she would keep the meeting confidential at Tustun, except for letting Matt's secretary, Maria, know."

"Donald Busby and Brian Glascock don't know about it?" Ben asked.

"No," Ralph said. "Elsie assured us of that. So did Maria."

Matt looked at Ben. "The port in Cartagena is probably the offloading point for shipping illegal drugs from Columbia, right?"

"Right," Ben said. "It contributes to our big domestic problem." He stood and walked over to a small suitcase in the corner. He opened it to reveal several sets of tactical communications gear. "Here's how we'll communicate tonight. This system has the range to reach Cartagena. We're using extra boosters."

"Ralph and I will take every benefit we can get." Matt grinned.

Dan glanced at his watch. "If my gut feeling is correct, you'll need every benefit."

After a few more minutes of discussion, the four new arrivals moved back to a small kitchen and grabbed sandwiches and drinks from a refrigerator.

"Dan's gut feeling might be right," Butch said, glancing at Matt.

"Think it might be a trap?" Matt asked, as he sat and placed his Coke and sandwich on a small round table in front of him.

Butch nodded. "It's a good place for one."

"However, the request for the meeting makes logical business sense," Ralph said. "We put out a lot of feelers."

"So, you aren't suspicious?" Kevin asked.

"I wouldn't say that." Ralph said. "I'm suspicious of everything. If we get surprised, it's our own damned fault."

••••

Later that evening, Matt glanced out a window of the private jet as it touched down on a runway at Rafael Nunez International Airport in Cartagena. He felt a rush of adrenalin. He knew he was ready for any challenge they might encounter.

The jet taxied to a stop in front of a secluded hangar.

Matt glanced at Kevin. "Is this another one of your CIA assets?"

"Yes," Kevin said. "The CIA has private hangars at most major airports around the world."

The pilot stated the ground temperature was 81 degrees as the four men exited the plane. Each man wore a Hawaiian-style shirt over his pistol.

They walked toward a black Hummer. The driver waited for the four men to be seated and then sped toward downtown Cartagena.

After a short ride, the driver parked in an area close to San Pedro Claver Square. "I'll wait here," he said.

Kevin nodded and gestured for the other three men to follow. He walked toward the art museum.

Ralph glanced at Matt. "Stay alert. This is the real thing."

"I think we're ready," Matt said.

Ralph narrowed his eyes "We'll see."

In front of the old museum framed by the glow of multiple lights, Kevin gestured to Butch. "Take the lead and watch for trouble."

Butch moved through the large double doors. In a few moments, the four men stood in the doorway of the designated conference room.

Matt glanced at the six men already in the room. One was sitting. The others stood along the wall behind him. All six men wore loose tropical-style shirts.

Ralph stared at the chubby man sitting at the small round table. "Are you Benito?"

"That's my name," the chubby man said. He jerked a thumb at the men behind him. "My business associates."

Ralph greeted the men along the wall with a slight wave and, without taking his eyes off them, said, "I believe we have a scheduled meeting."

"Are you Ralph Gibson?" Benito asked.

"Yes," Ralph said. He studied Benito for a moment and stepped closer to the table.

Butch moved beside Ralph and stood to his right. Kevin and Matt moved to Ralph's left. The four Americans faced Benito and the men standing behind him.

Benito flashed a broad smile. He stared at Ralph for a moment and then gestured toward a chair across the table from him.

Ralph eased into the chair.

"You're a cocoa bean grower?" Ralph asked.

"That's why I'm here," Benito said, flashing an even bigger smile.

Out of the corner of his right eye, Matt saw Butch change his position. The way Butch moved reminded him of a jungle cat ready to pounce. Remembering the display at the firing range the other day, he felt a wave of gratitude Butch was there.

Matt studied the five men standing behind Benito. There was no doubt they were thugs, but, perhaps, more professional than he had at first thought. They all had blank expressions and seemed comfortable with the situation.

Fighting to stay calm, Matt knew they were in big danger. Benito might run a business, but the people behind him certainly weren't typical businessmen. He concentrated on the training he had completed, but this was a little different. He had a strong feeling that he would need to employ his latest skills, and soon. Thank God Butch was with them!

"How much land do you farm?" Ralph asked, looking at Benito.

"None," Benito said.

Matt tried to look relaxed and stay ready to react at the same time. He was finding that tough to do. Despite his best efforts, he was beginning to tense up. He'd had plenty of practice, but the targets would now be shooting back.

"Then how do you produce all the crops?" Ralph asked.

"I don't."

"Then why did you tell me you produced a lot of cocoa beans?" Ralph asked.

Benito furrowed his brow and gave an acid grin. "I lied."

Matt thought it was the most evil grin he had ever seen.

Ralph slowly pushed his chair back about a foot. "Then why have this meeting?"

Benito shrugged. "Maybe I just wanted to meet stupid Americans."

Ralph looked at the man across the table. "So, this isn't a regular meeting?"

"Regular for us," Benito said. He laughed. "There are some people who don't like you meddling in Colombian affairs."

"Who?"

"They don't want to be identified," Benito said. "We take care of complications for them, complications like the four of you." He continued to smile. "Thanks for coming and goodbye."

Benito moved his hand toward his belt. The thugs behind him did the same.

Matt's heart pounded as he reached for his Glock 19. There was no way to practice for a real-life situation. His appreciation for actual battle experience immediately went up a notch.

Before any of the six men could raise their weapons, Butch had his Heckler & Koch USP pointed in their direction. He waved it back and forth at each of their heads. "I wouldn't do that if I were you."

One of the thugs continued and immediately dropped to the floor when Butch fired.

"Drop your pistols to the floor and then freeze or die." Butch extended his pistol forward.

Matt, Kevin, and Ralph also had their pistols pointed at the thugs.

Benito gasped loudly as he dropped his Walther PPK pistol on the table and raised his hands high.

The four remaining thugs behind Benito all dropped their pistols and raised their hands.

Butch moved toward the standing mobsters with the quickness of a big cat on the hunt and herded them over to the side.

"All of you standing get on the floor, belly down," Butch said.

Kevin collected the discarded pistols on the floor and put them in a pile on the table.

"You bastards, we'll get even," Benito muttered. "You won't get away with this."

Kevin placed the barrel of his Glock against Benito's head. "I'm just going to ask once. Who's your boss?"

"He calls himself Panther. That's all I know. I swear."

Matt noted Benito started to sweat profusely.

"Where does he live?" Kevin asked.

"Don't know."

Kevin pressed the barrel of his pistol harder against Benito's temple.

"I don't know. I swear it. I don't know!"

Kevin glanced at Butch. "We'll let the professional interrogators take it from here."

"No argument from me," Butch said.

Kevin seemed to have another thought. He turned toward Ralph and Matt, who were standing by his side. "You guys want to ask any questions?"

Ralph gestured to Matt.

Matt looked directly at Benito. "Ever hear of Jack Worthington?"

"No, never," Benito mumbled as he shook his head vigorously.

Matt could tell Benito was lying, but after repeated questions, he couldn't get anything out of him. However, Matt had noticed a flash of recognition from the other thugs whenever he mentioned Jack's name. He turned toward Kevin. "Okay, shoot them all. They don't want to give us any information."

Kevin pointed his Glock 17 at a mobster on the floor who had his head turned toward him.

The mobster blurted out, "Jack Worthington was down here a lot asking a lot of questions. He wanted to buy a lot of land, and he wanted a good deal."

"Who came with him?" Ralph asked.

"A large group always came. Benito is the only one I know."

"Were there any women in any of the groups?" Matt asked.

"Always one, sometimes two," the mobster said.

"Did you catch their names?" Matt asked.

"One was called Catalina. That's all I know."

After some more questioning yielded no further information, Ralph glanced at Matt and the two CIA agents, "Guess we can wrap up here."

Kevin nodded and spoke into his tactical mike, "Tell our local agents to send a cleanup team to the art museum. We'll wait until they arrive." He gave Ben a full report.

After finishing his conversation, Kevin turned toward Matt and Ralph. "I made sure our local assets were standing by. I wanted help to be close at hand if we needed it."

Butch left for a few moments and then came back into the conference room. "Everything looks all clear at the moment outside."

"Ben reported the same thing," Kevin said. "The Hawkeye is scanning the buildings around us. No threats are obvious."

Matt glanced at Ralph. "We can add this to our list of business meetings that didn't go so well." He grinned.

"You can say that again." Ralph returned the grin just as eight men carrying MP5 rifles rushed into the conference room.

"We'll take it from here," the leader said to Kevin.

Kevin nodded. "It's all yours."

Ralph looked at Matt. "Too bad we didn't have a real discussion with Benito. I was hoping to get a lot of clues about who killed Jack."

"At least we got some," Matt said. "Apparently someone named Panther is some type of boss down here, a woman involved in this is named Catalina, Benito is part of the picture down here, and Jack apparently visited a lot to try to make some deals."

"I'll pass that on to the interrogation team," Kevin said. "They'll work at trying to squeeze out some more useful information." After he spoke to the leader of the eight CIA agents who had rushed in, he turned toward the doorway and motioned the other three to follow.

Chapter 11

At CIA headquarters in McLean, the night duty officer received an urgent call from a support group at NSA.

The agent from NSA said, "We believe some of your assets are about to be ambushed."

"Based on what?"

"Ten minutes ago, we intercepted a call from southern Florida to a location in northern Florida. The exact location of the originating call has not been determined, but we know it was from the general area around Miami."

"Where did the call go to in northern Florida?"

"It went to the general area of Jacksonville. The call was on a secure line, so we couldn't get the entire conversation. We were able to decrypt parts of it, however."

"Go on," responded the CIA duty officer.

"Based on your earlier request to monitor calls from Miami, and using the fact sheet you supplied us, we were able to determine your party including Kevin Brown is targeted for an ambush."

"By whom?"

"Not determined, as yet."

"When and where?"

"Tonight, mention was made of San Pedro Claver Square."

"Any other information?"

"Nothing more."

"Thanks for the tip, I'll alert our team now."

The CIA duty officer consulted his extensive, but well organized, instructions for handling various crises. He had a lot of new information.

In a few seconds, after a quick check of some personnel data, he picked up his phone and dialed the secure landline for Craig Parker, head of a special investigation unit for terrorist threats.

"Mr. Parker, I'm sorry to disturb you after hours, but I have an emergency situation that concerns some of your agents."

"What's the emergency?" Craig asked.

"Kevin Brown and his party in Colombia are going to run into an ambush."

"When and where?"

"Sometime tonight, don't know when. San Pedro Claver Square was mentioned. That's in Cartagena, Colombia."

"I know that. Who's behind the ambush?"

"Undetermined. There was a phone call from the vicinity of Miami to a location in Jacksonville."

"When was the call placed?"

"Several hours ago, but the information was just partially decrypted fifteen minutes ago, sir."

"Any information on weapons?"

"No, sir."

"Any other details?"

"Some names mentioned were Kevin Brown, Matt Baker, and Ralph Gibson. NSA is still working on decrypting the whole recorded conversation."

"Let me know as soon as you get more facts."

"Yes sir."

"Thanks." Craig disconnected.

••••

Craig looked at his watch and did a quick time zone calculation. Realizing that seconds could matter, he grabbed his secure satellite phone and punched in a number.

"Come on! Pick up!" Craig muttered.

He listened to the second ring and hoped that he hadn't received the information too late for it to do any good.

Kevin answered.

"Where are you?" Craig asked, knowing that Kevin would know it was him because of the caller ID feature they had on each of their tactical phones.

"We're about to leave the art museum in Cartagena."

"Are you still inside?"

Yes," Kevin said. "We just had a skirmish in here. No problems for us. Local assets are mopping up."

"What kind of skirmish?"

Kevin gave him the details.

"Might not be the ambush I'm worried about."

"What do you mean?" Kevin asked.

Craig explained.

"Might be something else all right," Kevin said.

"They could be waiting outside for you."

"Ben's getting a direct transmission from a Hawkeye overhead. He'll inform us if any danger is spotted."

"Hawkeyes have infrared, don't they?"

"This one does for sure."

"All of the buildings have flat tops around there, if I remember right."

"That's correct," Kevin said. "The Hawkeye should spot anyone on a roof."

"What if they're down a story or two?"

"Don't think any of the buildings have many floors. Three stories, maybe four at the most."

"I don't like it," Craig said.

"Me either."

"And I'm not sure the skirmish you've finished would be described as an ambush."

"No argument with that."

"So, it looks like you could have another problem in the making."

"I'll give Ben a call and ask him to check things again," Kevin said.

"Tell him to check everything damned well."

"Roger."

"Those bastards down there might be smart," Craig said.

"I'm proceeding on that basis."

Craig hesitated for a moment. "And remember, San Pedro Claver Square was mentioned in the intercepted conversation."

"Got it," Kevin said. "We're ready to leave. I'll check with Ben before we walk outside."

"Keep me posted," Craig said.

"I will."

After Craig heard Kevin disconnect, he sat on the edge of his bed and thought more about the situation. The anxiety was a little too much to go back to sleep anytime soon.

He glanced again at his watch and then decided to call his counterpart, Gary Stennis, over at the FBI. They had each other's home phone number for this exact type of situation.

Craig punched in a number on the phone he still held in his hand. He heard Gary answer almost immediately.

"I was about ready to call you," Gary said.

"About the ambush?"

"Yeah, Ben alerted me. He had just heard from Kevin."

"So, you have all the details?"

"Damned right," Gary said. "Those bastards we're facing seem to be well organized."

"The intercepted call was from Miami to Jacksonville. Do you think this has some connection to the murder of Jack Worthington?"

"I'm convinced that's part of the picture," Gary said, "and I have some new information." He went on to explain.

••••

In the CIA hanger at the airport in Bogota, Ben heard Kevin's voice in his tactical communications earpiece.

"Found any problems for us yet?" Kevin asked.

"No," Ben said. "How do things look from your perspective?"

"Everything looks okay, but I don't want to take any chances."

"I'll inform you the second we spot anything significant."

"Thanks. I'll let you get back to work." Kevin disconnected.

Ben stared at a large monitor and glanced at one of the technical experts. "How long ago were these pictures taken?"

"Ten seconds ago, sir."

"Is the Hawkeye still over San Pedro Claver Square?" Ben asked.

"Yes sir. It's circling the area," an assistant said.

Ben looked at several of his technical experts. "Any suggestions?"

After seeing each one shake his head, Ben turned toward Dan. "If assassins are there, we should have some way to find them. Don't you think?"

"The infrared devices can penetrate several floors down," Dan said. "We're getting some readings, but it's impossible to tell if any images represent assassins."

"Anyone on the rooftops yet?" Ben asked.

"No."

Ben stood and started to pace. He didn't want to overlook anything. After a few moments, he stopped and glanced back at Dan. "How far out from the museum are we checking?"

"One quarter mile, lots of readings, but no one on rooftops."

Ben rubbed his chin, a habit he had picked up when he was thinking hard. He looked at the technical experts in the control center. "I want a map of the area where the Hummer is parked, and I want photos of all the buildings around it."

"I suggest we select places we think are best for an ambush."

"In process," Ben said as he checked his watch and turned fully toward Dan. "Know anything about the drug business in Cartagena?"

"Quite a bit, that's another reason I'm here." Dan narrowed his eyes. "I didn't want to give you a long story earlier. What do you want to know?"

Ben pointed to the map he had just received from the technical experts. "Here's where our Hummer is parked. Do you know if there's any significant drug activity in this area?"

Dan studied the map for a moment. "Several drug kingpins used to operate out of this general location. He looked at Ben. "If I were conducting an ambush, I would be in one particular place."

"Where's that?" Ben asked.

Dan pointed to a spot on the map. "On top of a building right here."

"Why?" Ben asked.

"Best field of fire, best cover too."

Ben rubbed his chin and stared at the map for a moment. He glanced at Dan. "And no one is on top of the building now?"

"Not yet," Dan said. "At least the Hawkeye hasn't picked up anyone."

"Something odd about this," Ben said. "If they're going to ambush our guys from that building, they should already be up there."

Dan shrugged. "Maybe they're somewhere else. But on top of that building is where I would be."

"I agree," Ben said. "I'll move the Hummer and give Kevin a heads up." He reached for his secure satellite phone.

••••

In Cartagena, Kevin stood just inside the front doors to the museum as he heard Ben's voice boom over his tactical communications unit. He listened for a few moments and then asked, "And you're sure there's no one on the roof of the building close to the Hummer?"

"Nobody at the moment," Ben said, "but I'm moving the Hummer as a precaution. It's coming your way. If it's okay with you, the driver will pick you up in front of the museum."

"We'll be ready," Kevin said. He looked at Ralph. "Are you still hoping to start some real business meetings tomorrow?"

Ralph nodded. "That's my plan if the villains around here allow it."

Matt noted the cleanup-team had completed their job. Two men had put the dead body in a bag and were carrying it toward the front doors. Two other men were escorting the other five thugs outside.

Kevin waited about a minute and waved the other three in his group forward.

When they walked out the front of the museum, Matt saw three black Hummers pull away. As the cleanup-team was leaving, he scanned the area. No other people were visible.

"I have a bad feeling." Butch glanced at Kevin. "I'll look around some more." He quickly disappeared into some nearby shadows.

After the three of them took cover, Matt scanned the area again, nothing. He glanced at Kevin just as Ralph poked him in the side.

"Over there." Ralph pointed down the street.

A figure was slowly moving toward them.

Even though the figure was about a hundred yards away, Matt could tell it wasn't Butch.

Matt saw more figures behind the first one. They were mostly staying in the shadows and coming closer.

Kevin drew his Glock and pointed it toward the oncoming figures. More appeared.

In less than two seconds, Matt and Ralph also had their Glocks pointed toward the approaching figures.

"Let them get a little closer," Kevin said, "Wait for me to shoot first and then let go with everything you've got."

Matt stood ready to fire. He wondered what Butch was doing.

••••

In the CIA control center in Bogota, Ben pointed to one of the monitors.

The CIA private jet was in flames at the Rafael Nunez International Airport in Cartagena.

"What the hell just happened?" Ben asked.

"Don't know, sir," one of the technicians answered. "We had one of our monitors dedicated to the jet. I saw nothing unusual."

"Any communication with the pilots?" Ben asked.

"No sir." The technician said. "No response."

"Damn," Ben said. He keyed his tactical communications unit. "Your jet just blew up at the airport. No contact with the pilots."

"What happened?" Kevin asked.

"Unknown at the moment," Ben said. "We're continuing to monitor the area. The Hawkeye had them under surveillance the whole time."

"You didn't see anything?"

"Not until the explosion."

"How bad is it?"

"Real bad, the whole plane is engulfed."

"And no communication with the pilots?"

"None. I'm guessing the worst."

"Damned."

"My feeling too," Ben said.

"We're standing outside the museum—"

"Are you there? What's happening?" Ben heard gunfire.

No answer.

Ben fought back panic. He didn't currently have a good image from the Hawkeye. He looked around the control room and shouted, "Kevin's team is under attack."

"I'm here." Kevin's voice boomed over Ben's earpiece.

"What the hell is going on?" Ben asked.

"Had some incoming fire."

"Any casualties?" Ben asked, noting concerned faces around the room.

"Yeah, but none of us," Kevin said. "We took down five of the six attackers. Butch is chasing the other one. Any new intel?"

"Not at the moment, use your best judgment," Ben said.

"I'll get back to you as soon as Butch finishes his current task."

"Roger."

Ben looked at Dan and asked, "Anything new on the jet explosion?"

"No," Dan said. "Whoever did it was damned good. We've reviewed the recorded video, not a trace of anyone around the plane."

"Missile?"

"Possibly," Dan said. "We should know more in a few minutes."

••••

In Cartagena, Butch decided to capture the fleeing assassin and try to get some information. He closed on the fleeing man and made a running leap, he targeted the backs of the assassin's legs, just below the knees.

The assassin, seeming to sense Butch's movement at the last second, dipped down and to his left.

Butch delivered a glancing blow to the assassin's back with both feet.

After being deflected, Butch landed in an awkward position but bounced back upright without any delay.

The assassin went down, but not hard. He recovered fast and went on the offensive. He charged toward Butch and lashed out with the heel of his right foot towards Butch's left hip.

Butch avoided contact by rapidly sliding to his left. The assassin's foot flew by inches in front of him.

Another martial arts guy, Butch thought. He dropped into a combat fighting stance and prepared for another attack.

"What's this all about?" Butch asked. He didn't expect an answer, but he thought it wouldn't hurt to see if the assassin said anything that could end up being of value.

The assassin remained silent and reached for something inside his belt. A pistol appeared in his right hand and was rapidly being moved into firing position.

Butch snapped his right elbow leftward full force into the assassin's right temple.

The assassin collapsed immediately, not getting off a shot. The pistol clanged on the pavement.

Butch saw Kevin, Ralph, and Matt run up.

"Looks like you won," Ralph said.

Despite the circumstances, Butch gave a quick smile. "I always do." He looked at Kevin. "What do you want to do with him?"

"Some of the local assets are collecting the dead bodies behind us as we speak. They'll be over here in a few more minutes. Our plane has been blown up."

"Do Ben and Dan know how that happened?" Butch asked.

"They're still investigating," Kevin said. "We'll leave in the Hummer as soon as the local security gets here."

....

In Bogota, Carmen watched Ricardo enter the office they were using as a control center.

"You're back. Change your mind?" Carmen asked.

"There's no big rush," Ricardo said. "I can be at the airport in less than thirty minutes and eliminate the CIA control center fast. I wanted to check the latest intelligence. Did they get Gibson and his group in Cartagena?"

Carmen kept his gaze on Ricardo. "I haven't heard. I'll check." He reached for his secure satellite phone.

Ricardo settled into a chair. "Thought you were watching things?"

Carmen punched in a number. "We don't have any surveillance equipment in this office for Cartagena. We're only focused on the airport here." He heard Juan pick up.

"Do you have a status report on Cartagena?" Carmen asked.

"I was ready to call you," Juan said. "Most of it is a disaster."

"What happened?" Carmen saw Ricardo lift an eyebrow.

"Most in the first group were captured. The second group also failed, might all be dead," Juan replied. "Moles don't have any additional info yet."

Carmen noted Ricardo was leaning forward.

"Details are sketchy," Juan said. "I had one man hanging back to watch what was going on. He reported American agents arrived and escorted five of the original group in the museum out in handcuffs. The other left in a body bag. My lookout isn't sure about the last group. He thinks they might all be dead."

"How many were in the second group?" Carmen asked.

"Six also."

"Ricardo's in here with me," Carmen said. "I want to give him all the details. Can you hold?"

"Let me talk to him."

"Juan wants to talk to you," Carmen said. He handed the phone to Ricardo.

Ricardo took the phone. "I'm here." He listened for a minute and then handed the phone back to Carmen.

"I'm back," Carmen said.

"Ricardo knows everything you know plus a couple of additional items," Juan said.

"Oh?"

"We blew up the jet that Gibson and his group flew to Cartagena." Juan gave a thin laugh. "At least we made sure they wouldn't be flying back in it."

"So, Cartagena wasn't a complete disaster for us after all?"

"At least we salvaged something."

"Do you think Gibson and his group will be coming back down here right away?"

"I'm sure of it," Juan said.

"How are they traveling?"

"I just got a report from one of our moles. CIA agents there are using one of their Hummers to drive them back to Bogota."

Carmen remained silent for a few moments and waited for Juan to continue.

After Juan didn't say anything, Carmen asked, "What's the other item you mentioned?"

"I've set up another ambush."

"For the Hummer?"

"Yeah." Juan gave that thin laugh again. "The bastards will get what's coming to them one way or the other."

"Where?"

"I'm blocking the road they're on; roadblock's just north of Medellin."

"How do you know they're going that way?"

"The logical choice, it's the shortest route and it's the best road."

Carmen remained silent.

"I have some lookouts along the way," Juan said. "I'll know as soon as the Americans are spotted."

"How do you plan to take them out?"

"A group with AK-74 rifles will greet them when they stop for the roadblock. The AK-74 has a higher muzzle velocity and a higher rate of fire than the older AK-47's," Juan said.

"Why not use a rocket launcher and demolish the Hummer?"

"Not available on short notice, concentrated fire from the AK-74's should work okay."

Carmen hesitated for a moment. "What about their control center at the airport here in Bogota?"

"What about it?"

"Still want Ricardo to take it out?"

"I've given Ricardo a change in plans," Juan said. "Under the circumstances, I thought I needed to take over. He can fill you in."

"Anything else?" Carmen asked with a touch of irritation.

"That's all for now. I'll keep you posted."

Carmen heard Juan disconnect. After putting his phone down, he looked toward Ricardo. "What are your new orders?"

Chapter 12

While traveling south from Cartagena, Kevin brought everyone up to date on what Craig had just told him about another ambush. He instructed the driver to pull the Hummer over to the side of the road and stop.

"Guess Panther, whoever he is, remains determined to get rid of us." Matt looked at Ralph. "I think we've stirred up a bigger hornets' nest than we expected."

Kevin spoke into his tactical communications unit.

"What's up?" Ben asked.

"Craig informed me about another ambush. Can you position the Hawkeye over Medellin and look for any signs of trouble along our route?"

"We have a full moon tonight, so we won't have to depend entirely on the infrared. Hold on for a moment."

After a few seconds, Ben said, "The Hawkeye is in range and scouring the main route, the one you're on. If anyone has an ambush set up, we should be able to spot it. Hold on while I check." There was a brief silence. "The Hawkeye spotted your Hummer. We have the exact position.

There's a roadblock a mile south of you just outside Medellin."

"Roger," Kevin said, "anything else?"

"The Hawkeye will continue to scan the area around the roadblock. I'll keep you posted."

"Roger, I'm going to get a helicopter for us."

Kevin grabbed his secure satellite phone and punched in a number. Once he disconnected from his call, he glanced around at his group. "We're getting a chopper. It's flying out of Medellin, should be here in fifteen minutes."

"Where will it land?" Ralph asked.

"It won't," Kevin said. "It's going to hover and drop a rope ladder." He focused on the driver. "You stay with the Hummer. As soon as we take off, drive it back to Cartagena."

The driver gave a thumbs-up.

A faint sound of rotors grew in volume. The chopper soon hovered about thirty feet off the ground, ten yards from the Hummer.

Kevin gave a wave to the driver of the Hummer, and his group of four ran for the nylon ladder dangling from the helicopter.

The four men kept their heads down and coped with the wash from the rotor as they scrambled into the chopper.

After they buckled up, the helicopter ascended.

There were enough seats for all of them, with one extra. The pilot appeared to be a no-nonsense guy who wasted no time. He pointed to four pairs of binoculars, four thin bulletproof vests, and four SIG 556 rifles (with attached sound suppressors) stacked on and around the spare seat.

"Good job." Kevin looked at Ralph and Matt. "The SIG 556 uses NATO 5.56mm rounds and can fire 900 rounds per minute. It weighs 7.8 pounds and is a little over a yard long, 37 inches to be exact. You can see it has two pistol grips."

Ralph and Matt each nodded.

Kevin kept one of each item and passed the others along.

"Take us up the highway," Kevin said to the pilot. "We'll find those bastards. They have a fight on their hands."

Butch glanced at Kevin and raised his binoculars. "I'll take the right side of the road you take the left."

They flew at an altitude of about 500 feet, making it easy, with binoculars, to spot figures on the ground and not being so low as to attract unwanted attention.

Matt glanced at Kevin. "We probably should concentrate on the big curve in the road. I'm guessing that's where they'll be. It's the logical place."

Kevin peered through his binoculars at the suggested location. "Good call. I see several dim lights moving, probably flashlights."

"I think we can sit down in a clearing ahead that's highlighted by the full moon. It looks like a big parking area of some kind." Butch pointed. "It's about a half mile past them." He looked at Kevin.

Kevin gave a thumbs-up and looked at the pilot. "You got it?"

"Yes sir."

Butch slapped a fresh magazine into his SIG 556. "Ralph, you and Matt hang back. Kevin and I will handle the situation. We're experts with these rifles and it's our job. You haven't trained with them, but I'm sure you can handle them if you need to. We want you to have some extra firepower if you need it."

"Bullshit, no one is going to prevent Matt and me from getting those bastards." Ralph looked at Kevin. "From the intercepted phone calls, we know Matt and I are the main targets. We'll both be safer in the future if we eliminate this group of assassins. Besides, I've fired this rifle before."

Matt nodded. "I agree. Ralph and I are the main targets. We're in the game too." He glanced at his rifle. "Give me about thirty seconds of instruction and I'm good to go."

"You're not agents with our training. I would be negligent to involve you directly at this point," Kevin said.

"Remember we've had a lot of training and, besides, we've already had a damned lot of action," Ralph said, "and don't forget, we're also in great physical condition."

Matt looked at Kevin. "That's right. We don't want to stay behind at the chopper."

After glancing at Butch, Kevin looked back at Ralph and nodded.

"Okay, you have a point. You're both in."

Kevin gave the details of his plan as the helicopter landed. Ralph noted the pilot also had a SIG 556 to defend himself if he needed to.

Glancing at the pilot, Kevin said, "Keep the blade rotating, we might need to get out of here in a hurry."

The pilot nodded as everyone activated their tactical communications gear.

Kevin and his group of four vacated the helicopter.

Matt noted the vegetation was somewhat sparse for a jungle area, but there would be ample cover. There were rocks and shrubs scattered among some large trees outside the cleared area where the helicopter landed.

"Fan out in a horizontal line," Kevin said, "five yards apart, so we can still see each other. Let's move fast and close on them from behind. Matt, you and Ralph are on the ends. Butch and I are in the middle. Follow my signals."

Weapons ready, they moved forward at a steady pace.

"They'll certainly have automatic weapons, be extra cautious," Butch said. "Get low and be ready to drop to the ground fast."

A burst of automatic fire followed almost immediately. The foursome dropped to the ground.

"Check in," Kevin said into his tactical mouthpiece.

Three voices responded.

"Anyone hit?" Kevin asked.

Each reported no injuries.

Kevin whispered, "Ralph, you and Matt were on the ends where the shots started. How did you avoid being hit?"

"The bullet-proof vest helped," Ralph replied. "I took a couple of glancing hits on it, works like a charm."

"Same here," Matt whispered. "I see some of them, two behind a small boulder to our right. I have a good shot at one to the far right."

"Okay. I've got a good bead on one further left," Kevin said. "Butch and Ralph hold tight. Matt, let's coordinate our fire."

"Roger."

"Fire on the count of three. One, two," Kevin said.

Two distinctive pops ensued on 'three'.

Both targets jerked and slumped over. Their weapons clattered down the side of the rock they were on.

Kevin whispered into his mike, "Nice shooting, Matt. You performed like a pro."

"Hard to miss with a SIG 556 at this range when you have a full moon for improved visibility," Matt said.

Kevin rose into a low crouch and waved the other three forward.

Within a few seconds, Kevin asked, "Did you hear that voice?"

"Negative," Butch said.

Ralph and Matt also replied they heard nothing.

"Ah, I see some type of equipment, probably a communications unit, at the foot of the boulder ahead not far from me. That's how I heard it. Someone's checking," Kevin said. "Watch out for more assassins."

"The leader is probably checking with his outpost," Matt said.

Butch spoke into his mike, "Some more might be close. Stay on your toes."

While staying about five yards apart, they all converged on the boulder the first two assassins had been behind.

As they reached the boulder they dropped to the ground and crawled the last few yards to the top. Matt could see the original two ambushers on the ground on the other side. Each was obviously dead.

Matt scanned the area and saw three figures approaching from the north about 30 yards away. "We're getting more company."

"Stay still and let them get within about 10 yards," Kevin replied. "I don't want to let any get away."

"They stopped about twenty yards down the hill from us," Matt said. "The visibility is good. I see three heads showing above the top of a boulder."

"Butch you take the one on the end to our left. I'll take the one on the end to our right. Matt, you take the one in the middle. Ralph, be prepared to shoot anyone we miss. Everyone, stay ready to fire and let's get a little closer." Kevin crawled forward.

Continuing to crawl forward, Matt eased to within ten yards of where he had seen the three assassins peeping over the top of the boulder. Taking a calculated risk, he rose into a kneeling position.

Matt saw three rifle barrels rise over the top of the boulder. The barrels were followed by the assassin's head. Matt aimed and fired at the one in the middle. He saw the head jolt backwards. The metal rifle barrel clanked on the stone.

The other two heads also jerked backwards, and their rifles nosily slid down the boulder they were behind.

"We got them," Butch said. Keeping his SIG 556 ready for action, he stood and ran toward the boulder the assassins had fallen behind.

Matt also stood and ran. He lagged a few yards behind Butch. Kevin and Ralph followed close behind.

"They're all dead." Butch carefully scanned the area and glanced up at Matt. "You got the one in the middle right between the eyes."

"I've had plenty of practice with a pistol for that. It was easier with a rifle," Matt said.

Everyone stayed alert and continued to scan the area. Kevin removed his secure satellite phone from a pocket and called Ben.

In a few seconds he glanced at the men around him. "Ben tells me the Hawkeye is zeroed in on us and, by using infrared, has verified there are only nine bodies in the area. That means the four of us and the five dead assassins are the only ones around."

"It's good the dead bodies continue to give off heat for a while," Matt said.

Kevin told Ben they would get back in the chopper and go directly to the control center. He asked Ben to alert the local group of CIA agents in Medellin to take care of the cleanup.

They checked all five dead assassins for ID (there was none) and then walked back toward the helicopter.

"I might be a little sore tomorrow," Ralph said. "I haven't practiced the low crawl in my workouts."

Matt grinned. "I'm a little lax on that myself."

"You guys did really well," Kevin said, "especially under the circumstances."

"We have a lot of unfinished business. Someone is putting a lot of effort into eliminating us." Matt hesitated for a moment. "We need to find out who Panther is, and fast."

After notifying the pilot they were returning, they approached the helicopter.

••••

On the way to Bogota, Ralph leaned toward Matt and spoke just loud enough to be heard over the helicopter noise. "There seems to be a lot more international involvement in Jacks' death than I thought. This whole situation has become a lot more intense than I expected."

"I think being down here with the FBI and CIA gives us the best chance to put all the pieces of the puzzle together," Matt replied. "The training we completed is paying dividends. I think we're doing the right things and we're probably going to pick up some valuable information before it's all over, like we planned."

"Yeah, if we stay alive," Ralph said.

"Seeing things firsthand down here gives us a better chance to solve the mystery of Jack's murder," Matt replied. "Most likely, we'll recognize the significance of certain things better than anyone else. This might also help us put all the pieces together on the business side."

Ralph nodded. "You're probably right."

"Speaking of putting all the pieces together, when was the last time you talked to anyone in Jacksonville?" Matt asked.

"I'm confident Elsie's looking after things," Ralph said. "She assured me she would contact me if any issues came up. If she and Maria need any more security, she knows to call Justin. I'm sure Justin will try to get in touch with me immediately if he hears anything from Elsie or Maria."

"There's no telling what Donald and Brian are up to. I'm not sure Elsie can keep up with them."

"Elsie will watch them like a hawk. I asked Maria to do that too. I have a lot of confidence in both." Ralph punched Matt are the shoulder. "Let's see if we can find out who in the hell Panther is and what he's up to."

••••

In the CIA control center at El Dorado International Airport in Bogota, Ben continued to study the main row of monitors. In a few moments, he glanced at Dan. "What's the latest from the Hawkeye?"

"First Hummer's heading back north toward Cartagena," Dan said. "Three other Hummers went to the ambush site from Medellin. Cleanup-team is on the job."

Ben narrowed his eyes. "Where's the helicopter?"

"Ten minutes out," Dan said.

Ben walked over to the technicians. "Anything new from the UAVs?"

A technician shook his head. "No activity around the fortress we spotted earlier."

Ben walked closer to Dan. "There's something suspicious about that."

"About no activity around the fortress?"

Ben nodded.

"Think they know we're watching it?"

"I'm sure they suspect we're watching." Ben stared at Dan. "Any further thoughts about why they built something like that?"

Dan shook his head. "Still can't think of any logical reason."

Ben massaged the back of his neck as he glanced at one of the monitors. "Chopper's coming in."

Ben and Dan charged for the door and waited in front of the hangar while the helicopter settled on the tarmac and the passengers got out.

"You guys had a bit of action," Ben said, as the foursome approached him.

The helicopter quickly lifted off and flew in the direction of Medellin.

Kevin nodded. "A bit more than we expected."

"A hell of a lot more in my opinion," Ralph said.

"I suspect the bastards we encountered got a lot more action than they expected too." Butch grinned.

Matt also grinned and punched Butch on the shoulder.

Ben waved the group inside.

"You guys hungry?" Dan asked.

"Damned right," Ralph said, as everyone else nodded.

"Fridge is stocked," Ben said. "Help yourself. When you're finished, join us in the control room. We'll compare notes and review our plan of action."

The four men nodded as they walked toward the kitchen area.

After relaxing for a moment and digging into roast beef sandwiches, Ralph glanced at Matt. "It was obvious from the start we might be dealing with some vicious people. I just didn't know how vicious and how large the scope was."

"You guys are really good, by the way." Kevin looked at Ralph and Matt. "You've certainly upheld your end of things."

"Damned good shooting from you guys," Butch said.

"Either of you feel like you're in over your head?" Kevin asked.

"I've acquired the right mindset now," Matt said. "I feel relatively comfortable."

Ralph nodded. "Ditto, I now have more confidence. Matt and I know we can both rise to the occasion when we need to."

"We're all being targeted," Kevin said. "We have a leak somewhere. Someone is giving out inside information on what we're doing down here and where we're going to be."

Ralph turned and looked directly at Matt. "Got it figured out yet?"

"I'm sure we all have one obvious conclusion in mind," Matt said, as the four men stood and walked toward the control room.

Chapter 13

Just outside of Bogota, Carmen reacted to the ringing sound on his secure satellite phone in his makeshift control center. He checked his watch. It was almost 10:00 PM. The caller ID showed that it was Juan. Carmen picked up the phone.

"What's up?" Carmen asked.

"Ricardo still there?"

"He left over an hour ago," Carmen said. "As planned, he's heading for the airport."

"Good, I suspect Gibson and his group have returned there."

Carmen listened to Juan's explanation of the latest events and then said, "Damned, we haven't had much luck so far."

"Our luck will change. Ricardo will come through for us. He always has."

"This group with Gibson seems to be pretty good.'

"Shouldn't be any problem for Ricardo, he doesn't have an equal on the planet."

Carmen remained silent.

"Ricardo will take care of the immediate problem," Juan said. "Then, I think we should step up the activity at the fortress."

"Anything you want me to do?"

"I thought while you were over there you could take care of some family business. You, Omar, and I are equal partners, after all."

"What do you have in mind?"

"There's a big shipment of cocaine tomorrow morning from one of the cartels, one in Medellin," Juan said. "They're getting too pushy, demanding too big of a cut. We can't tolerate that. I want to knock them off."

Carmen hesitated. "You don't expect me to do that, do you?"

"Not personally, Ricardo will take care of it." Juan chuckled. "I want you to set up the hit and then continue to operate the control center. Monitor things until we've taken care of the matter."

Carmen took a deep breath and exhaled. "Okay, I can do that."

"Ricardo at the airport yet?" Juan asked.

Carmen glanced at one of the monitors. "About five minutes away."

"So, he's wearing the tracking device."

"He didn't want me calling and asking questions at critical times; so, he agreed to wear it."

"I hope he also has the tactical communications gear on."

"Yes," Carmen said. "It's for him to talk to me, or for me to alert him to some critical new situation he needs to know about."

Juan chuckled. "Sounds like Ricardo. He doesn't want to be answering questions about where he is or other mundane stuff like that."

"We had that conversation when we first devised our strategy," Carmen said.

"Keep me posted."

"Will do."

Carmen heard Juan disconnect and he leaned back and took another deep breath, exhaling slowly. He hoped Juan was right about Ricardo being the best. Gibson and his group needed to be eliminated and the sooner the better.

••••

Along with Ralph, Kevin, and Butch, Matt walked into the control room from the kitchen area. Matt noted Ben and Dan were both staring at a large monitor on the wall.

"Anything happening at the fortress?" Kevin asked.

"No." Ben turned and looked at Kevin. "There's been nothing going on there since we've been watching it."

"Are the UAVs still in the air?" Butch asked.

Ben nodded. "We have a couple of new ones up there now, equipped with infrared. The Hawkeye's back in the area too."

"The fortress was obviously designed for warehouse operations." Matt gestured toward a monitor showing a side view. "Even has a large door for the trucks to go in and out on the first level."

"This place was mentioned in some of Jack Worthington's notes," Ben said. "Somebody needs get inside and check it out."

Matt nodded. "My opinion also."

Ben started to comment but was interrupted by a slim dark-complexioned figure.

"Move and you're dead." Ricardo, hidden from the technicians by a row of filing cabinets, glared at the six men standing by the monitors. "If you don't do as you're told, you won't remain in this world."

"How did you get in here?" Kevin asked.

"It's easy when you know how." Ricardo grinned and trained his silenced 9mm Heckler & Koch USP at Butch's head. "Reilly you keep standing. Everyone else get flat on the floor."

Kevin, after dropping to the floor, looked at Ricardo. "Who are you?"

"He goes by the name Ricardo. We've met before." Butch showed no expression.

"I'm somebody you don't want to mess with." Ricardo kept his pistol pointed at Butch's head. "And you, mister badass, don't try anything. I'm an expert at dealing with your type."

Butch remained silent as the other five lay flat on the floor.

"You think you're good, but I know better." Ricardo looked directly at Butch and sneered.

Butch didn't comment.

"Now put your hands straight up. Stretch those arms." Ricardo held his pistol steady, still aimed at Butch's head.

Matt watched Butch comply with the instructions while Ricardo holstered his Heckler & Koch USP.

"Okay, you can lower your hands," Ricardo said. He kept his grin. "Anytime you're ready." He held his right hand a few inches from the pistol in the fast draw holster on his right hip and wiggled his fingers. "You have a reputation for being the fastest gun on the planet, but I know that's not true. I know I'm the fastest and I'm going to prove it, fair and square."

Butch remained motionless and made no comment.

"Come on, you chicken or something?" Ricardo asked. He narrowed his eyes and stared at Butch.

Butch didn't move and remained silent.

Matt noted Ricardo's intense gaze was focused on Butch's right hand.

Knowing Ricardo was concentrating entirely on Butch starting his draw Matt slowly positioned himself on his left side and eased his pistol out of the holster on his right hip. He carefully pointed it at Ricardo.

"I thought you'd at least have enough guts to try." Ricardo sneered. "I thought—"

A loud bang ensued, and Ricardo dropped limply to the floor.

Matt scrambled to his feet and lowered his Glock 19. Everyone else also stood as a group of technicians rushed around the filing cabinets.

"We're all okay," Dan said.

The technicians stared at the body on the floor.

Giving a sharp exhale, Butch walked to where Ricardo was lying. A large pool of blood had already formed.

After Ben made a quick call on his secure satellite phone, Butch shrugged. "I guess we'll never know who was the fastest." He looked at Matt. "Thanks, Ricardo was damned good. I'm not sure I could have beaten him."

"His ego clouded his judgment. I knew he was concentrating hard on you starting your draw," Matt said. "I figured that gave me a good chance to do something."

"You're getting a lot better, but that still took a lot of guts," Butch replied. "Thanks again. Chances are you saved my life."

Matt nodded and gave a slight smile. "Glad I could help."

Butch focused his gaze on Matt and Ralph. "Ricardo's bosses were mainly after the two of you. We're all lucky Ricardo tried to satisfy his big ego first."

"Yeah," Ralph said, "damned lucky."

Ben instructed the technicians to return to their stations and glanced at his watch. "After the cleanup crew finishes and we have some additional security in place, we'll meet in the conference room. We still have a big job in front of us."

A five-man crew arrived within ten minutes. Ricardo was taken out in a body bag and two men stayed outside as additional security.

"There's activity at the fortress." Ben gestured toward the monitors, infrared pictures were streaming in.

"Trucks are going through the side door," Matt said. "Probably offloading drugs, looks like about ten people."

"Busy as hell too," Ralph said. "Look at them scurry around." He gave a slight shrug. "Guess we know where we're going next."

Dan pointed toward the monitor. "They're leaving. No need to rush over there."

"We need to do some planning first anyway," Ben said. "We also need to figure out who Panther is. Maybe he was Ricardo. We'll huddle in the conference room early tomorrow morning."

····

In Miami, Juan glanced at his secure satellite phone. It was ringing. The caller ID showed it was Carmen. Juan answered.

"Bad news," Carmen said.

"What now?"

"Ricardo didn't succeed."

"How do you know?"

"The tracking device showed him not moving for a while at the airport and he's now downtown, still not moving. He didn't report anything, and he doesn't respond to my calls. The conclusion is obvious."

"Damn."

"Yeah."

"Hard to believe Ricardo failed," Juan said. "He's always been reliable."

"Maybe he ran into something unexpected. I halted the work at the fortress about twenty minutes ago when I knew things had gone bad at the airport."

"Ricardo knew all about the CIA security measures. I doubt he was surprised by anything. Let me check something. I'll call you back in a few minutes." Juan disconnected.

Juan punched in a number and got an immediate answer. He went through his security routine and asked, "Know anything about what's happening in Bogota?"

"Quite a bit," the person said. "What do you want to know?"

"Everything you know."

Juan listened for several minutes.

"And that's the latest," the person said. "I got an update five minutes ago."

"Keep me posted on how things develop."

"You can depend on it," the person said.

Juan disconnected and then punched in the number for Carmen.

"What did you find out?" Carmen had a touch of concern in his voice.

"You're right: Ricardo's dead, but we have to move on," Juan said. "I'm guessing the Americans are going to make a move on our main warehouse tomorrow."

"The fortress?"

"We knew they had it under surveillance with a Hawkeye and some UAVs," Juan said. "It seems they noticed our activity and then noticed we left."

"What should we do now?"

"The cartel that's been giving us trouble, the Medellin Cartel, is scheduled to drop off a load of drugs at the fortress tomorrow morning. I'm going to send a group to wipe them out along with any Americans who are stupid enough to show up."

"Is this the best time for that?"

"Yes," Juan said. "I'll take the shipment tomorrow to another location and then blow up the fortress. It's no good to us now."

"What do you want me to do?"

"Nothing now that Ricardo is dead."

There was a brief silence.

"Come back here as soon as you can," Juan said. "Having you over there in Bogota hasn't worked too well anyway. We have a lot of new planning and coordination to do."

"Such as?"

"I don't want to get into that over the phone. After you get back, we'll sit down and evaluate things."

Chapter 14

The next morning at the CIA control center in Bogota, Kevin looked over his coffee mug at Ralph and Matt. Ben, Dan, and Butch also sat at the table where they were meeting.

"Do you know anything about this fortress other than what was in Jack Worthington's notes?" Kevin asked.

Ralph shook his head.

"I had a conversation with Justin Mason earlier today," Ben said. "He found some notes Jack had made about the fortress in the files of Donald Busby."

"How does Justin know they're Jack's notes?" Matt asked.

"Jack's handwriting," Ben said.

Matt turned toward Ralph. "Elsie should have called you."

"Maybe she's planning to," Ralph said. "We'll see." He looked back at Ben. "Did Justin mention what Donald had to say?"

"Donald told Justin he didn't remember filing the note. He mentioned Jack gave him a lot of things to file and he didn't always read them." Ben studied Ralph for a moment. "Have you talked to Donald since you've been down here?"

"No," Ralph said. "Only Elsie and Maria know where we are."

Ben nodded slowly. "Justin told me Jack's note indicated the fortress was a staging area for critical supplies."

Ralph and Matt exchanged glances.

"Hard to believe Jack would be involved in illegal drug trafficking." Ralph gestured with both palms out.

"Is Justin convinced the note is authentic?" Matt asked.

"His experts confirmed its Jack's handwriting," Ben said.

Kevin looked at Ralph. "Do you think you and Matt should head back to Jacksonville?"

"I think it's better to go along with you," Ralph said. "We want to see the fortress firsthand, and you know we're well initiated in handling tough situations."

"We agree." Butch looked at Matt. "Even though Ricardo was concentrating on me, how did you pull that off?"

"Just being a good analyst," Matt said. "I concentrated on how I could get my Glock into firing position. Before I flattened on the floor, I positioned every movable part of my body to support what I did."

Matt explained the details.

"Interesting how you didn't attract his attention while getting your pistol into position," Kevin said.

Matt shrugged. "His concentrating hard on Butch's right hand gave me a huge advantage."

Butch gave a thumbs-up.

"We'll take some local agents with us to the fortress." Kevin looked at Ralph and Matt. "We'll all be in assault gear with assault weapons."

"I'm sure the bastards will be expecting us. They seem to have constant access to inside information," Ralph said.

Kevin frowned. "Yeah, it looks like they have some high-placed moles."

"Some might be in the FBI." Ben replied. "We have several active investigations on that."

"We'll be prepared for the worst," Kevin said. "That's why we'll all be in assault gear. Craig is convinced we have at least one mole in the CIA."

Matt nodded. "I think you have several."

Ralph glanced at Kevin. "What are you going to do about the moles?"

"We have investigative teams just like the FBI does," Kevin said. "We're trying to find them. For now, I'll use some misdirection like you did at Tustun."

Everyone gave Kevin a curious stare.

"I'll call Craig and tell him to circulate the information we're going back to the United States immediately." Kevin gave a slight shrug. "Maybe the moles will report that."

"Think Panther could be a mole?" Matt asked.

"I hope we soon find out," Kevin said.

••••

In Miami, Juan looked across his desk at Carmen. "I'm glad my private plane was fueled and ready to go. I like it much better when we're discussing issues face to face."

"It was a quick trip, and I got to rest on the way back." Carmen looked directly at Juan. "I guess we both agree running a control center isn't my strong suite."

Juan took several puffs from his pipe. "Going forward, I think you and I can handle things well enough from Miami." He glanced at his watch. "More action is coming up soon."

"At the fortress?"

"It's going to be the last stop for Gibson and his whole group." Juan gave Carmen a knowing smile.

"I thought you told me on my flight here that Gibson was going back to Jacksonville this morning?"

"I did." Juan continued to smile. "That's what our mole at the CIA told me."

"Gibson's not going back to Jacksonville?"

Juan leaned over and emptied his pipe. He reached for his tobacco container. "Another mole got the true story. Kevin Brown called his boss at CIA headquarters and asked him to circulate the story they were returning this morning."

Carmen nodded.

"I listened to a recording of the conversation," Juan said.

"How did you get that?"

Juan savored a puff of his cherry-blend. "Our money buys the best technology along with the right expertise."

Carmen raised an eyebrow.

"We also have moles in other places," Juan said. "Our mole in the CIA office in Bogota told me they're supplying people and some extra gear to support Brown and his group storming the fortress this morning."

Carmen grinned.

Juan glanced at his watch. "We should have a group of assassins in place at the fortress as we speak."

"Tell me more about the situation there."

Juan started to speak just as the phone on his desk rang. It was his secure line. He stared at the caller ID and smiled. "I think we're about to know more."

Carmen sipped his coffee while Juan was talking.

After Juan finished his conversation and disconnected, he looked at Carmen. "It's not going to be easy for us this morning."

"How so?"

"Brown's group is going to be in full SWAT gear."

"Can we handle that?"

"Depends," Juan said. "I don't know the credentials for this particular group of assassins at the fortress."

"They should at least give the Americans something to think about."

"By the way, I had the illegal drugs removed from the fortress last night."

"All of them?"

"The fortress is cleaned out except for numerous stacks of wooden crates with various supplies. I had to empty out the big trucks to make room for transporting the drugs."

"Where did you take the drugs?"

"Cartagena," Juan said. "We have a new warehouse nestled in an industrial area. It shouldn't stand out. And it's only a few miles from the docks."

"Are you planning to reactivate the fortress later?"

"No, I'm going to blow it up," Juan said. "I have an observer with a good vantage point down there. We'll see how well our assassins do first."

Carmen nodded slowly.

Juan savored a long puff on his pipe. "Our moles will keep us informed. We'll make sure Brown's group is eliminated one way or the other."

••••

Later that morning in the Columbian jungle southwest of Bogota, twelve people in camouflage dress disembarked from three Hummers parked a quarter mile from the fortress.

Under the outer camouflage layer, each SWAT team member wore a suit of the newly issued lightweight 'nano-armor,' a tungsten disulfide-based nanocomposite material over five times stronger than steel. The short-sleeved suits provided extra protection from neck to knee.

"Weapons check," Kevin said.

Each team member carried a submachine gun, a Heckler & Koch MP5/10 A2 with an integral suppressor (a 'silencer'), ready and loaded with a 30-round magazine. It could fire 800 rounds per minute in full-automatic mode.

The A2 variant had a fixed stock and weighed only 5.6 pounds, unloaded. Most MP5's fired 9 mm ammunition, but the CIA's custom models delivered a bit more power using 10 mm rounds.

Although each team member had two spare full magazines, they set their weapons on semi-automatic or single-shot fire mode. Since at least some of the upcoming action would take place inside a building, the danger of ricochets made default use of a multi-shot firing mode inadvisable.

In addition to the MP5/10, each team member carried a silenced automatic pistol: a custom Springfield Armory Tactical Response Professional, Model 1911-A1 which used a .45 ACP round. The two-pound seven-ounce pistol had two safeties, one to block slide action and the other to prevent discharge unless the grip was firmly held.

Each team member also carried four grenades in vest pockets, two M84 stun grenades (flash-bangs) and two MK3A2 concussion grenades.

One stun grenade, used in the right way, would incapacitate a roomful of opponents for much longer than the time needed to take control of the room. The detonation blinds with a one million-candle power flash and deafens with a 170+ decibel bang. Anyone looking in the direction of the flash loses use of his eyes for at least five seconds. The bang affects the targets' inner ears, causing temporary disorientation and dizziness of varying duration.

Every team member also had tactical communications gear, night-vision goggles and helmet-mounted infrared flashlights. If the electricity was cut off, they still could navigate in dark areas.

After everything was checked, Kevin waved the group forward through the woods. He soon approached the fortress and walked toward a side door. There was no opposition yet.

Kevin turned the handle. As expected, the door was locked. He grabbed a small kit from a vest pocket and removed a pick. In a few seconds he and the others eased cautiously through the open doorway and looked for cover inside the fortress.

With the group spread out and crouching behind stacks of large wooden crates inside the back door, Kevin surveyed the area. A pungent smell hung in the air. He couldn't quite identify it.

They were in a huge room with a high ceiling and no windows. About a hundred stacks of wooden crates dominated the space.

A wide stairway was prevalent in a distant corner. A bank of elevators dominated a sidewall close to the stairway.

••••

An observer, strategically located on a rocky ridge several hundred meters from the fortress, raised his binoculars.

He studied the intruders for a moment and then grabbed his secure satellite phone and punched in a number.

It was time to alert everyone.

The leader of the group inside the fortress took the call and then announced to his team, "They're here."

"Do we wait for them?" one assassin asked.

"Of course." The leader raised his AK-74 into firing position.

"How soon should we start shooting?" another assassin asked.

"As soon as they're close enough for you not to miss. You make the decision," the leader said.

••••

"Get lower," Kevin whispered into his tactical mike as he crouched and moved toward a better vantage point. He stopped and surveyed the situation.

Matt was a few yards to the right of Kevin. He peered around the corner of a row of stacked boxes and studied his surroundings.

Within seconds, Matt pulled back and whispered into his mike, "Movement up ahead."

Kevin peered out from another corner. "Two heads showing about fifty yards down the aisle. They're behind some crates close to the stairs. Matt, target the one on the right. Three seconds." He gave a hand signal and started to count. "One thousand, two thousand…"

Two soft pops sounded.

One man fell out into the open, motionless.

"Got one, at least, Matt and I will check. Butch you take two men and check upstairs. The rest of you hold position." Kevin signaled Matt and moved out from the stack of crates.

Both men ran a zigzag path toward the enemy combatant lying

motionless in the open.

••••

"What the hell!" The assassin leader, from his vantage point on top of the crates, saw two of his men sprawl on the floor below him.

The leader keyed his communications unit. "Spread out and get the truck ready to leave. I'll join you in a minute. I have a little unfinished business." He crawled across the top of the stacked crates toward the other side of the warehouse area and then dropped to the floor. He spoke into his communications unit. "They took out two of our men. I'm going to extract some revenge before we depart."

"Roger."

••••

Matt reached the downed enemy combatant who had fallen in plain view. He saw the other one had fallen behind a crate; both were dead.

After crouching behind a large forklift, Matt glanced at Kevin on his left.

"There's another guy moving this way," Kevin said. "Watch my back." He stepped out from the corner and leveled his rifle at the enemy combatant. "One mistake and you're dead."

After a stunned glance at Kevin, the enemy combatant dropped his AK-74 and raised his hands in the air.

"Lose the pistol," Kevin said. "Left hand, two fingers, that's right. Now drop it and step away."

Kevin gestured for Matt to join him. "I've got the one I saw. Careful, there may be more."

Within seconds, Matt closed on Kevin's position.

The assassin leader stood motionless.

Matt glanced at Kevin. "Someone else is coming."

When Kevin shifted his gaze to Matt for an instant, the assassin moved with lightning speed and unleashed a karate-style kick. Kevin's rifle went flying.

Matt realized that he couldn't help immediately because of their relative positions. Kevin was too much in his field of fire.

After his foot connected with Kevin's rifle, the assassin leader tried to recover his balance. Kevin stepped forward and slammed a forceful Karate punch just under the assassin leader's lower right rib cage.

The assassin reeled from the blow, but it didn't take him out of action. He snarled and unleashed a straight punch toward Kevin.

Kevin moved to his right.

The assassin's punch hit nothing but air.

Kevin countered with a punch of his own. He connected.

The assassin leader went down. Kevin dove at him, but the assassin leader squirted away and rolled toward his discarded AK-74.

He grabbed it with a quick move and swung the barrel toward Kevin.

Matt stayed ready to help, but Kevin was staying too much in his field of fire. He didn't have experience or training in this type of situation, but he knew instinctively he could hit the wrong one if he fired.

The assassin leader tightened his finger on the trigger.

Kevin drew his pistol from his holster in less than a second and fired.

When hit with the 45-caliber slug the enemy leader dropped straight down and his AK-74 clanged on the concrete.

Matt watched the action; then, scanned the area again. "Shit."

"What?" Kevin turned.

Two enemy combatants about thirty yards away were charging from the back entrance, coming toward them with rifles pointed.

Both enemy combatants fired.

The bullets went wide.

It was the only chance they got. Kevin (still holding his pistol) and Matt (aiming his rifle) fired at the same time.

Both enemy combatants sagged to the floor.

"They thought they were going to surprise us," Kevin said.

Matt nodded. "We aren't that easy to surprise." He and Kevin scanned the area as Ralph and two local CIA agents rushed up.

"All clear from our direction," one of the local CIA agents said.

Butch's voice came over the tactical communications units. "All clear upstairs, we're coming down."

••••

Back in Miami Juan picked up his ringing phone.

"No one is communicating. We lost the fortress. Everyone is dead or running," the outside observer said on his secure satellite phone, as he lowered his binoculars.

"Running?" Juan asked.

"Saw a truck leave, loaded with our men."

"Leader still down there?"

"Doesn't answer."

"Any of our men still in the building?"

"I'll check again, wait one." Within seconds, the observer was back on the line with Juan. "No one answers."

"Destroy the place," Juan said. "You have the detonator."

"Roger."

••••

Matt heard a ticking noise, and his internal alarms went off.

"We need to get out of here," Matt said into his tactical mike. "They're going to blow this place up."

Kevin yelled into his tactical mike. "Everyone, get out of the building as fast as you can. Move the Hummers now. We'll rendezvous at Checkpoint One."

"Go out the open loading door," Kevin continued yelling into his mike. "Move it."

Twelve people charged toward the large opening and bolted out of the fortress.

Matt and Ralph kept up with the rest of the team as they spread out and charged up the road, heading north toward the checkpoint.

Within less than a minute, Matt heard the explosion and glanced back.

A giant fireball rose behind them. Flames enveloped the fortress and nearby forest and were spreading fast.

Continuing to run as fast as he could, Matt heard massive amounts of debris falling behind him.

Luckily all the members of the team were far enough away.

Matt felt a sense of accomplishment. He and Ralph had easily kept pace with all the highly trained warriors. His and Ralph's athletic background and exercise routines were paying off.

Chapter 15

At the CIA control center in Bogota, Dan and Ben stared at a row of monitors in the hangar they occupied. The fireball stood out in bold relief.

"I'm sure there's nothing left of that place." Ben gestured toward the fireball on the monitor. "Good thing the team got away in time."

"That was damned close, too damned close," Dan said. "It's a good thing Matt quickly figured things out."

Ben nodded.

"Still need the Hawkeye?" Dan asked.

"Were they able to follow that truck?"

Dan shook his head. "Lost it."

"I need to talk to my boss." Ben fished his secure satellite phone from a pocket and punched in a number. "There's something I need to check."

Ben finished his conversation with Gary Stennis and walked over to Dan. "There's a lot going on back home."

"Such as?"

Ben explained.

"So, we know for sure Panther is involved in the current situation?"

Dan asked.

"Consider that a fact."

Dan gestured toward one of the monitors. The CIA team is at the rendezvous point with the Hummers. "Are you going to let Kevin know about Panther right away?"

Ben nodded and spoke into his tactical mike, "Kevin, you wrapping up?"

"Yeah, we're heading back to the control center."

"Did you discover anything of interest inside the fortress?" Ben asked.

"No, not enough time."

"Can you see the fireball from your current location?"

"Yeah, and we can feel the heat too. It's probably going to be a few days before anyone can inspect the ruins."

"Are you going to let the local CIA agents take care of that?"

"Right," Kevin said. "We're heading back to you."

Ben stared at one of the monitors and saw the three Hummers moving.

"Is there something you want me to do before you get here?" Ben asked.

"Can't think of anything."

"I have some news for you," Ben said. He explained what Gary Stennis had told him.

"I suggest you release the Hawkeye, pull in the UAVs, and start packing up," Kevin said. "I want to leave for home as soon as possible. I think we can make more progress from there."

"Roger." Ben gave a sarcastic chuckle. "This hasn't been a luxury vacation down here anyway."

"From what you just told me," Kevin said. "It's going to be even more dangerous back home."

••••

In Miami the next morning, Juan savored a long puff on his pipe and looked at Carmen.

"For the most part, things have been a disaster in Columbia," Juan said.

"I don't know why you destroyed the fortress." Carmen gave a slight shrug. "Seems like we could still find a use for it?"

Juan shook his head. "Not with it being constantly watched by the CIA."

"It cost us a lot of money," Carmen said.

"Trust me, I did the right thing." Juan narrowed his eyes and pointed the stem of his pipe at Carmen. "And money is not a problem for us. Omar added another twenty billion US dollars to our operating budget."

"Oil profits?"

"I didn't ask."

Carmen shrugged. "Too bad Gibson and his group survived the blast. Our observer down there reported they all got out."

Juan took a couple of quick puffs on his pipe. "We can't afford to waste any more time before setting up the partnership with Tustun."

"Have you talked to Donald the last couple of days?"

Juan reached for his secure phone. "We'll see if he knows anything about what Gibson's planning to do next."

"Think Donald could have Brian Glascock knock him off?" Carmen asked.

"Not a good idea, at least not now. We don't want any of our partners at Tustun to come under any suspicion," Juan said. "We need someone else to take care of that problem." He punched in a number on his secure phone.

"Donald, how are things up there?" Juan asked.

"Are you concerned about something in particular?"

"No," Juan said. "Gibson back in the office?"

"Yeah, he's back from Louisiana."

"Louisiana?"

"Yeah," Donald said. "He's been over there a few days checking out some property for growing sugarcane."

"What makes you think he was in Louisiana?" Juan asked.

After a slight hesitation, Donald asked, "Do you know something I don't know?"

"Yeah, I do." Juan chuckled. "He and Baker were down in Colombia along with some FBI and CIA agents. Guess he doesn't trust any of you."

"Justin Mason is conducting a murder investigation."

"He's the Jacksonville police chief?"

"Right and he went through my files."

"Did he find anything?" Juan asked.

"Some of Jack's notes on Colombia."

"You should have destroyed those."

"Jack sent me a lot of things. I forgot they were there."

"Did you have anything to do with Worthington's death?" Juan asked.

"No," Donald said. "Did you?"

"Of course not, Worthington was useful to us."

"I'm sure we're all suspects," Donald said.

"Keep me posted on any developments." Juan took a long puff on his pipe. "And keep an eye on Gibson. We must know what he's doing."

"I'll get back with you later," Donald said. He disconnected.

Carmen gave Juan a pensive look. "So, what did he say?"

Juan took several puffs of his cherry-blend and then explained.

"Sounds like we could have some problems from all that, right?" Carmen stared at Juan.

"Maybe, but I don't think so."

"Oh?" Carmen raised an eyebrow.

"We didn't kill Worthington, and I don't think Donald did either," Juan said.

"You're leveling with me?"

"Like I told Donald, Worthington was valuable to us. His being dead paints us in the corner we're in now," Juan said. "Gibson will never go along with the deal we're offering. He must be eliminated."

"Hope we have better luck than we did in Colombia."

"No shit."

"Any specific plans?"

"Yeah," Juan said, "I'll fill you in later. I have a few people to check with first."

"More assassins?" Carmen asked.

"Good ones," Juan said, "top professionals."

"Ricardo couldn't get Gibson, think they can?"

"Our chances are going to improve. Trust me." Juan narrowed his eyes and looked directly at Carmen. "Things are going to become much more dangerous for Gibson and Baker up there in Jacksonville."

Chapter 16

The next morning at FBI headquarters in Washington DC, Ben arrived on time for his scheduled meeting with Gary Stennis and Paul Becker, the FBI Director.

When Ben walked through the doorway into Paul's office, both men were waiting for him.

Paul waved Ben to a chair and studied him for a moment. "You just finished a bit of an unusual assignment, huh?"

"Yes sir," Ben said. "Never thought I would run a CIA control center in a foreign country. Good experience, though."

Paul narrowed his eyes. "At least you came out alive."

"That's the good part," Ben said. He noted Paul and Gary were both staring at him.

"The fact somebody went to such lengths to try to kill all of you is significant." Paul leaned forward. "Tell me the whole story of your experience in Columbia, from the beginning. I want all the details."

Ben told the complete story.

Gary looked at his boss. "The more we find out, the odder this thing gets. We know someone with the codename Panther is heavily involved, but none of the current trails we're following lead to Columbia or to Miami."

So, you can't trace the name back to Juan Medina or Carmen Flores?" Paul asked.

"Correct," Gary said.

"It's still logical for Panther to be one of them," Paul said.

"That's right, given their nature, their interest in Tustun, and their previous involvement with Jack Worthington," Ben said, "but no trails lead to them at the moment."

Paul's gaze rested on the men in front of him. "Any suggestions about what we should do next?"

"I have new data from Kevin. It originated with something the NRO found," Ben said. "The CIA combined intelligence data from several organizations, the National Security Agency among them."

Paul leaned forward. "Get to the point."

"The CIA has just discovered a new warehouse in Cartagena that supports the illegal drug trade."

"How large?" Paul asked.

"Over 200,000 square feet," Ben said. "We have satellite photos."

"Why did the NRO train satellites on that precise area?" Paul asked.

"Kevin mentioned some recent tips from CIA agents on the ground there prompted the scrutiny," Ben said. "And NSA has intercepted calls referring to shipments from Cartagena to JAXPORT."

Paul looked at Gary. "I want a specific plan with objectives and resource requirements before I give the green light to take any further action down there."

Both Ben and Gary nodded.

"I'll set up a joint meeting with the CIA." Paul looked at Gary. "Hang tight. We have some more things to discuss."

Gary nodded.

Paul gestured to Ben. "We'll let you get back to Jacksonville. Plan to stay in close touch."

"Yes, sir," Ben said. As he stood and walked toward the door, he had a strong feeling the team that had just returned from Columbia was about to see more action down there.

••••

At Tustun in Jacksonville, Maria, her black hair framing a pleasant olive-colored face, smiled at the sandy-haired man as he walked toward the open doorway of Ralph's office.

Ralph sat at the round conference table in the corner and waved Justin toward an empty seat. Matt was already there, with a coffee mug in front of him, matching the one in front of Ralph.

Justin cleared his throat. "I'm making progress. I've been through a lot of Jack's files and some more interesting facts have popped up."

After apologizing for interrupting, Maria asked, "Coffee?"

Justin nodded. "Black."

Maria turned back toward the coffee pot on the credenza by her desk.

"Jack went to Colombia five times and to Mexico two times in the last year," Justin said. He looked up as Maria walked over with a steaming mug of coffee and placed it on the table in front of him.

"Thanks."

Maria nodded and immediately left the room.

"When going to Columbia, Jack always flew into either Cartagena or Bogota," Justin said. "In Mexico, it was always Monterrey."

"In what order did he make the trips?" Matt asked.

"Two trips to Cartagena first. Then three in succession to Bogota," Justin said. "He made two trips to Monterrey after that."

Ralph slowly shook his head. "Didn't realize it was that many trips, guess I wasn't counting."

"It's going to take a while longer to sort everything out." Justin looked at Matt. "I could use some help. You have a reputation as an expert analyst."

"We'll both help," Ralph said.

"That will be appreciated." Justin smiled. "I have good detectives working on this, but the two of you have inside knowledge on many related things."

Ralph gestured toward Matt. "I've assigned him full time to this case and I'm spending a lot of time on it too. I'm letting Donald continue to run the company, at least for the short term. Our new chairman, Chuck Milton, isn't scheduled to show up for another week."

Justin nodded.

"Does international oil play a part in what you know?" Matt asked.

"No," Justin said. "Both legal and illegal drugs are the focal points of what we've discovered so far."

"So, the oil thing might be a cover?" Ralph asked.

"That seems to be the case," Justin said. "The financials are twisted up in a big maze. A lot of FBI and CIA financial experts are working on it."

"Any opinions from them?" Matt asked.

"They think various transactions at the World Bank are smack dab in the middle of moving the drug money."

"Is anyone else helping the FBI?" Ralph asked.

Justin narrowed his eyes and gave a slight smile. "Some experts at RAND are helping the CIA investigate the offshore financial arrangements. They're sharing their findings with the FBI."

"So, it's a joint effort, and a big one?" Ralph asked.

"Yes," Justin said, "and they want Matt to participate as much as he can. In addition to his being an expert analyst on general matters, they know he's also an expert financial analyst." He looked at Matt. "You should be hearing from them soon."

Matt nodded.

Justin gave a slight shrug. "Everyone at Tustun has been scrutinized and we know a lot about all of you. That's a basic part of the process with this being a murder investigation."

"I'm glad Matt will be involved in more of the analysis going forward," Ralph said.

"Tustun has wired several million dollars to the World Bank in the past year." Justin looked directly at Ralph.

"Not possible," Ralph said. "I would know about that."

"It wasn't direct." Justin explained the details.

Ralph shook his head slowly. "I'll be damned."

"That folder in Jack's office with a lot of maps of Mexico..." Justin took a sip of coffee. "Each map had an area circled. Those maps were labeled 'Mexico,' but it turns out they were maps of certain areas in Colombia."

"You told us those maps had two different dollar figures for each circled item?" Ralph asked.

"Yes."

"Any new insights on what the numbers mean?" Matt asked.

"Not yet," Justin said.

Ralph glanced at Matt. "You have any fresh ideas about the numbers?"

"I'll dig back into it as soon as I can." Matt grinned. "I've been a little busy on some other aspects of this lately."

Ralph returned the grin.

Justin took another sip of coffee and then turned fully toward Ralph. "Remember, one of the numbers was five hundred billion dollars."

"Large number, I'll admit," Ralph said. "But remember, Jack was a visionary. Sometimes he could be a bit of a dreamer."

Matt nodded.

"Don't forget we did a thorough investigation of Jack's finances," Justin said. "We thought he might have had some money problems, but we found the opposite."

"Has anyone proven Jack was getting paid off?" Matt asked.

"Not yet," Justin said, "but from what we know now, it looks bad for him."

••••

In Miami, Juan sat at the desk in his office and pondered the implications of what he had discussed with Carmen. Things were becoming even more complicated.

Juan lit the tobacco in his pipe and savored a few long puffs. To properly camouflage their drug trafficking, it was essential to partner with an American company. Tustun was the best candidate. Things were complicated, but he now had a plan to move forward.

When a familiar noise interrupted his thoughts, Juan picked up the phone on one of his secure private lines. He knew who it was by the caller ID.

"I got your email," Omar said.

"Do you have an assassin who can get the job done?"

"You have access to more of those resources than I do."

"I just need one, a real good one," Juan said. "I don't have any better choices than the ones who've already failed."

After a moment of silence, Omar leaned forward, "I know one who might be of good use. She's done some good work for me here in Saudi Arabia."

"She?"

Omar chuckled. "I've become more of an equal-opportunity employer in these modern days. Do you have a problem with hiring a female assassin?"

"Not if she's good enough."

"She'll be expensive. What's the job?"

"I'll give you all the specifics later. I still have some decisions to make."

"Have you decided when and where you'll need her?"

"Jacksonville, Florida," Juan said, "and as soon as she can get there."

"You want her to communicate with you using this number?"

"That should work."

"I'll take care of it. If I don't call you back, you can expect to hear from her within the next few hours."

"Good," Juan said. He heard Omar disconnect.

Juan gazed at the ceiling for a moment and savored every puff of his tobacco. Feeling satisfied with his plan, he grabbed his secure satellite phone and punched in a number. He heard Carmen ask, "What's up?"

"You still want to be informed on new tactics?"

"Of course," Carmen said.

"I've hired a female assassin from Saudi Arabia."

"You trust a female for this type of work?"

"Of course, if Omar recommends her. He has the bigger bias."

"So, what will she do?"

Juan explained the details of his plan which included sending a couple of men from Colombia for insurance.

"You'll get no argument from me," Carmen said. "Nothing else has succeeded. We must eliminate our obstacles at Tustun so we can move ahead with our plans."

"I'll keep you informed." Juan disconnected.

....

At the FBI headquarters in Washington DC, FBI Director Paul Becker sat at a large table in a conference room that had been converted into an operations center of sorts. Gary Stennis, their head of investigations for domestic threats, and Dan Maxwell, the main technology specialist reporting to Gary, sat across the table from him.

Now working in close cooperation with the CIA, Paul decided to expand and formalize a main objective of their joint project—stopping the shipment of illegal drugs into Jacksonville, Florida.

Paul's gaze focused on both men sitting in front of him. "When do you expect the next shipment of drugs into JAXPORT?"

"Dan and I were working on that prior to this meeting," Gary said. "We're keeping a close watch on the port in Cartagena. We think it will be the origination point for the next shipment. It has been before."

"Think you should give Ben an update?" Paul asked.

"He already knows exactly what we're doing," Gary said. "I'll give him another call after Dan and I finish our meeting at CIA Headquarters."

"I've decided to go to the meeting too," Paul said. "I need to get more involved in the details on this one." He glanced at his watch. "We'll go together. I'll drive. I'll meet you at my parking space in twenty minutes."

••••

In Miami, Juan leaned back in his desk chair. There was a new problem. He grabbed his secure satellite phone and punched in a number.

"Has something changed?" Carmen asked.

"Yeah."

"What?"

"Got more intelligence data from some of our moles."

"Bad news?"

"We might have some competition," Juan said.

Carmen's voice went up an octave. "Go ahead and tell me what you're talking about."

"Another cartel is interested in Tustun."

"Who?"

"They call themselves NEUEXP. It's short for Nourishment and Energy Universal Exports."

"Never heard of them."

"Hang on, I'll get Omar on the line," Juan pressed a few buttons and the man in Saudi Arabia answered.

"Ever heard of NEUEXP?" Juan asked.

"Dangerous group," Omar said. "They operate out of Saudi Arabia. I've run across them several times in my oil business, ruthless bunch. I advise avoiding them at all costs."

"Carmen, are you still there?" Juan asked.

"Yes."

"Might be hard to avoid them," Juan said. "They might be competing with us for Tustun. They're in the food and drugs business too. Besides legal drugs like Morphine and Codeine they manufacture a lot of illegal drugs."

"How did you discover that?" Omar asked.

"Some things the CIA just uncovered. Our mole let me know," Juan said. "Also there has been activity in the past where Tustun benefitted from some illegal drug trafficking by NEUEXP and the associated money laundering."

"Jack Worthington?" Omar asked.

"Our mole thinks so," Juan said. "I'm going to call Donald."

"What if he's involved with NEUEXP?" Carmen's voice had a touch of concern.

Juan was silent for a few moments. "I don't think he is, and he might have some helpful information."

"Why do you think he's not involved?" Carmen asked.

"I don't have time to explain. Take my word for it," Juan said. "I'm pretty sure he's not. Despite NEUEXP, I'm going ahead with our plan to take over Tustun. I'll keep both of you up to date."

"Is Chuck Milton on board at Tustun yet?" Omar asked.

"Should start next week," Juan said. "I need to get busy. I'll keep both of you fully informed." He disconnected.

••••

When the threesome from the FBI arrived at CIA headquarters for their meeting with Joe Frank, they were escorted immediately to a conference room, Dan noted Craig and Kevin were already there, so was Butch.

Joe gestured to Craig as soon as everyone was seated.

Craig moved to the front of the room while Kevin inserted a DVD into the computer network server on the table.

Photos of the warehouse under surveillance in Cartagena, along with related intelligence data, displayed on four different large screens built into two of the walls. After reviewing all the information, Craig looked around the room. "Any questions?"

"Any signs of imminent large shipments?" Paul asked.

"Not yet," Craig said.

"Wonder why they're waiting?" Gary asked. "Think they know what we're doing?"

"It does seem they're waiting on something," Craig said. "NSA picked up a call from Miami into this area a short while ago."

"Did they get a specific location?" Paul asked.

Craig shook his head. "The call was encrypted, advanced

algorithms."

"No exact location on either end?" Gary asked.

"Just know it was from somewhere in Miami coming to somewhere in the Washington DC area."

"Could be those guys in Miami at DUISONZ," Gary said. "They might have a contact up here, maybe a mole."

Paul frowned. "We need to find out if it was to any of our offices?"

"We've decrypted some of the call," Craig said. "NEUEXP was mentioned, so was Tustun."

Joe looked at the FBI agents. "NEUEXP is an international cartel with their headquarters in Saudi Arabia, from where they export oil. They also have offices in Venezuela, Colombia, and Mexico, from where they export legal drugs. Their full name is Nourishment and Energy Universal Consortium."

"We've found links from them to the Gulf Cartel in Mexico," Kevin said. "We're continuing to watch things."

"Think there's a connection to the warehouse you're watching in Colombia?" Paul asked.

"We don't think so," Kevin said. "We think whoever runs that warehouse is a separate group, but we'll see."

Joe studied Paul for a moment. "Ralph Gibson and Matt Baker are working with you in an official capacity, aren't they?"

"Yes," Paul said. "Any concerns about that?"

"How much do you know about them?" Joe asked.

"We did a thorough check before we brought them aboard. We needed the cover of their business activity," Paul said. "They've already proven capable of defending themselves, as you probably know."

Joe nodded. "I heard about their exploits in Colombia." He jerked a thumb toward Butch and Kevin. "Direct from these guys."

"Gibson and Baker have also been checked out by Justin Mason," Paul said.

"The Jacksonville Police Chief?" Joe asked.

Paul gave a quick nod. "He's conducting a murder investigation."

Joe narrowed his eyes. "The Jack Worthington thing, right?"

"Right," Paul said. "Mason assures us that Gibson and Baker are clean, plus he's known them for a while and vouches for their character."

"Both men are single, aren't they?" Joe asked.

"Yeah, both have had girlfriends on and off. Mason told me he checked into that too, no significant issues were found. Mason's very thorough." Paul chuckled. "He mentioned both men were exercise nuts and liked to take their business issues home with them. Guess there aren't too many females on the planet who wouldn't get tired of that after a while."

Everyone gave a slight nod and grinned.

"Didn't I hear something about Baker discovering some funds were being sent to the World Bank from Tustun?" Joe asked.

"Yes, and he gave us a lot of information about how the transfers were done," Gary said. He gestured to Dan.

Dan explained the details.

"So, we don't know who at Tustun is transferring the funds, we just know how they're doing it?" Craig asked.

"Right," Gary said. "Dan and I know Matt is still investigating the situation. We'll check with him later today to see if he's made any further progress."

Joe looked at Kevin and Butch. "Any new leads from Colombia as to who was trying to knock Gibson and Baker off?"

Kevin shook his head. "Someone named Panther is directly involved. Ricardo Garza was involved but he's been eliminated. Juan Medina, Carmen Flores, and Omar Karam are also in the picture."

"Gibson and Baker are still improving their weapons skills," Gary said. "We just put them through some of our facilities in Quantico again."

"I can vouch for them," Butch said. "They're both pretty good. Matt Baker might have saved my life in Bogota." He explained.

Joe leaned forward. "We need to find the connection between NEUEXP and Tustun."

"We also need to find out exactly who's trying to knock Gibson and Baker off," Paul said, "and, along that line of thinking, we need to find out who Panther is."

Gary nodded. "It looks more and more likely the murder of Jack Worthington is directly connected to what's still going on."

"I think Donald Busby is involved in at least some of these issues," Dan said. "Justin Mason's investigation should turn up something real soon and I'll bet my last dollar Todd and Brenda Fisher are also involved in some way."

Joe narrowed his eyes. "This is quite a tangled mess and constantly becoming more entangled."

After a little more discussion, everyone stood, shook hands, and walked out of the conference room.

Things were indeed a complex entangled mess, Dan thought. They needed to make some progress, and soon.

Chapter 17

The next morning in Jacksonville, Justin Mason walked toward the round mahogany conference table in Ralph's spacious office at Tustun.

Matt was already sitting there with Ralph. Steam from hot coffee rose out of the mugs in front of the two men.

Justin settled into a chair at the table where a full coffee mug was already placed for him. Maria had been busy.

"Have you gathered any more facts relating to Jack's murder?" Ralph asked.

"Possibly," Justin said. He took a sip of coffee. "Dan Maxwell called just before I came over here. I think we're about to make some progress."

Ralph and Matt both leaned forward.

"Ever heard of NEUEXP?" Justin asked.

Ralph shook his head.

"The name rings a bell, give me a moment." Matt glanced at the ceiling. "That name was involved with some wire transfers from here to the World Bank." Matt snapped his fingers. "A NEUEXP account was one of the accounts listed in the transfers."

"Who in the hell are they?" Ralph asked.

Matt turned slightly toward Justin. "I have the same question."

"The acronym stands for Nourishment and Energy Universal Exports," Justin said. "They're headquartered in Saudi Arabia."

"Damn odd name." Ralph reached for his mug.

"The nourishment part refers to food products and legal drugs they ship out of Venezuela, Colombia, and Mexico," Justin said.

"What's the energy part," Matt asked.

"NEUEXP is a big producer of oil," Justin said.

Ralph narrowed his eyes. "In Saudi Arabia?"

Justin nodded and relayed the details Dan had given him.

Matt studied Justin for a moment. "So, we don't yet know much about NEUEXP's full international operation?"

"That seems to be the case." Justin's gaze focused on both men sitting across from him. "Dan told me both the FBI and the CIA are working hard on this. We should know more soon."

Ralph raised an eyebrow and stared at Matt. "You should have told me about this NEUEXP thing."

"There are a lot of wire transfers, most legit, but some questionable. I'm still looking at those," Matt said, "didn't want to bother you with any unnecessary details."

Ralph grunted. "Under the circumstances, you don't need to worry about bothering me with too many details."

Matt gave a short nod.

Ralph kept his gaze on Matt. "Have you found any evidence Jack was getting paid off?"

"There's no definite proof." Matt shrugged. "Jack had hundreds of investments, and some are paying off big. They were all set up for direct deposit into Jack's main account. I haven't had time to complete a thorough analysis of all the thousands of details."

Ralph grinned and leaned toward Justin. "Don't forget we've both been a little busy sharpening other skills."

Justin returned the grin. "I guess you still don't want any bodyguards, right?"

"Not yet," Ralph said." He jerked a thumb toward Matt. "This guy's pretty damned good and I'm close to matching his skill level."

"Let me know if you change your mind." Justin glanced at Matt and Ralph. "Incidentally, both the FBI and the CIA agree with your assessment of your skills. That's a big reason they want to keep you aboard."

"It all started with their need to use our business activity for cover," Ralph said. "That fit perfectly with what Matt and I needed to do, so we ended up joining forces."

Justin gave a thumbs-up. "Ben told me you and Matt could take care of yourselves as well as anyone else he knew, except maybe for Butch."

"I don't want to go back to South America without Butch," Ralph said, "no matter how well Matt and I can defend ourselves."

Matt chuckled. "Yeah, I second that motion."

After a moment of silence, Ralph looked at Justin and asked, "DUISONZ is still in charge of the security at JAXPORT?"

Justin nodded.

Ralph shook his head. "Juan Medina and Carmen Flores have to be tied somehow into the illegal drugs coming into the port, too many coincidences."

After a brief pause, Justin said, "I haven't yet found anything bad on the Fishers, but I'll continue to investigate."

"Brenda's still here in Jacksonville," Ralph said. "She's going through what's left of Jack's things."

"Is anyone supervising that activity?" Justin asked.

"Elsie," Ralph said.

Justin took a sip of coffee. "Guess that's logical."

"Elsie keeps me well informed," Ralph said. "She's more particular about Jack's things than Brenda. In fact, she goes ahead of Brenda and sorts through everything."

Justin raised an eyebrow. "Why do that?"

Ralph shrugged. "She's always been protective of Jack. Maybe she wants to make sure Brenda doesn't find anything embarrassing."

Justin glanced at Matt. "Are you aware of anything specific that throws suspicion for Jack's death on Donald Busby?"

"Nothing other than the association with Juan Medina and Carmen Flores," Matt said. "I'm still looking hard for something though."

"Lot of coincidences regarding Brian," Ralph said. "Along with Donald I suspect him too."

Justin nodded. "He was the last person known to see Jack alive."

"If there's anything there, I'll find it," Matt said.

Justin leaned forward. "The FBI and CIA are giving everything plenty of scrutiny. They have all the necessary resources."

"I doubt they have our motivation," Matt said.

Ralph nodded and looked directly at Matt. "Speaking of motivation, let's spend the rest of the afternoon at the gun club."

"Yeah, no need to get stale," Matt said, "especially since we seem to be somebody's favorite targets."

"Somebody like Panther, maybe?" Justin asked.

Ralph nodded. "Any guesses about Panther's identity?"

Justin took a deep breath and leaned back in his chair as he slowly exhaled. He then said, "I have a feeling you guys are going to find out before I do."

••••

In Miami, Juan felt a degree of satisfaction; his next offensive against Ralph Gibson was in motion. The female assassin had already contacted him. She was in Jacksonville and preparing for her work.

Juan punched in a number on his phone.

A familiar voice came over the line, "Yes."

"I need information on Gibson's schedule for the next day or two."

"He doesn't always keep Maria fully informed."

"Mainly, I need to find a way to verify where he's going to be tomorrow night," Juan said.

"I'll see what I can do."

"Get back to me as soon as you've gathered some information. I have some people I need to keep informed."

"I'll make it as quickly as I can."

As soon as Juan disconnected, his phone rang. He recognized the caller ID and answered.

"Has the female assassin contacted you yet?" Omar asked.

"Yes, she's in Jacksonville."

"Good. What about the other two assassins you mentioned earlier?"

"They're there too," Juan said. "I'll make sure they hook up. One of our moles at the FBI is working on finding out where Gibson will be tomorrow night."

"What about Baker?"

"Gibson's the important one. We can take over Tustun without disposing of Baker."

"It would be better to get him too."

"We will, if they're together," Juan said. "We'll see how things work out and make decisions as we go."

"We need to be successful this time."

"I'll keep you informed." Juan smiled as he disconnected. Confidence flowed within him. They would certainly take Gibson out real soon, and probably Baker too. He expected them to be together most of the time now.

••••

At CIA headquarters in McLean, Craig drummed his fingers on his desk and glanced at Kevin. "We've got to find that mole."

"Or moles," Kevin said.

"NSA intercepted another call from Miami into this area about an hour ago."

"Encrypted?" Kevin asked.

"Advanced algorithms, better than before," Craig said. "NSA has no information from the conversation."

"Still no exact location on either end?"

"We just know it was from somewhere in Miami coming to somewhere in the Washington DC area."

"Why do you think it was to a mole?"

"That's my guess," Craig said. "The caller in Miami has some very advanced technology. They're very rich or they're backed by someone with a lot of money."

Kevin stared at Craig. "DUISONZ has a lot of money, so does NEUEXP."

"Could be either one or both."

"Think they could be in cahoots?" Kevin asked.

"Possible."

"We need to find out who's involved. There must be a way with all our capability."

Craig jutted out his jaw. His eyes narrowed. "There's one damn big problem."

"What?"

"The bastards we're looking for probably have a bigger budget than we do," Craig said. "They can afford the best and the newest technology money can buy. They can also pay big bucks for expert help."

Kevin leaned forward. "NSA also has advanced technology. That's how we've detected the calls. If our technology were any less advanced, we wouldn't even know about the phone calls."

Craig exhaled slowly and focused a steady gaze on Kevin. "The bastards in Miami apparently have installed new algorithms. However, NSA assured me they would keep working on the transmission data. They're installing some new algorithms too."

••••

That evening, Matt settled into a lounge chair in his den. He thought about the practice he and Ralph had completed an hour previous. They had practiced synchronizing their fast draws while firing at simultaneous targets.

When his cell phone beeped, Matt glanced at the caller ID. It was Ralph.

"Are you available for dinner tomorrow night?" Ralph asked.

"Where do you have in mind?"

"St. Augustine, thought we would enjoy the atmosphere, lot of good restaurants there," Ralph said.

"Did you know it's a sister city to Cartagena, Colombia?" Matt asked.

"No," Ralph said. "You analyze everything, don't you?"

Matt chuckled. "Some people don't like that characteristic of mine."

"Well, in my case it's encouraged," Ralph said. "In fact, that's the reason for dinner tomorrow night. I want to discuss more details about some things you've analyzed."

"Why wait until tomorrow night?"

"It's a bit late right now and I'm tired. Also, I need to prepare for some company meetings tomorrow on some other issues," Ralph said, "meetings last all day, routine company business, but still important for me to be there."

"Dinner's fine with me. I don't have anything planned."

"O.C. White's okay with you?"

"Yeah, love the seafood."

"I'll pick you up at your house at six tomorrow evening," Ralph said. "Roger."

"I think Donald's going out of his way to avoid me. I haven't seen him around the office. He's up to something for sure."

"He's spending a lot of time with Brenda, sorting through Jack's things."

"Elsie's still going through everything first, isn't she?"

"Yeah, far as I know," Matt said. "I stop by Jack's office several times a day, doors are open. Elsie's been in there most of the time."

"Elsie's a real fireball," Ralph said. "It's good she's there." He paused. "Were Donald and Brenda in there too?"

"Not every time, but most of them. Why don't you confront Donald with some things?"

"He'll deny any accusations. Confronting him will backfire if I don't have proof," Ralph said. "Can't make my move too soon, but I'll bet he and Brian are in this thing together."

"I'll spend most of my time tomorrow to see if I can come up with any specifics on what Donald is up to."

"Be careful. I don't want to tip our hand."

"Most of the recent Tustun financial transactions I need to analyze fall into Donald's area," Matt said. "Due to my business responsibilities, I have a good reason to be checking with him."

"It's going to be interesting if he has any connections to NEUEXP."

"Or to any of the funds-transfers to the World Bank," Matt said.

"Yeah, that's a fact. We'll discuss all that tomorrow night."

Chapter 18

In Saint Augustine at seven o'clock the next evening, Matt and Ralph walked toward O.C. White's Restaurant, located near the city yacht marina and the historic Bridge of Lions.

"Thought we could both use a change of scenery," Ralph said, "and things usually aren't too crowded down here on Thursday evenings."

"Works for me," Matt said.

"I had a long meeting with Elsie today. During the discussion, she requested some information on the current plans for growing cocoa beans in Colombia."

"What does Elsie have to do with that?"

"She had found some old notes in her desk from Jack." Ralph shrugged. "She told me she had taken some dictation from Jack a month ago about that very subject. Curiosity overcame her. She wanted to check the accuracy of a few things."

Matt raised an eyebrow. "That brings up all sorts of questions."

"I know." Ralph gave a dismissive wave. "I told Elsie she didn't need to worry about any aspects of growing cocoa beans in Columbia. I would handle it. I have the notes now. There was something even more interesting, however."

"What?"

"Donald was in the meeting, and he also wanted the notes, pretty badly too," Ralph said.

"But you kept them?"

"Yes." Ralph grinned. "I had to remind Donald I outrank him."

Matt nodded as they walked into the restaurant. They had chosen not to eat in the patio area. Once seated with menus in hand, they took a moment to scan the choices.

The waitress appeared. "Would you gentlemen care for drinks or appetizers?"

Ralph glanced at Matt and then shook his head. "I think we're ready for the main course."

They ordered the Maryland Blue Crab Cakes with a choice white wine—a 2001 French Chardonnay. They chatted about trivia while the waitress poured the wine and returned with the meal.

Ralph looked at Matt. "You mentioned a couple of interesting things on the way down here. Care to elaborate a little bit more?"

....

The assassin from Saudi Arabia crouched on top of a low building beside the O.C. White's parking lot, across the narrow street on one side of the restaurant.

Good angle, she thought, as she adjusted the features of her SIG SG 550-1 sniper rifle.

After pulling the adjustable butt-plate snug to her right shoulder, she angled the rifle downward. She pointed the barrel toward the front of the restaurant. Peering through the scope of her laser-sighting device, she could see the small red dot on the main door into the restaurant.

She didn't need the high magnification of the usual sniper scope; this was short range.

It should be a snap, she thought, but she still wanted to use the laser. It was a bit of a crutch for her.

••••

After they finished the crab cakes and wine, both Ralph and Matt ordered decaf.

"Best to stay alert now days," Ralph said. "You're carrying your Glock, I assume."

Matt grinned. "A bit late checking on that, aren't you?"

Ralph shrugged. "I figured you had it. I just got the urge to check."

The waitress approached with the decaf.

"I want to have a chat with Elsie," Matt said after the waitress left.

"About those notes on growing cocoa beans?"

"That and a few other things," Matt said. "I think she can fill in some gaps we have in our current information."

"Okay, but be careful. I don't want to rile her up. I know she has a temper."

After they finished their coffee and Ralph took care of the bill, they strolled toward the front of the restaurant.

Ralph gave Matt a quick stare as they left the back section of the dining area. "Any gut feelings?"

"About what?"

"Danger."

"Why ask now?"

Ralph gave a slight shrug. "It's dark outside and you have good intuition."

Matt stopped inside the door. "Being paranoid might be safer." He glanced at Ralph. "Did you tell anyone we were coming here tonight?"

"Just you," Ralph said, "on the phone last night." He stared at Matt for a moment. "Feeling anything?"

Matt shook his head. "My intuition isn't that good, just pops up on occasion. However, we could be extra cautious and play it safe."

"Any recommendations?"

"Let's check and see if we can leave from another door," Matt said, "just in case."

••••

The assassin saw her two targets standing just inside the front glass door. She thought about taking them out now, but she wasn't sure what kind of glass she would be shooting through. It might be strong enough to deflect or even block the bullets.

She held her fire and waited for them to come out.

"What are the bastards doing?" She muttered as she they moved away from the door. The thought struck her like a hammer. They're going out another way!

She sprang to her feet. She would come back later for the case and accessories. She raced down the fire escape. They were going to go out the side entrance—she was sure of it. She had checked the exits earlier. It was the only other way out.

She rushed behind a dumpster about ten meters from the side door of the restaurant. Good, they're not out yet. She took the scope off the GF 550 and put it in a side pocket.

••••

When they got to the side door, Matt glanced at Ralph. "You can best detect movement in the dark out of the corners of your eyes."

"I know that." Ralph reached out and turned the knob and started pushing the door open.

"Wait a second." Matt closed the door. "Close your eyes a moment so we can better adjust to the dark when we get out." He hesitated and opened his eyes. "On second thought, let's go out the front." He turned back toward the front door.

Ralph followed. "One question, why?"

"I did some quick analysis."

••••

In the alley, the assassin saw the door open a little and then close. She waited a moment, nothing.

What the hell are they doing? Puzzled, she readied her rifle and stared at the door.

She frowned. She was a great shot from a prone position, but not so great shooting on the run. She racked her brain. What should she do? If they were coming out here, they were taking their time.

After deciding to move out to the street, she planned to find a position to watch both exits.

••••

As they again reached the front door, Ralph gave Matt a curious look.

"They tried to knock us off in Colombia and failed." Matt shrugged. "They have a good information network. They knew where to find us down there and they might have found us here. A sniper out front could see us through the door. I'm betting our turning around was detected."

"I get it," Ralph said. "If someone was out there, they moved to cover the other door."

"That's my guess. I think this is our best option, everything considered."

Ralph pursed his lips. "Let's go for it."

Matt turned the doorknob. "To play it as safe as possible, we need to spread out after we clear the doorway."

Ralph nodded as they hurried through the open doorway and separated fast.

Crossing the street to the parking lot, Matt stayed as much in the dark as he could. He stopped in a dark spot in the graveled area. He could see Ralph was now on the same side of the street, but about ten yards away.

Matt regretted they didn't have communications gear, a careless oversight. They had concentrated too much on relaxing. He moved out of the dark spot and signaled Ralph to move toward him. Ralph complied.

••••

The assassin got into her new position just in time to see both of her targets rush out the front of the restaurant.

She tried not to overreact.

Going north toward Bridge Street and staying in the dark, she rushed to the other side of Marine Street and toward the parking lot. Being a former Olympic sprinter and staying in top condition came in handy.

....

As they drew close to Ralph's Jaguar, Matt suggested they stop and crouch in a dark area.

"Some lights must be out, sure as hell is dark," Ralph whispered.

"The only light is right over your Jag. Someone might have staked it out."

"We should be very cautious."

"Something's up, those other lights were working when we parked."

"I'm glad you were paying attention," Ralph whispered, "Let's stagger our approach, I'll go first. Wait about ten seconds and I'll have the car started."

"Roger."

Each man drew his Glock and attached a silencer. If they had to fire, they didn't want to attract attention.

....

There they are, crouched down in the dark. The assassin raised her rifle and aimed.

No, she couldn't see the targets well enough. Careful to make no sudden movements, she stood in her dark hideaway and eased toward her targets.

One of the targets bolted toward the Jaguar. She felt a wave of panic. They must not get away. She must not fail.

Even though she was a seasoned professional, she got caught in the emotion of the moment. Moving fast, she raised her rifle and pointed it toward Gibson. He wasn't getting away this time. She was better than those guys in Colombia.

Her target was now fully visible, having moved into the better-lit area around his car.

••••

Matt saw a figure with a rifle to his right, visible out of the corner of his eye. Matt aimed and fired twice. A rifle clanged on the concrete.

There might be more, Matt thought. He scanned the area and then joined Ralph who was already hovering over the felled assassin.

"This woman took two bullets in the upper chest, no body armor, dead for sure." Ralph looked up at Matt.

After detaching the silencer, Matt holstered his Glock and picked up the rifle. "It's obviously some type of sniper rifle."

Ralph inspected the corpse. "Middle Eastern features, might be connected to one of the oil cartels."

"Maybe connected to DUISONZ or NEUEXP," Matt said.

"Damn right." Ralph detached his silencer and shoved his Glock back in the holster. He grabbed his phone and punched a digit. He talked for a few moments then disconnected. "Ben told me the FBI will take care of the body. A local team should be here within 5 minutes."

Matt nodded just as two men materialized from out of the shadows.

"Hold it right there." The swarthy men stepped forward and leveled their weapons at Matt and Ralph.

Matt noted a silencer on the front of each rifle barrel. He knew no one outside the parking area would hear any of the shots.

"I've called the FBI, they're here." Ralph looked at the street.

After taking a quick glance behind them, the men glanced at each other. They seemed to dismiss the concern.

The first man stared at Matt for a moment. "We're not falling for that crap, *gringo*." He pointed his rifle at Matt's head.

Ralph grinned and continued to stare at the street.

One of the swarthy men frowned and took another look behind him.

The other man did the same.

Matt knew he and Ralph had practiced this same type of thing at the shooting range multiple times. He hoped the hours they both had spent practicing would pay off.

Deciding this was their best chance and hoping Ralph felt the same, Matt drew his pistol with smooth efficiency and fired at the man on the right.

The man went down, but so did Ralph. Matt fired at the other man, who dropped.

Matt looked down at Ralph, who had grabbed his right arm. Blood seeped between his fingers.

Matt wrapped a clean handkerchief around the flesh wound.

"I think your shot distracted the one who shot at me," Ralph said. "Luckily the bullet just grazed my arm."

Matt started to comment just as three men rushed up and flashed ID.

"Are you guys Baker and Gibson?" the first FBI agent asked.

"Yes sir," Matt said.

The first agent picked up one of the AK 74 rifles and inspected the corpses. "These men are professionals." He looked at Matt and Ralph. "I heard you guys were good, but this is amazing."

"This other one is a woman," the third agent said, "appears to be a professional also."

The first agent inspected everything while the other two agents moved back into the shadows and stayed on alert. There was no crowd to control. No one had reacted to the gunshots, probably due to some temporary loud traffic.

One of the agents inspected Ralph's wound and applied a tourniquet. "I've seen worse, but you'd better check with your doctor anyway."

Ralph nodded.

"You guys can go," The first agent said. "We'll take it from here. Ben told me he didn't want you around when we start attracting attention."

"So, we won't get any credit for our skills." Ralph grinned.

The first agent returned the grin. "Guess not, too bad." He gave a dismissive wave and turned to the other agents. "Let's get busy. The necessary crew and vehicles should arrive within a few minutes."

Ralph tossed his keys to Matt. "You drive."

••••

In Miami, Juan disconnected from his call and glanced at the man sitting in front of him.

"What did you find out?" Carmen asked.

"Bad news, our assassins are dead, all three of them. The woman failed and the two men I sent to back her up did too."

Carmen shook his head slowly and made no comment.

"We might have some problems on this one," Juan said.

Carmen raised an eyebrow. "Oh?"

"The two men can be tied to DUISONZ, fingerprints...."

"Exactly what happened?"

"Tell you in a moment. Our mole had the complete FBI report." Juan stood and walked to the wet bar.

"He got access to it rather fast," Carmen said.

"That's because he filled it out." Juan replied. "He told me something else." He poured a glass of bourbon and walked back to his chair. "The FBI is coordinated with the CIA on this and they're all going to come after us."

"How do they know we're behind this?"

"Omar assured me the female assassin was the best. I figured the probability was high she would succeed." Juan gave a slight shrug. "But I decided to use some men from our main DUISONZ security force at JAXPORT to back her up anyway, just a safety precaution."

"You should have told me earlier you were planning to use DUISONZ security. You're supposed to keep me informed on everything."

"I had a lot of confidence in the female based on Omar's recommendation," Juan said. "And our two security guys were the best we had, a step above the assassins we used in Colombia. I thought telling you was an unnecessary detail."

"So, what do we do now?"

"Move our operations to another location." Juan reached for his secure satellite phone and glanced at Carmen. "I'll alert Omar."

Chapter 19

The next morning at Tustun, Maria, her black hair flowing to her shoulders, walked into Ralph's spacious corner office.

"What happened?" Maria asked, staring at the sling on Ralph's right arm.

Ralph explained.

"What did the doctor tell you?" she asked. Her dark eyes appeared mysterious.

"He told me I'll be fine."

Maria gave a broad smile.

"Thanks," Ralph said. He noticed that Maria was staring at him. "I'm fine, really."

Maria nodded slowly and left just as Matt was coming in.

"I would've been glad to pick you up," Matt said.

"Thanks, but I prefer to drive. I can take my arm out of the sling when I need to." Ralph looked directly at Matt. "I feel great, and the Doctor told me I would be fully functional in a few days.

Matt reached into a coat pocket and removed a stack of index cards.

"Organized my notes," Matt said.

"Thought you kept them in your computer?"

"I do," Matt said. "I sometimes jot things down on note cards and use an old technique that still comes in handy."

"How so?"

"It gives you a lot more flexibility in categorizing things," Matt said. "I started using this in college. A professor recommended it for debate preparation."

"Can't you do that in the computer?"

"Much of this stuff is subjective, intuitive. I can shuffle the cards around quickly."

"Any more insight into what's going on?"

"I don't think NEUEXP is working with DUISONZ."

Ralph raised an eyebrow.

"Nothing conforms to any logic they would use if they were in cahoots. Sometimes they work against each other."

"How do you figure that?" Ralph asked.

"I don't think you want a detailed explanation."

"Summarize."

"The final conclusion is based on a combination of inductive and deductive reasoning," Matt said. He gave examples of where some transactions at JAXPORT by DUISONZ worked against NEUEXP and vice versa.

"So where does that leave us?"

"We're dealing with more than one large organization that's shipping illegal drugs into JAXPORT," Matt said.

"I think we already knew that." Ralph gestured toward the cards. "Any other conclusions?"

"DUISONZ and NEUEXP are both using multiple branches of the World Bank."

"Laundering money?" Ralph asked.

Matt nodded.

"Is someone at Tustun involved?" Ralph stared at Matt.

"Yes," Matt said. "Don't yet know who, but there are some clues."

He looked at one of the cards. "Every transaction to the World Bank has a direct connection to something Jack did."

"Any transactions since Jack's death?" Ralph asked.

"Some.'

"How is that possible?"

"All the transactions deal with things Jack set in motion."

"So, someone else is creating the transactions now?"

"Yes."

Ralph leaned forward, intent.

"I think it's someone who worked very closely with Jack."

"Donald?" Ralph stared at Matt. "I was always skeptical about Jack confiding in Donald and Brian so much."

"I think it's someone else."

Ralph hesitated a moment and then asked, "Okay, how did you come up with that one?" He raised a hand. "And don't tell me it was from induction or deduction."

"Those were the dominant analytical processes, but I also use stochastic processes in probability analysis. It's also called 'random walk' which deals with predicting things that don't follow any known pattern or conform to any known criteria, like predicting where a drunk would wind up after walking away from a bar and roaming around city streets."

"What does it do for us in this situation?"

"It tells me neither Donald nor Brian are the culprits," Matt said. "Trust me. You don't want the details about my logic."

After hesitating, Ralph asked, "Then who is it?"

"I don't know yet, but I'm closing in."

....

At the FBI headquarters in Washington DC, Paul Becker, FBI Director, shifted his position and drummed his fingers on the conference table in the makeshift operations center designed to facilitate working with his cohort at the CIA, Joe Frank.

After staring for a moment at several rows of monitors along two walls, Paul glanced at the other two men in the room. The room was reserved exclusively for use in the ongoing war on illegal drugs and the recent related events taking place on that front, including the activities at JAXPORT.

Gary Stennis sat across the conference table from him, as did Dan Maxwell.

Paul focused a steady gaze on Dan. "So, you're going back to Jacksonville for a meeting with Tustun tomorrow morning."

"Yes sir," Dan replied. "Kevin Brown and Butch Reilly are going with me. The meeting was Ben's idea. He and Justin Mason thought it would be good for some of us to meet with Ralph Gibson and Matt Baker to compare notes firsthand."

Paul nodded and then asked, "Those assassins in the St. Augustine incident, any ID?"

"Not yet, a lot of our analysts are working on it along with all the other stuff," Gary said.

Paul's gaze took in both men. "I got a call an hour ago from the NSA Director. He told me they were close to decrypting those phone calls that came from somewhere around Miami to this area. He thinks they'll nail down the exact locations on both ends and he expects to have the data by tomorrow."

"Great, that should help with our meeting in Jacksonville. It should provide at least a few more answers," Dan said.

••••

In Miami, two men departed the city on a private jet.

"So, you took a few extra billion last year and built new offices in Colombia?" Carmen glanced at Juan.

"A small office in Cartagena and a larger one in Medellin, both are under a different company name," Juan said.

"Again, this is something you didn't tell me."

"I was going to, but I've been a bit preoccupied. Anyway, you know now."

Carmen looked directly at Juan. "You've had this corporate move planned for a while, right?"

"It's always good to be prepared," Juan said. "I've felt for a good while that we might need a bug-out strategy. Now we're executing it, a disaster recovery plan, so to speak."

There was a brief silence.

Carmen narrowed his eyes. "Who do you think knocked off Worthington?"

"It might really have been a suicide," Juan said. "However, my guess is that it was someone from NEUEXP, whoever they are?"

"How do you figure that?"

"NEUEXP might have already been setup within Tustun," Juan said. "They might have reached a point where they didn't need Worthington anymore."

"Maybe Worthington got in their way?"

Juan nodded. "I suspect that was the case. I plan to check back with our sources in Washington to see if I can get more details about the murder investigation."

"Is our new office completely set up in Colombia?"

"Yes."

Carmen frowned. "Do you think the Americans are coming after both of us?"

"For sure," Juan said. "We both made the trip to Jacksonville." He stared at Carmen for a moment. "And it's well known we both represent DUISONZ."

"Think they'll find out about Omar?"

"Doubtful."

Carmen rubbed his chin. "At least I'll be back in my homeland now."

••••

Kevin Brown drove north on George Washington Memorial Parkway. Late afternoon sunshine filtered through thick clumps of trees on both sides of the road, creating a warm pleasant scene, one that contrasted with his feelings.

Craig had summoned him to a meeting in Joe Frank's office.

Soon after turning off on Chain Bridge Road, he pulled up to a gate at CIA Headquarters. The guard scanned his ID and waved him through. Kevin entered the main building and ran his ID through the appropriate slot on the security unit. In a couple of minutes, he arrived at Joe Frank's office.

Joe gestured toward a round conference table, surrounded by four chairs, one of which was occupied. Kevin popped into a chair next to Craig. Joe settled into one of the two remaining chairs.

"We have some new angles on things you need to keep in mind down in Jacksonville." Joe gave Kevin a long look before he nodded to Craig.

"Joe and I have completed some recent meetings with some of our congressmen," Craig said. "We're drawing a lot of scrutiny about our activity within the United States." He leaned toward Kevin. "Since we have a joint project going with the FBI, we still want you to go to Jacksonville. We just…"

Joe's secure phone rang. He raised his hand to signal everyone to wait for a moment while he answered.

After a brief conversation, Joe disconnected and looked at Craig and Kevin. "That was Paul Becker. He called about the same thing we're talking about."

"Our working domestically with the FBI?" Craig asked.

"That's the subject," Joe said. "Paul agrees with me that the circumstances allow us to push a few boundaries."

"So, the meeting in Jacksonville is still on?" Craig asked.

"Both Kevin and Butch are still fully approved to be functional members of the combined taskforce in Jacksonville," Joe said. "Paul just wanted to make sure we were on the same page."

Craig rubbed his chin and glanced at Kevin. "Are you flying down with Dan?"

"Yes," Kevin said, "and Butch is too. We'll fly on an FBI plane."

Joe's gaze took in both Craig and Kevin. "Good luck moving forward." He stood and gave a wave of dismissal. "We need a breakthrough on the illegal drug trafficking. We must justify our participation down there in Jacksonville."

"I get the message loud and clear," Craig said, as he and Kevin stood and turned toward the doorway.

••••

In Jacksonville, Matt turned his Mercedes into his driveway.

The late afternoon sun was still above the treetops, casting long shadows across his front yard. After punching a button on his garage door opener, he eased the car into its normal parking spot.

In need of a break, he had left work earlier than usual. The peaceful drive home was a good start, being ahead of the usual rush hour traffic made a difference.

He settled into a lounge chair in his den.

Some things he had discovered late that afternoon just didn't make sense. Given a little more time, he was confident he could figure out what was going on. He had always been a talented problem solver.

He mulled over new information about the World Bank Group (WBG).

WBG was a family of five international organizations responsible for providing finance and advice to countries for the purposes of economic development and eliminating poverty.

But was Colombia a country that needed help?

He mulled over the facts. A thought flashed in his head that it would be a good idea to grab some index cards, but he decided to organize things in his head for now. He leaned back and mentally sifted through the facts.

The five organizations that made up the WBG were: International Bank for Reconstruction and Development (IBRD), International Development Association (IDA), International Finance Corporation (IFC), Multilateral Investment Guarantee Agency (MIGA), and International Centre for Settlement of Investment Disputes (ICSID).

Matt reflected that the label 'World Bank' was the usual reference to the activities of the IBRD and the IDA, whereas the World Bank Group was all five institutions. The main problems he had uncovered were within the IFC, so that made it a WBG issue.

Jack had been involved with a lot of transactions with the IFC just before his death. Matt shook his head slowly and continued to organize his thoughts.

The International Monetary Fund (IMF) and the World Trade Organization (WTO) also showed up in the process Jack had been using. There were even joint projects tied into what the IFC labeled 'technical cooperation projects.' There was a broad scope of these technical cooperation projects, and the goals were often convoluted.

Matt ran his fingers through his dark brown hair. Most of the time, these projects were funded by donor countries or by the IFC's own budget.

Saudi Arabia showed up several times as a donor country for certain private sector projects, some were in Colombia.

Very suspicious, these private sector projects, Matt thought. He could figure it out. Logic was something he thrived on.

Matt had noted transactions from both NEUEXP and DUISONZ appeared in the data. Many of the transactions involved Saudi Arabia and Colombia in some combination. Some, however, involved Mexico and the United States.

He scratched his head. He had advanced degrees in Finance, Mathematics, and Engineering. He was confident that, given the new data, he could figure this out. He let his mind wander across the facts he had stored in his head.

A few transactions involving NEUEXP were initiated at Tustun. The other transactions to the IFC involving NEUEXP had been initiated in Saudi Arabia or Colombia. All the DUISONZ transactions had been initiated in Florida or Mexico.

Matt started a new line of thought just as he was interrupted. He picked up his ringing phone. He knew by the caller ID it was Ralph.

"Got things figured out yet?" Ralph asked.

"It's pretty complex."

"Maybe we can make some real progress in our meeting tomorrow."

Ralph hesitated for a moment. "On second thought, I'd like to get a jump start on tomorrow."

"What do you have in mind?"

"Are you available for a discussion?" Ralph asked

"I guess so, where?"

"Have you eaten yet?"

"No, but I'm going to be thinking about that pretty soon."

"What if I pick up some steak sandwiches at Fireman's Subs on the way over to your house?"

"Sounds good," Matt said.

"What do you want to drink?"

"I have plenty of milk and cokes here, if that works for you."

"See you in a bit," Ralph said. "I discovered some new stuff, and I prefer to not talk about it over the phone."

Matt heard Ralph disconnect.

Less than thirty minutes later, Matt saw Ralph's green jaguar turn into his driveway. He opened the front door. The steak sandwiches smelled great.

Matt gestured toward the breakfast room table.

Ralph nodded. "Perfect."

"I'm getting milk," Matt said, stopping at the refrigerator.

"That works for me too." Ralph put the bag of subs in the middle of the table.

Matt approached the table with two large glasses filled to the top. He settled into a chair across from Ralph and grabbed a steak sandwich from the bag. It was still hot. He noted Ralph was already eating his.

"So, what did you find out today?" Matt asked.

"Harrell dropped by my office. In passing, he mentioned Tustun had some new security equipment he installed last month."

"Brian's the Security Director. Why didn't he tell you?"

"He normally just keeps Donald informed on the security issues." Ralph shrugged. "I guess that's normal since Donald's his boss."

Matt took a bite of steak and then asked, "Where is it?"

"In Elsie's area," Ralph said, "just outside Jack's office."

Matt raised an eyebrow. "What does Elsie say about it?"

"Elsie told me Jack had ordered it. She didn't know what he had in mind, but Jack and Brian had watched Harrell install it when it arrived. She also told me no one had been using it."

Matt looked over his sandwich at Ralph. "Since Harrell works for Brian, do you still trust him?"

"I still peg him as an honest guy." Ralph said. "I think he tries hard to do his job." He shrugged. "I don't think he's in cahoots with Donald and Brian."

"Don't know of any reason to argue." Matt shrugged and looked at Ralph. "Was Harrell going to check the equipment when he left your office?"

"Yeah," Ralph said. "He mentioned it's a sophisticated online computer system, the same setup that some big banks use for wiring money, encrypting software, the works. He told me it's being used a lot. That's why he needed to fine-tune it."

"Why did Elsie tell you no one was using it?"

Ralph shrugged. "Maybe she never saw anyone, maybe it can be operated remotely." He finished his first sandwich and reached into the bag for another.

"Think Elsie's involved?" Matt asked.

"Why do you keep bringing that up?"

"This new equipment seems a little suspicious," Matt said. "She should have mentioned it to you."

"I asked her about that. She told me she hadn't paid any attention to it since it had been installed. I never noticed the equipment." Ralph stared at Matt. "You ever notice it?"

"Never paid attention to the equipment around Jack's office," Matt said. "Elsie has several duplicating machines, several binding machines, and several computer consoles. Jack demanded a lot of support."

Ralph chuckled. "Some analyst you turned out to be."

Matt gave a slight shrug. "Hindsight's always 20/20." He reached into the bag for the last sandwich. "Are you going to talk to Elsie tomorrow?"

"I thought we both would after our scheduled meeting with all the law enforcement."

Matt nodded.

After he had thrown the empty bag and wrappers in the trash, Matt put the glasses in the dishwasher and waved Ralph toward the den. They settled into two comfortable leather-covered lounge chairs.

"Most of the latest DUISONZ transactions to the IFC were sent from Miami, probably from Juan Medina," Matt said. "A few were sent from Mexico; the rest were sent from here."

"Now who's the IFC?"

"International Finance Corporation, we've been calling it the Word Bank." Matt gave a slight shrug. "It's a part of the World Bank Group. I'll explain later."

"Donald and Brian have to be involved in the transactions from here, right?"

"That's my opinion."

Ralph studied Matt for a few moments. "Found any connections to Jack's death yet."

"I'm uncovering a lot of clues," Matt said. "I need a little more time to connect the dots."

"Any good guesses or gut feelings right now?"

"Yeah, several."

"Involving Medina and Flores?" Ralph asked. "Or is it Donald and Brian? Or is it all of them?"

"Concerning Jack, I don't think it's any of them," Matt said.

"How do you figure that?"

Matt explained.

"Who do you think it is?"

"It could be Elsie."

Ralph laughed. "Again, I've known Elsie for a long time and I'm sure Jack had her well checked out when he hired her."

"I'm not positive she's involved, but there are a lot of clues indicating she is." Matt went on to explain.

Ralph leaned back in his chair. "I've heard enough for tonight. My head is spinning." He stood and turned toward the front door "Maybe we'll get this ironed out in the meeting tomorrow."

"Thanks for the sandwiches," Matt said with a grin.

Ralph returned the grin and gave a dismissive wave.

Chapter 20

In Columbia the next morning, Juan puffed on his pipe in route from Cartagena to Medellin and looked out the window of his custom-built jet. The smell of the cherry-blend permeated the luxurious cabin.

Carmen leaned forward in his heavily padded swivel lounge seat. "You told me this is a BBJ3?"

"A custom version," Juan said. He smiled at Carmen. "It comes in handy."

"Nice plane," Carmen said. "I was preoccupied with other thoughts and didn't comment on it yesterday, but I noticed some of the features."

"BBJ stands for Boeing Business Jet. The BBJ3 is based on the 737-900ER. The 'ER' stands for extended range."

Carmen nodded slowly and then asked, "Exactly how does Omar feel about our current situation?"

"He's concerned, but he agrees with what we're doing. He's aware the CIA is coming after us."

Carmen glanced out his window for a few moments; then, turned toward Juan. "Do you think we're safe down here?"

"I think we'll be okay if we're careful and pay off the right people."

....

In Jacksonville, Matt walked with Justin toward the Tustun boardroom. They walked down a hall lined with mahogany paneling.

After they entered the boardroom, they shook hands with the five men mingling around a large coffee service. Ben and Dan from the FBI were there along with Kevin and Butch from the CIA. Ralph was the other man.

The morning sunshine filtered through the partially closed blinds and contributed toward a comfortable atmosphere.

Matt noted the flower arrangement in the middle of the table was low enough to not block anyone's view. Elsie was an expert decorator, he thought.

When everyone was seated at the table, Ralph waited a few minutes for everyone to relax and get a few sips of hot coffee then he gestured toward Matt. "He'll share his analysis with everyone first. We'll proceed from there."

Matt repeated the facts and opinions he had given Ralph the previous evening.

"That matches what I've concluded," Justin said. "I have just one thing to add." He explained.

"That's hard to accept," Ralph said. "Why would Elsie have any reason to get involved with something like this?"

"Money, a huge amount of money," Justin said. He nodded toward Kevin.

"Our analysts uncovered several offshore numbered accounts that we traced back to Elsie," Kevin said.

Ralph raised an eyebrow.

"A couple in the Channel Islands and one in the Isle of Man," Kevin said. "The Channel Islands are the islands of Jersey and Guernsey off the coast of England, located in the English Channel. There are some smaller islands in the mix, but they're considered a part of the bigger islands.

They're all closer to France than Great Britain. They're thirteen miles from the northern coast of France and 85 miles from the southern coast of Great Britain."

"Some of the islands like Jersey are where they raise cattle?" Ralph asked.

Kevin nodded. "These islands have provided a variety of tax havens, immune to inquiries from foreign authorities. I think that's why Elsie has been using them."

"But not immune to the CIA." Matt shot Kevin a knowing look.

Kevin smiled. "We have our methods. However, the financial community on the islands has tightened up. They're much better regulated now, and they tend to cooperate, for the most part, with foreign authorities."

"Where's the Isle of Man?" Ben asked.

"North of the Channel Islands, it has a central location in the Irish Sea between Northern Ireland and Great Britain," Kevin said. "The financial community operates, for the most part, the same as it does in the Channel Islands."

"It's hard to believe Elsie would be involved in this. Do you think someone might be trying to frame her?" Ralph asked.

"Elsie has withdrawn some of the funds," Kevin said. "We verified a lot of things. She bought a huge mansion on Great Abaco in the Bahamas. We have satellite footage of her there."

"How long ago?" Ralph asked.

"Last weekend," Kevin said.

Ralph frowned and shook his head. "It's still hard to believe."

"It's certain she's involved." Kevin looked at Ralph. "I'm sorry."

Ralph turned toward Justin. "Did you know all this?"

"I got the evidence from Kevin earlier this morning," Justin said. "It fit with a few things my detectives had uncovered."

Ralph glanced at Matt. "Guess you were right." He narrowed his eyes. "Elsie must be involved in the IFC transactions that originated from here."

Matt nodded. "It looks like Elsie has been helping launder the money from illegal drug trafficking."

Ralph scanned the faces around the room. "What about Donald and Brian?"

"We're not sure yet if they're involved in this one," Ben said. "At least we have no evidence of their direct involvement."

"That's hard to believe." Ralph shook his head. "What about Jack's murder?"

"Elsie," Justin said. "I had several conversations with her yesterday and had another meeting earlier this morning, things started coming together."

"Why would she murder him?" Ralph asked.

"Maybe Jack discovered what she was doing and confronted her," Justin said. "She seems to be a very resourceful lady." He gestured toward Ben and Kevin. "Their two agencies dug up a lot of history. The first twenty years of her life were a bit checkered."

Ralph raised an eyebrow.

"Long story, we'll give you a full report later," Justin said. "Let me just say that her father operated a drug cartel in Mexico while she was growing up. Her real name is Catalina Ramirez."

"She must have covered up her sordid past rather well," Ralph said. "I remember Jack doing a thorough background check."

Kevin nodded. "She had a lot of money to concoct a new identity."

"She must have run out of that money and needed a big payoff," Matt said.

Ralph looked at Justin. "Are you going to arrest her this morning?

"Soon as this meeting is over," Justin said.

Ralph hesitated. "It's going to be hard to concentrate on anything else."

Justin put both hands flat on the table and pushed into a standing position. "Well, let's go make an arrest. At least we now know about Catalina Ramirez."

••••

Upon their arrival in Medellin, Juan and Carmen were met at the airport by two members of their new security team.

After a short exchange of pleasantries, a large black limo headed in the direction of downtown, toward the new office building.

While they motored toward downtown, Carmen glanced at Juan. "Do you plan to try to make any deals with Tustun from down here?"

"I've been advised it's too big of a risk," Juan said.

"Who did you hear that from?"

"Panther."

"By the way, exactly who is Panther?"

"No one seems to know."

"Does Panther communicate with Omar too?"

"Quite often, according to Omar."

Carmen hesitated a moment and then asked, "And Omar doesn't know who he is either?"

"I've pressed him on that, and he insists he doesn't."

Carmen shook his head slowly. "Strange."

"Why do you say that?"

"It seems like some of us would know."

"Panther probably doesn't want to take any chances on being exposed, no matter how small the risks," Juan said as the limo came to a stop.

••••

Ralph led the way out of the conference room and walked toward Elsie's desk, Justin and the others followed close behind.

Bringing up the rear of the procession, Matt fished out his cell phone and punched in a number. There was no answer.

"She's not at her desk," Ralph said, as they approached the area outside of what had been Jack's office.

Everyone stopped except for Matt; he rushed over toward a body slumped in a far corner. It was Harrell.

Justin and each of the Federal agents grabbed their phones and punched in a number.

Matt felt Harrell's pulse. He was alive. Harrell's eyelids fluttered when Matt slapped him on his left cheek. "Ouch," Harrell said. He rubbed his chin.

Eight policemen rushed in. One started conversing with Justin. The others spread out and scanned the area.

Matt looked at the group around him. "I tried to call Harrell a few moments ago and got no answer. We now know the reason."

"Twenty of my men secured the building before we started our meeting," Justin said. "She must still be here." He gestured to his men. "Search it."

Ralph made a call also and instructed Maria to get the word out for Tustun employees to help with the search.

Harrell staggered to his feet and braced himself with his right hand on the wall. He looked at Matt. "That lady packs a punch."

"Don't know if I would call her a lady now days," Matt said. "How did it happen?"

"I was milling around the area when she bolted from her desk toward that door." Harrell pointed. "I was directly in her path, and I guess she considered me a threat."

"You're trained in several martial arts techniques, aren't you?" Matt asked.

"Simply put, she's better than I am," Harrell said.

Ralph walked over to Matt. "It's my fault."

"How do you figure that?"

"You were really close to nailing this down last night," Ralph said. He gestured with both palms out. "I should have given you more credit. I should have called Justin last night. I just couldn't bring myself to believe Elsie murdered Jack."

Justin walked over to Ralph and said, "Just got a report, we don't think she's in the building."

"How could she get out?" Ralph asked. "We know she was here when we started the meeting." He stared at Justin. "You told me you had the foresight to position your men around the outside of the building in case they were needed."

"We'll keep looking, but it appears somehow she's given us the slip." Justin stared back at Ralph for a moment. "I suggest we go back to the conference room and finish the meeting. We can use it as a control center for a while."

"Fine with me," Ralph said.

Kevin glanced at Butch. "Go ahead and look around some."

Butch nodded.

"You sure you're okay?" Ralph asked, glancing at Harrell.

Harrell rubbed his chin for a moment and nodded.

"Then I suggest you join us for a bit." Ralph turned and walked back toward the conference room. Everyone followed.

Justin looked at Ralph. "Maybe you should give Glascock and Busby some kind of explanation. Say whatever you want, but I suggest you keep them out of this."

Ralph nodded and made a couple of short calls.

"Anyone have any bug detection equipment available?" Matt looked around the room.

"I can get some." Harrell looked at Matt. "I won't let Brian know." He rushed out of the room and returned in a couple of minutes. Everyone had remained silent except for whispered conversations in the far corners of the room on their cell phones.

"Check the flowers," Matt said.

Harrell flipped a switch on a long wand that he carried and swept it over the batch of flowers on the middle of the table. He got a hit. He reached into the bouquet and extracted what looked like a fly. "This is it."

Harrell smashed the fly and then looked at Matt. "How did you figure that out?"

"Deduction," Matt said.

Ralph narrowed his eyes. "She must be damned good at escape and evasion."

"Apparently so," Butch said, entering the room. "She's gone for sure."

Justin looked at Ralph. "I heard you blame yourself a few minutes ago. I think she would have gotten away even if we had gone after her last night. This woman is one slick operator. Let's call her by her real name Catalina from now on."

Everybody nodded.

"I had no idea who we were dealing with," Ralph said.

"Well, I suggested we come back in here to compare notes." Justin ran his fingers through his hair. "I think I've disclosed everything I know so we can move on to anything else we need to address."

"NEUEXP has connections to Mexico," Dan said. "But all the evidence we have at this time supports their being a legitimate global corporation." He hesitated for a moment. "I mentioned NEUEXP because of, uh, Catalina's family ties."

Matt nodded. "NEUEXP is based in Saudi Arabia, but they might have more activity in Columbia and Mexico than we realize."

"That was my primary thought," Dan said.

"It's worth checking into further," Ralph scanned the faces around him, "especially since we were planning to expand our business into Mexico."

"Remember, Jack was doing a lot of analysis involving Mexico," Matt said, "Jack or Catalina, or maybe both."

After receiving a call, Justin glanced at the men around him. "My men have completed a thorough search. She found some way to get out." He looked at Butch. "You were right. She's gone."

"Lot going on we didn't know about." Ralph looked around the room. "We might have just stumbled into the biggest surge of deception we can imagine."

"And DUISONZ and NEUEXP are both involved," Matt said.

Ben looked at Ralph. "Those male assassins who tried to knock you off in St. Augustine were employed by DUISONZ. They were part of DUISONZ security at JAXPORT."

Ralph raised an eyebrow. "When did you find that out?"

"A few seconds ago," Ben said. He held his phone up.

"Is anyone going after Medina and Flores right now?" Ralph asked.

"Dan and I are waiting on some high-level decisions," Ben said.

"We'll keep everybody informed."

Ralph glanced at Justin. "Any more questions for Harrell?"

After seeing Justin shake his head, Ralph told Harrell he could go. "Suggest you see our company doctor, just in case."

"Right," Harrell mumbled as he left the room.

"Let's discuss the port situation," Ben said. "That's an important issue that has to be dealt with."

Ralph nodded and discussed the shipping arrangements Tustun was engaged in, including the imports of legal drugs from South America."

"Will you increase shipments of legal drugs into JAXPORT?" Ben asked.

Ralph gestured to Matt. "You've done all the business analysis."

Matt explained Tustun's imports would triple in volume if all the plans were implemented.

Ben glanced at Dan. "Have you run across anything that would throw any suspicion toward Busby and Glascock?"

"Nothing yet," Dan said.

"I'm always suspicious of those two, hard evidence or not." Ralph gestured to Matt.

"There's nothing solid against Donald and Brian I've found yet." Matt said. "Both Ralph and I will keep a close eye on things."

While they ended the discussion, Ralph suggested they concentrate on going after Catalina. No one disagreed.

••••

Soon after arriving at their new headquarters in Medellin, Juan sat with Carmen at the round conference table in his office and glanced out the window at the sunshine.

He had given up a few things, but not much when compared to the big picture. He could do without DUISONZ. He would concentrate on creating a new front company to handle things. Counting Omar's and Carmen's contributions, his revenue from oil and drugs was now over 50 million American Dollars a day.

"What's the name of our new company?" Carmen asked.

Juan shrugged. "Haven't decided yet."

"The sign on the building was Roinzex Enterprises."

"Had to have a purpose for the building," Juan said. "A large building with no name on it would draw a lot of attention." He pursed his lips. "I introduced that name around here a few years back, set up some business for crop growing."

Carmen nodded.

"I might continue with that name, don't know yet." Juan stared at Carmen for a moment. "You have any suggestions?"

Carmen shrugged. "I like the name okay. It's neutral. It could be any kind of business."

Juan pointed toward a giant map of Colombia on the wall. "Watch this." He pressed a button under his desk. Multiple locations lit up on the map.

Carmen walked over to the map with Juan following right behind him. He studied it for a couple of seconds; then, pointed to a location in Cartagena. "Is that our new warehouse?"

"Yes," Juan said, "still secret too, at least as far as I know."

"The other locations are the farms used by Roinzex Enterprises?"

Juan nodded. "DUISONZ will no longer create any transactions. And we'll soon have more warehouses on the map."

"Isn't it dangerous to have a map like this in your office?"

Juan smiled. "You have to punch in a complex code to activate it."

"What are you going to use it for?"

"It will be useful for strategy meetings and other similar things." Juan hit another button under his desk. A large map of South America appeared on another wall. He hit the button again. The map changed to a map of the United States. After another press of the button, the map became a map of the world.

"Quite impressive," Carmen said.

"These other maps have the same capability of displaying highlighted locations as I demonstrated with the first map. I have this same setup in one of the large conference rooms."

Carmen nodded.

"I want to constantly improve our technology for drug trafficking." Juan grinned. "I want to buy some submarines."

"How will you get them?"

"I'll find a way." Juan smiled.

••••

In Jacksonville, Matt parked his Mercedes in the usual spot at home and eased into a lounge chair in his den. He had more thinking to do.

Catalina Ramirez was on the loose, whereabouts unknown. Was she still a threat?

Based on recent events, he was sure that he and Ralph were targets to be eliminated. Was Catalina in control of that activity? Did she have any connection to Panther? Maybe she was Panther?

He continued to focus on Catalina and felt his anger build. He was now sure she had something to do with Jack's murder. He would bring her to justice. The game wasn't over. Jack's death would be avenged.

When his thoughts were interrupted by a familiar sound, Matt reached for his secure satellite phone and answered.

"Got some new information," Ralph said. "Justin called about new data he received from the FBI. The phone calls from Miami were to the FBI and the CIA, and they were from DUISONZ."

"Not too big of a surprise after what's been happening," Matt said. "Medina and Flores have connections to some moles."

"Justin also discovered my office phone was bugged, along with yours and Maria's."

"Now we know how they knew our every move," Matt said. "We better have our home phones checked."

"Justin has already checked mine, no bugs. He's on his way over to check yours."

"Our home security is pretty good. Guess it was easier to bug our phones at work with Catalina, Donald, and Brian looking after things," Matt said. "I'm certain Donald and Brian have connection somewhere to the criminal activity."

"With all that analysis you've been doing, you still haven't been able to find anything concrete?" Ralph asked.

"Not yet."

After a moment of silence, Ralph said, "Ben also called and gave me some more news about Catalina."

"What?"

"She ran one of the drug cartels in Mexico when she was in her teens, and she was known as 'The Tigress'."

"Who discovered that?"

"RAND found out, don't know the details," Ralph said. "Once RAND had her real name, they were able to do a lot more research."

"Harrell might have done better if he was expecting her to be a tigress."

"Maybe."

"She's probably Panther, makes more sense now."

"Yeah," Ralph said. "But whether she's Panther or not, we can't allow her to get away with this. No one can murder Jack and think we're going to forget about it. We'll track her down."

Chapter 21

The next morning in Columbia, Juan sat in his new office in Medellin and looked over his desk at Carmen. "Omar should be arriving in a few minutes."

"Why does he need to come here?"

"He has some things he needs to discuss with us."

"Saudi Arabia is a long way off and we have secure lines. Why not do a conference call?"

Juan chuckled. "Omar likes to get in your face on some issues. Besides, I think he got tired of sitting around."

"What's the topic?"

"He wouldn't tell me." Juan lit his pipe and took a puff. "He mentioned he had some sensitive things to discuss, and some new ideas. Omar is much more paranoid than we are, maybe that's good."

Carmen shrugged and didn't comment.

"Our moles informed me the National Security Agency has intercepted some of our calls and picked up more information about us," Juan said.

"You told me nobody could break our encryption."

"They must have made some improvements. It's probably a good thing Omar is coming here to discuss things."

Carmen started to comment just as Omar walked in.

Juan stood and waved Omar and Carmen toward the round conference table in a corner of his office. All three men settled into chairs.

Omar took a deep breath, exhaled slowly, and then said, "We need to make our next shipment into JAXPORT immediately."

Juan narrowed his eyes. "Why the big rush?"

"Some things have changed," Omar said. "We must act before all of our secrets are discovered."

"What has changed?" Juan asked.

"I'll get to that in a moment," Omar said. "We need to move quicker than the Americans can react."

"We're prepared to fully load a ship." Juan leaned back in his chair. "The warehouse in Cartagena is well stocked."

"I know," Omar said. "And I'm telling you to get moving."

"Considering everything we moved from the fortress, we actually have an oversupply," Juan replied. "We can move a fleet of trucks alongside the warehouse and load up fast."

"How long to load up?" Omar asked.

"With the right crew, eight hours," Juan said.

Omar nodded. "How long to get the trucks in position?"

"We have to pull them from various places," Juan said. "They can all be at the warehouse in two days."

"We should start immediately to get the trucks into position. They should be ready to start loading the ship as soon as it docks."

Juan rubbed the back of his neck for a moment. "This is a bit of a surprise, but I won't argue."

Omar grinned. "I brought several surprises." He punched a number into his secure satellite phone. "Come on in."

A tall slim lady, clad in a sleek black pants suit, strutted through the door. She stopped, saying nothing, and stared at the three men in the room.

"I believe you knew this lady as Elsie Farmer, Jack Worthington's secretary." Omar chuckled. "Let me introduce Catalina Ramirez. She's on our team, always has been. She just needed to maintain the utmost secrecy."

Omar proceeded to explain her background and the discussion he had engaged in with NEUEXP in Saudi Arabia.

Catalina took a seat at the conference table.

Juan looked directly at Catalina. "Are you Panther?"

"Even if I were, I wouldn't admit it," Catalina said.

Omar gave both Juan and Carmen a hard look. "Panther's identity has been a well-kept secret for a long time, and it needs to stay that way. Catalina is one hell of a fighter and we're lucky to have her on our side, damned lucky."

"Are we going to partner with NEUEXP?" Juan asked.

Omar nodded. "Chuck Milton has inside knowledge. He'll help on that."

"Do you have more surprises?" Juan asked.

"To be precise, two more," Omar said. "I think the four of us should supervise operations in Cartagena. We need to hurry things along. We'll make sure all necessary items are included in the next shipment." He looked at Juan and Carmen. "Have you ever heard of the SIG 556 rifle?"

Both Juan and Carmen shook their heads.

"It weighs 7.8 pounds, is only 37 inches long, and fires 900 rounds per minute, NATO 5.56 rounds," Omar said. "It's Swiss made for law enforcement."

"Do you have one?" Carmen asked.

"I have several of them." Omar gave a sly grin. "I brought four with me. The right amount of money opens a lot of doors. I thought they might come in handy while we supervise operations at the warehouse."

Juan and Carmen listened while Omar gave the details.

Catalina walked over to the credenza and poured a cup of coffee. She stood by the window and looked out while she sipped it.

Juan figured she already knew the details.

••••

Ralph, Matt, and Harrell (who had received an all-clear from the company doctor and was fully on the job) sat across the large boardroom table from Ben and Justin.

"You swept the room again for bugs, just in case?" Ralph asked.

Harrell nodded. "It's all clear."

"Ben and I have found no damning evidence yet on the Fishers," Justin said. "DUISONZ is a client of the Fishers, but that's not illegal. We'll continue to investigate."

Ralph glanced at Matt. "You found nothing suspicious about the Fishers in all your analysis?"

"Nothing that would refute what we just heard," Matt said.

Ralph stared across the table at Ben and Justin. "What about Donald and Brian?"

"Long story short, Justin and I have found nothing solid yet," Ben said.

Justin nodded.

Ralph hesitated for a moment and looked at Harrell. "You work for Brian. Maybe you've seen something."

"Nothing that's out of line with normal corporate security policy," Harrell said.

Ralph kept his gaze fixed on Harrell. "Keep your eye on things. My door's always open if you have any concerns."

Harrell nodded.

Ralph looked at Ben and Justin. "Looks like this situation might have another round or two."

"At least one investigation might be ending. We know who the likely murderer is." Justin glanced at Ben. "I'm in more of a support role now."

"The FBI is in a similar role for apprehending Catalina," Ben said. "We don't think she's in the country. Craig Parker is leading the search for her."

"Should Matt and I stay directly involved?" Ralph asked.

"Yes, we still need your inside knowledge on all this," Ben said.

"Not to mention Ralph and I are both battle tested." Matt grinned.

"That helps," Ben said. "I'm certain you'll have more battles coming up. It's best you stay alive."

Ralph turned toward Ben. "Speaking of that, I want to request some more training at your facility in Quantico."

"I'll go you one better," Ben said. "Craig Parker made arrangements for you to go through some new advanced training at a CIA facility. This training will be useful if we repeat the experience we had at the fortress."

"So, we're still partners with you and the CIA?" Ralph asked.

Ben nodded. "Kevin designed the training scenario."

"When's the training?" Matt asked. "And how long does it last?"

"It's scheduled for tomorrow morning and it lasts for six hours," Ben said. "Our best intelligence sources tell us we need to move quickly."

Chapter 22

Early the next morning, at a CIA training facility in McLean, Ralph and Matt wore SWAT team gear and stood in a large dome. A replica of a city street, dark except for a few streetlights, stretched out before them.

The instructor, a short trim man, swung a hand in a sweeping motion. "This facility simulates all conditions, including wind and rain." He studied Ralph and Matt.

"Ever used a SIG 556 before?" the instructor asked.

Ralph and Matt both nodded.

"But just for a brief time," Ralph said.

"Well, you're going to use one again." The instructor handed each of them a rifle with a short stock and two pistol grips.

Ralph and Matt held their rifles and listened to the instructor.

"At the CIA, we use this weapon on a lot of our missions." The instructor looked directly at his two new students. "Any questions?"

Ralph and Matt both remained silent.

The instructor glanced at his watch. "Let's see how well you can use it. Set it for semi-automatic fire." He motioned for both men to spread out on the street.

The instructor turned and climbed a ladder to a high platform.

Matt stood on a sidewalk on the right side of the street. Ralph stood on the other side, directly across from him. The streetlights dimmed.

Faint silhouettes of large structures loomed on both sides. A fine mist fell from the simulated night sky as Ralph and Matt moved down the dark street.

Matt held his silenced rifle in ready position and scanned the training area, the size of a city block. A target popped up to his left. He fired, got it.

For several minutes, Matt picked off targets. He moved down the street, alert and reacting fast. He thought he was doing okay, maybe not great, but okay.

"Hold it," a voice from the darkness shouted.

Bright light flooded the street. The instructor waved his hands and hurried over to where Matt was standing.

"It's not the damned jungle." The instructor glared at Matt. "City streets are different. Do better or you're going to die."

The instructor, who looked fit enough to take on a new mission himself, glanced over at Ralph. "The same applies to you." The instructor shook his head. "You didn't even see the last target."

"Where?" Ralph asked.

The instructor exhaled. "Rooftop, to your left." He frowned. "Move your head from side to side. You can best detect movement out of the corners of your eyes."

Ralph shrugged. "I've heard that before. Guess I wasn't scanning right."

"Damn right you weren't," the instructor said. "In this situation, keep rotating your head. The technique might save your ass."

Ralph nodded and the instructor glanced over at Matt.

Matt also nodded. He knew he had to adjust to this scenario—fighting on city streets in dim light.

The instructor scowled. "You'd be dead in a real situation. Keep performing like this and you'll get your ass shot off." He turned and stomped off, glaring back over his shoulder.

Matt suppressed a grin. The instructor was intimidating, but using a teaching method he was becoming used to.

"Let's see some improvement." The instructor climbed to the platform. The lights dimmed again.

Matt moved forward, turning his head from side to side. There, to his right, on the rooftop. He aimed and fired, got it.

As he moved forward, Matt hit target after target. He had it now. After nailing twenty more targets in a variety of locations, rooftops, alleys, windows, doorways, he felt he had mastered this exercise. Every target went down in less than a second.

"Halt." Lights came on. The instructor strolled out, appearing relaxed this time. "Better, you did okay for this part." He studied both men for a moment. "Now let's see if your expertise with the pistol is still okay."

The instructor held out his hands for the rifles. Both men handed them over.

"You have ten minutes to change back into the clothes you wore," the instructor said, glancing at his watch.

Ralph and Matt scampered toward the locker room.

Ten minutes later they were back. Each wore casual clothes with a sports coat. Each had a Glock 19 in a holster toward the back of the right hip.

"You have full magazines?" the instructor asked.

Both men nodded.

The instructor handed them some extra magazines; then, turned and ascended the steps to the platform. He looked down at the two men. "Any final questions?"

Each shook his head.

The training area again became a dark city street.

Matt moved forward. There, to his right, on the rooftop. He drew and fired. The target went down. He continued for several minutes, eliminating target after target.

The additional practice lasted a couple of hours before the instructor called a halt and descended from the platform.

Ralph and Matt moved to the middle of the street.

"You're both good enough to stay alive, don't get too cocky though." The instructor stared at the two men. "Attach the silencer and put the Glock in the front of your belt. We'll get a few more hours practice with a different method."

••••

The late morning sun bathed the area as Kevin Brown drove into CIA Headquarters. He had just completed a meeting with the DEA in downtown Washington DC.

As he strolled into the designated conference room, Kevin glanced at his watch; he was the last one there, but he was on time. He grabbed an empty seat and looked around the table. Paul, Gary, Dan, and Ben were there from the FBI. His bosses Joe and Craig were there, as was Butch. Having finished their training, Ralph and Matt were also there.

"There's an opportunity to make a significant dent in the illegal drug business," Joe said. "Let's take advantage of it." He nodded toward Craig.

"We have more intel from NSA and NRO," Craig said. He glanced at Kevin. "DEA have anything new?"

"Same intel we already had," Kevin said. "We've synced up."

Craig nodded and pushed a button in from of him. A satellite view of the drug warehouse under surveillance in Cartagena came into view on a large wall monitor.

"We know a ship is en-route there," Craig said.

"Do we know anything about their schedule?" Matt asked.

"They're scheduled to start loading the illegal drugs on the ship at noon tomorrow." Craig fixed his gaze on Kevin. "Your team will close the operation down."

"Have you considered using our assets stationed in Cartagena?" Kevin asked.

"Joe Frank and Paul Becker both think your team must lead the mission for several reasons," Craig said. He went on to explain.

"Think they'll be waiting for us in Cartagena this time?" Matt asked.

Craig frowned. "We hope not. We've done everything possible to keep this operation secret."

"We've kept it under wraps at the FBI too," Paul said. He glanced at Ralph and Matt. "We also nailed a mole in our offices, getting a lot more specifics from NSA helped make the ID."

"We'll use the same team as before," Craig said, "except we'll supplement it with more agents who work in Cartagena." He distributed packets of photos and intelligence information. After everyone scanned the data, he gave the details.

Kevin looked around the room. "Our overall team should be better than last time. We have more experience working together."

"I can vouch for Ralph and Matt," Butch said, "they're as good as most of our top agents."

"We have a satellite photo of Catalina Ramirez," Ben said. "She was spotted close to that warehouse we've been watching in Cartagena."

"Can you tell if she's directly involved in the drug trafficking?" Ralph asked.

"It's pretty obvious," Ben said. "She was with Medina and Flores."

"Anyone else in the group?" Matt asked.

Ben nodded. "Probably Omar Karam, Middle Eastern features. We're working on the ID."

Paul turned toward Ralph. "Do you need to go back to Tustun and take care of a few things since Elsie, err Catalina, isn't in place to help run things now?"

Ralph shook his head. "Jack always allowed people a lot of freedom to run their parts of the business. I've been doing the same thing. Maria is watching what's going on and she knows to keep me informed of anything significant."

"Is she comfortable doing that?" Paul asked.

"I think so," Ralph said. He gave a short laugh. "If she's not comfortable, she's a damned good actress."

"And she's watching what Donald Busby and Brian Glascock are doing?" Paul asked.

"Closely enough," Ralph said. "Harrell is constantly checking with her, and I've asked Justin Mason to meet with her at least once a day to see if she's okay with how things are going."

Paul hesitated a moment and leaned forward. "Okay, one more question. When is Chuck Milton going to show up?"

"The last I heard, he's going to take over the chairmanship next month," Ralph said.

"What's the delay?" Paul asked.

Ralph shrugged. "I'm not sure of all the details, but I was informed he still had some issues to wrap up relative to what he had been doing before he got the offer to replace Jack."

"And what had he been doing?" Paul asked.

Ralph narrowed his eyes. "Do you suspect something?"

"Just answer the question," Paul said.

"I don't know exactly what he was doing," Ralph replied. "I just know I was informed earlier by our Board of Directors that he was selected to replace Jack."

"And someone on the Board of Directors is keeping you informed?" Paul asked.

"Yes," Ralph said, "various ones at various times."

Paul nodded slowly. "Okay, enough on that for now."

Ben glanced at his watch. "We need to be at the airport in about three hours." He looked at Ralph. "Are you sure this works for you and Matt?"

"Damned right it does," Ralph said. "Matt and I want to bring Jack's killer to justice as soon as possible. That remains our number one priority."

••••

In Medellin, Juan looked around the large table in the conference room in his new headquarters. He and Carmen sat across from Omar and Catalina.

Omar announced he wanted to ensure they were all in agreement on every detail before they left for Cartagena to supervise loading the ship that was scheduled to take the cargo to JAXPORT.

Juan waited for Omar to review the details and then asked, "So we're only going to supervise moving the drugs from the warehouse at the port onto the trucks?"

"That's right, we have plenty of extra security at the docks who'll supervise moving the drugs from the trucks onto the ship," Omar said.

Juan glanced at Carmen and then looked back at Omar. "I haven't been able to reach our mole in the CIA for two days now."

"Have you had that problem before?" Omar asked.

"A couple of times," Juan said. "He was on some critical assignments, and he always called me as soon as he was back on regular duty."

"I wouldn't worry about it," Omar said. "Two days isn't much time to complete a critical assignment. You'll probably hear from him soon."

Catalina looked at her three cohorts. "You can bet Ralph Gibson and Matt Baker will be back down here. I'm looking forward to knocking them off. They've caused me a lot of irritation for a lot of years."

••••

At Tustun, Donald Busby looked across the top of his desk at Brian Glascock.

"Are you okay with things right now?" Donald asked.

"There's a lot of uncertainty, but I don't have any big issues at the moment," Brian said. "I'll feel better when Chuck Milton gets aboard. He should provide a lot of guidance."

"Yeah, but in the meantime, we can keep operating like we always do. At least Gibson hasn't put any restrictions on us."

"Ralph knows better than to do that," Brian said. "Jack and Chuck made a few trips together. They probably agree on how to run a company."

"Why didn't you let me know Jack and Chuck knew each other?"

Brian shrugged. "Guess I didn't view it as a big item, and it hasn't come up before in any of our conversations."

"Think Chuck had anything to do with Jack's murder?"

"I'm guessing Elsie took care of all the details," Brian said.

"Well do you think Chuck had anything to do with it, or not?"

"Probably," Brian said, "but I wasn't always kept up to date about things."

"Elsie should have kept you better informed."

Brian nodded slowly. "Yeah, but that wasn't her style. She was good at keeping secrets and she was obviously reluctant to share much information with us."

Donald nodded slowly. "Tell me about it. Guess we should call her Catalina from now on."

Chapter 23

Early the next morning at Rafael Nunez International Airport in Cartagena, the unmarked private jet settled on the runway and taxied to a stop at the side of a large hangar. Six men deplaned and hurried to the command center, inside the hangar.

Kevin walked over to a familiar figure huddled with several local CIA agents over a large map.

"Everything setup and working?" Kevin asked.

"Yes sir," Emilio Rivera, the local CIA agent in charge of the command center said. "All computer systems are online, and the satellite feeds are coming in."

"We want to operate like we did in Bogota so Ben will take over for now." Kevin slapped Emilio on the shoulder "We're in a foreign country, but we're fighting a domestic threat. Illegal drug trafficking is killing us."

Ben shook hands with Emilio and then glanced toward the map. It showed a section of the port. Beside the map were numerous close-up photos.

Emilio reached for one of the photographs on the table. The

photograph showed a large truck being unloaded by eight men.

"Good you're in casual clothes, best for being in the city," Emilio said. "What weapons are you using with your civilian clothes?" He raised an eyebrow. "I'm just curious."

"Ralph and I are each carrying a Glock 19," Matt said.

"Why the Glock 19?" Emilio asked.

"Best combination of size, weight, and firepower," Matt said. "Magazine holds fifteen 9mm shells."

Emilio looked at Kevin. "Are all of you carrying a Glock?"

"Variety." Kevin shrugged. "Everybody picked their favorite for urban situations." He gestured toward Butch. "He has a Heckler & Koch USP. I have a Browning HP."

"Couple of Glock 22 pistols for us FBI types," Ben said, jerking a thumb at Dan.

Kevin glanced at Emilio. "Variety of holsters too, everyone's had training on the fast draw. Each person picked the equipment he thought would maximize his effectiveness."

Without expression, Emilio stared toward the whole group. "I'll lead my men and we'll all be in full SWAT gear. We'll go to the port first. We'll be ready to help if your team comes under heavy fire."

Kevin nodded. "We have full SWAT gear too. If we need it, we'll use it later in the mission." He glanced at Ben. "Speaking of that, are you ready to get started?"

Ben turned toward Emilio. "Give Dan and me a tour of the setup and we'll start preparing for the mission."

In a few minutes Ben and Dan returned along with Emilio. Ben motioned everyone toward the conference room.

After everyone settled into chairs, Ben gestured toward a large wall monitor. He pressed a button, and a map appeared.

The warehouse at the port occupied the center of the map.

Kevin narrowed his eyes. "We can be sure they have plenty of security around the warehouse."

"Right," Butch said. "There'll be a lot inside the warehouse too."

Kevin pointed to a spot on the map south of the warehouse. "We'll start out here. We'll keep good cover and work our way to the side of the warehouse."

Ben picked up a utility bag and put it on the top of the table. He opened it to reveal sets of tactical communications gear. He extracted the needed items and handed them out. After a short test, Ben said, "We're good on the communications. We're ready to kickoff."

••••

Later in downtown Cartagena, Matt scanned the area. He and Ralph walked down opposite sides of an alleyway, toward the warehouse. With sound-suppressors attached to the end of the barrels, their Glocks were now tucked behind the front of their belts and under their shirts.

Kevin and Butch were on an adjoining street. Ben, Dan, and Emilio were back in the control center. Kevin had the drug detection device.

"The setup is much like that last bit of training we had at the CIA facility, except we have daylight," Matt said.

Ralph nodded. "We'll probably have some activity tonight. Maybe Kevin had all this in mind when he set that training scenario up for us."

Matt spoke into his tactical mike, "Couple of men on the roof to our left."

"Yeah," Ralph said. "One's head and shoulders are visible; just see the head of the other. They seem to be curious about what we're doing."

"I have a feeling we're soon going to be applying our training." Matt glanced at Ralph. "There's another man to our left and I see a couple more a few yards behind him."

Ralph nodded.

Matt saw an assassin on a nearby roof stand and turn a rifle toward him. Another assassin also stood and swung his rifle in Matt's direction.

Matt figured the assassins stood to get a better field of fire. He drew his Glock, and two muffled pops filled the air. The men fell.

After ducking into the shadows and flattening against a wall, Matt noted with satisfaction that Ralph had disposed of two more. The whole thing took less than two seconds.

"See any others?" Ralph asked, glancing at Matt.

Matt shook his head and whispered into his communications unit. "Kevin, we just took out four assassins, any action on your street?"

"We knocked off five of them," Kevin said, "Don't see any more."

••••

Omar glanced at his three cohorts. "None of our security on the rooftops is responding."

"Not a good sign," Juan said. "Gibson and his group will probably show up inside the warehouse."

Omar shrugged. "We'll know when they get here. I have a surprise for them."

••••

In the CIA control center at Rafael Nunez Airport, Ben stared at the monitor and glanced at one of the technical experts. "How long ago were these pictures taken?"

"Ten minutes ago, sir."

Ben activated his tactical microphone. "Catalina entered the warehouse ten minutes ago along with Juan Medina, Carmen Flores, and Omar Karam. We're keeping up with their exact positions."

"Roger," Kevin said. "We're ready to enter. Do you have a fix on us?"

"Yes. You're at the northeastern corner of the warehouse," Ben said. "None of the body heat readings show anyone close to you. You're clear to enter."

"What's Emilio's status?" Kevin asked.

"He and his team are at the port. He wants to secure an area there before the trucks start to unload," Ben said.

"Roger," Kevin replied.

"The ship has entered the port area and should be docking in a few minutes. We're waiting for it. We can see the row of trucks from our location," Emilio's voice came over the tactical communications units.

"Kevin, are you sure the four of you don't need any help at the warehouse?" Ben asked. "Our latest readings show there are a lot of people in there."

"With Butch along, we can handle it," Kevin whispered into his mike. "Don't worry. We know what to do. There's a small door about ten feet away. That might be our best entrance point,"

"Good choice," Ben said, "no opposition in that area."

Once inside the warehouse, the team of four split into pairs and went to opposite walls.

Ralph and Matt, each with his silenced Glock 19 in hand, moved down separate aisles between large rows of crates.

Within a couple of minutes, Matt saw a figure coming in his direction.

He aimed and fired twice in less than a second. The figure dropped. A rifle bounced on the concrete floor.

"Got one," Matt whispered, as he moved toward the prone figure. Within a few seconds, he crouched down over the felled assassin.

"Dead," Matt whispered.

"No sign of anyone over here," Ralph said. "I'm joining you."

Matt picked up the rifle as Ralph walked over. "It's a SIG 556. We'll hang onto it."

"Yeah, Catalina and the others with her probably all have one," Ralph said.

••••

Ben spoke into his tactical microphone, "I see your images and I still see four images south of you. Are you going to try to close the warehouse down now, or should you wait for Emilio and his men?"

"We'll move toward the four images and try to capture them," Kevin said. "If we succeed, we'll discuss the next step with you."

"Roger," Ben said. "No new status on Emilio's operation. He's on our system, but we've temporarily lost contact."

Dan gestured toward one of the monitors. He removed a laser pointer from his pocket and put the red dot in the middle of four figures in the infrared image from a satellite. "Kevin's group is approaching the south end."

Ben studied the monitor for a moment. "Good thing the warehouse has a roof our cameras can penetrate."

Dan nodded and directed his laser pointer toward another monitor. "That's Catalina and her group."

••••

Omar detached his tactical communications unit and glanced at his three companions. "Carlos doesn't answer anymore."

"He's the lookout you posted in the middle of the warehouse?" Juan asked.

"Yes," Omar said, "looks like he's been eliminated."

Catalina released the safety on her SIG 556 and stared at Omar. "How much security do you have in here?"

"Not much, but I have a lot outside," Omar said. "Also, most of the workers with the trucks are armed with pistols and knives. They'll be of some help if they're needed."

"Why didn't you put more in here?" Juan asked.

"I thought we were going to be outside supervising loading the trucks," Omar said. "I wanted us to be safe out there. I thought Carlos would give us a warning if he saw anyone in here."

"Did you make that clear to him?" Catalina asked.

"I told him to use his best judgment as to what to do first, eliminate them or call me," Omar said. "Probably a mistake, remember, I'm not a seasoned battlefield commander."

Catalina frowned. "We'd better move outside and check on the trucks. We all should have tactical communications units."

"Yeah," Omar said. "Oversight on my part, didn't expect us to have this exact problem. I posted a lot of security around the area. They should have taken care of things."

Shaking her head slowly, Catalina moved her SIG 556 into ready position and walked toward the nearest exit.

....

Kevin waved his group forward. After stopping behind some large crates, they scanned the area. No immediate threats were apparent.

Matt reflected on the recent training he and Ralph had completed. Many aspects of this situation were familiar. Now he needed to reap the benefits. Holding his silenced Glock 19 in ready position, he peered around the corner of the stack of crates he was behind.

"What's our plan?" Ralph asked.

"Pincher movement," Kevin said. "You and Matt go to the right. Butch and I will move up the left side."

Before they moved, Matt heard Ben's voice in his earpiece. "Catalina's group is outside and moving in the direction of the trucks."

"We'll go outside, and we'll move that way too," Kevin said. He waved everyone toward the nearest exit.

....

Carmen looked at Juan as they approached the trucks. "We should find a safe place. This type of fighting isn't our forte."

Juan shrugged. "We have good firepower. We can make it."

Omar nodded. "And we have a lot of security around us out here. When Gibson and his group show up well kill them."

Carmen, hands shaking a little, pointed his rifle forward. "You want them to come to us?" Eyes wide, he turned his head and stared at Omar.

Omar nodded. "Of course I do. We should have an excellent chance to pick them off. I doubt Gibson and Baker have any experience in this type of thing."

"You could be wrong on that," Catalina said. "I know they were getting a lot of lessons." She looked at Juan. "I think you and Carmen should wait here. It's a place with a lot of cover. Omar and I will go on to the trucks."

....

In a few moments, Kevin said, "I've spotted two of them."

"Which two?" Ralph asked.

"Juan Medina and Carmen Flores," Kevin said, "Flores looks pretty nervous."

"We're closing on Flores and Medina now," Butch whispered.

Matt heard a couple of muffled pops coming over his communications unit.

"Two down and we're the proud owners of two more SIG 556 rifles," Butch said.

••••

Catalina turned toward Omar. "You hear that?"

"What?" Omar glanced at Catalina.

"Sounded like rifles banging on the pavement, thought I heard a couple of faint pops too."

"Think Juan and Carmen had a problem?"

"Possibly."

"What if they were shot?"

"Juan, Carmen, you there?"

No answer.

"I guess they didn't defend themselves too well," Catalina said. "If Gibson and Baker get close to me, I'll take them out."

"I'm glad you're capable of doing that." Omar pointed toward the line of trucks. "Let's keep going. They're starting to unload, and I have a lot of security around the trucks."

••••

Matt stayed in a semi-crouch as he moved forward. He scanned for any sign of Catalina.

"I have a fix on both Catalina and someone with her." Ben's voice echoed in Matt's earpiece. "They're behind the last truck in the convoy. No one else is close to them."

"Thanks," Matt replied, as Kevin waved all of them over to the side of a building, hidden from view of anyone around the line of trucks.

"Best we stay out of sight for a few moments more," Kevin said. "It looks like the trucks are getting ready to move closer to the ship that just docked."

••••

Omar peered around the corner of the truck he was behind.

Catalina turned and walked toward some buildings. "I can kill Gibson and Baker some other time when things are more to my advantage. I don't like staying here."

Omar peered around the corner of the truck again as Catalina began to leave. He scanned the street.

"There they are," he said. He pointed his SIG 556 and then fell backwards.

••••

Butch looked at Matt and said, "Not bad shooting."

"When someone points a rifle barrel at you, it's time to react," Matt said, just as the line of trucks started moving.

One body was lying in the street and no one else was around.

The four task team members rushed over to the body and Ralph grabbed the SIG 556. Now they all had one.

Ralph glanced at Matt. "Hard to tell exactly, but it looks like you hit him right between the eyes."

Matt heard Ben's voice come over their communications units. "Emilio's SWAT team has all the trucks under control. He's sending a team to the warehouse as we speak."

"Does he know our latest status?" Kevin asked.

"Yes," Emilio said. "I've been back on your system for a few minutes and monitoring your conversation. My team will take care of all the bodies."

"Kevin, as for your situation, we haven't reacquired Catalina," Ben spoke into his tactical microphone. "She apparently knows how to disappear."

"Based on her background that we now know about, she's obviously been an expert at that and many other things for a number of years," Matt said. "She's also the best I've ever known at keeping secrets in every way, actions, voice tones, expressions, everything. She's a master at deception."

"No argument there," Ben replied. "I hope we can catch her before she gets completely away. We'll keep scanning the area."

"We'll look around for a while." Kevin signaled everyone around him to spread out more. "If we don't find her, we'll go back over there. I think Emilio's team can take it from here."

"That's right," Emilio said. "I'll take care of everything, and I'll keep everyone appropriately informed as we complete our cleanup."

••••

Later in the temporary CIA control center in the hangar, six men sat around the table in the small conference room.

Ralph clinched his fist. "Catalina gave us the slip again."

"We tried everything we know, but we never reacquired her image on the cameras," Ben said. "She knows what she's doing."

Matt glanced at Ralph. "You'd think she'd be rusty on all this after spending twenty plus years as Jack's secretary."

"I guess she found a way to keep in practice," Ralph said. After a brief silence, he looked at Ben and asked, "Are we transporting the drugs back to the States or leaving them down here?"

Ben shrugged. "We'll probably leave them here; we've done this before. The newspapers will report a raid on drug traffickers by the government, an ordinary drug bust. The local top official will be thrilled to get credit."

"We're right where we want to be," Kevin said, "invisible to the public and politicians."

Ralph laughed. "That seems to be what Catalina is, invisible."

"We'll continue to do all we can to help," Butch said. "At least we know a lot more about her now. We'll track her down in due time."

"The FBI will continue the search from back in the states," Ben said. "For now, we're wrapped up down here."

Chapter 24

The next day at Tustun, Ralph and Matt sat with Justin and Ben at the round conference table in Ralph's office.

"Coffee?" Maria asked.

Everyone nodded.

Ben cleared his throat. "I got a news flash from the CIA just before I left my office. Catalina was spotted just outside Bogota last night."

Ralph raised an eyebrow.

"They lost track of her, though. She's slippery, but we already knew that," Ben said.

"Any guesses where she was headed?" Matt asked.

"Consensus is to El Dorado International Airport," Ben said. "She could be going anywhere in the world."

Maria brought in a tray with four mugs of coffee. She placed one on the table in front of each man.

Ben reached for his coffee and glanced at the other three men. "However, they never spotted her at the airport."

"She probably wore a disguise," Justin said.

Matt nodded. "And I'm sure she used another name."

"Dan studied all the details," Ben said. "He told me the CIA was expecting both of those things, but they still couldn't pick her up."

"She might have used a private plane," Ralph replied. "Well, wherever she is, we need to find her. Matt and I can't get any closure on Jack's death with his killer running loose."

Ben glanced at Justin. "Find any more guilty parties while we were gone?"

Justin shook his head. "Busby and Glascock still seem to be clean. I worked closely with Harrell and checked everything. Also, the Fishers still seem to be clean."

"I don't trust Donald and Brian," Ralph said. "I figure they're involved in Jack's death in some way."

Justin pursed his lips and leaned forward. "Maybe so, but the evidence I've been able to gather still indicates they've consistently pursued legitimate business interests."

"At least we took care of Juan Medina, Carmen Flores, and Omar Karam." Ralph scanned the faces around him. "We know for sure they were involved with Catalina. They might also have been involved in Jack's death."

"Any progress on the identity of Panther?" Matt asked.

"Not yet," Ben said, "but, we still have a lot of people working on that."

Ralph leaned back and took a deep breath. He scanned the faces around the table. "Any thoughts on finding Catalina?"

"We know her roots are in Mexico," Matt said.

Ben nodded. "Dan told me she still has family living in Monterrey."

Ralph stood and walked over to a window. He rubbed the back of his neck for a moment and then said, "Matt, I think you and I are going to take a little vacation in Mexico."

When Ralph turned back toward the table his mouth dropped open.

Matt moved his head slightly and saw Catalina standing in the open doorway. Her silenced Heckler & Koch USP was extended. She was in perfect position. Everyone was well covered.

Catalina stared at Ralph. "I'll make sure you get your little vacation to Mexico. You'll be in a box though."

"How did you get in here?" Ralph asked.

"Not difficult," Catalina said. "Don't forget I spent twenty-two years in this joint." She waved her pistol. "Don't try anything. These 9mm slugs carry quite an impact."

Catalina flashed a triumphant grin as she flipped a sign on the doorknob to read 'DO NOT DISTURB.' Keeping her pistol pointed at the people in front of her, she closed the door.

"Maria's alive but she's not in great shape. She's in a closet by her desk and she's unconscious, bound, and gagged." She looked directly at Ralph.

Ralph's eyes narrowed. "So, what do you want?"

"For all of you to die," Catalina hissed. "You all have it coming."

"You can't evade everybody for long," Ralph said. "The CIA is also in this chase. Somebody will get you."

"I'll deal with the CIA later." Catalina waved her gun at Ralph and gestured toward the empty seat at the table. "Sit down. I have some things to tell you before you die. I'm going to enjoy seeing your reaction."

As he walked back to the table, Ralph stared at Catalina. "You had it good here at Tustun. Why did you have to kill Jack?"

"I killed him for good reasons. The last time Jack and I went to Monterrey, he killed my father in an argument over some drug trafficking strategy." Catalina gritted her teeth. "He mistreated my family for years and then he started mistreating me too. Jack should have known I don't tolerate things like that. He was a fool and deserved to die. He had to be eliminated."

"Jack's death was a matter of revenge," Matt said.

Catalina flashed an evil grin. "You could say that."

"Are you Panther?" Ralph asked.

Catalina laughed and waved her pistol. "I guess I can admit to that now."

Ralph reached for his chair and pulled it back slowly before he eased into it.

Matt was glad Catalina seemed overconfident. He decided to try to get some useful information while he could. "How did you get involved with NEUEXP and DUISONZ?"

Catalina gave a slight shrug. "My family has always been in the drug trafficking business. We've always tried to develop a lot of useful connections to help us maintain good cover while we ran our operations."

"So, your family decided that Tustun would be a great intermediary for laundering drug money through the World Bank," Matt said.

"I thought of that little angle, not my family," Catalina snapped.

"Not a bad setup until Jack wanted to change some things," Matt said, "guess your father didn't agree with the changes?"

"You think you're pretty smart, don't you?" Catalina hissed.

Matt shrugged. "I'm obviously not very smart about avoiding problems." He looked directly at Catalina. "However, I'm curious about something. I'd really like to know the answer before I die."

"And die you will," Catalina said with a big laugh. She looked directly at Matt. "What do you want to know?"

"Who are these NEUEXP people?" Matt asked.

"I'm sure you know all about them, but that won't be a problem. NEUEXP is legit, except for a small group I work closely with," Catalina said. She grinned. "That group and a small group at the World Bank will never be discovered. They're too well camouflaged. We all keep secrets well."

Ben pushed his chair in slow motion away from the table.

"Hold it right there." Catalina pointed her pistol at Ben. "That's far enough."

Ben stopped.

Catalina narrowed her eyes and stared at the group. "Don't try anything." She waved her pistol. "I know all your tricks. Everyone freeze. I'll cut down the next one who makes any movement."

"We're going to die anyway," Ben said.

Catalina laughed. "You're smarter than I thought." She extended her pistol toward Ralph. Her finger tightened on the trigger.

"One more question before we die," Ralph said.

Catalina eased the pressure on the trigger and waved her pistol back and forth among the four men.

"What specifically did Jack have the argument with your father about?" Ralph asked.

"Jack brought Chuck Milton and Brian Glascock along with us on a lot of our trips to Monterrey. They were with us on our last trip there. My father thought there were too many people involved in all the secret stuff. Jack didn't agree." Catalina shrugged. "Their argument went on for a long time and eventually turned violent."

"Why didn't you kill Jack before all of you left Monterrey?" Matt asked.

Catalina narrowed her eyes and looked directly at Matt. "Jack promised to give me a large amount of money after we got home. I wanted him to stay alive long enough to give me the payoff, but he double-crossed me."

"Why did you poison him instead of shooting him?" Matt asked.

Catalina laughed. "You should be able to figure that out."

Matt nodded. "You obviously thought poisoning would be easier to get away with."

"Brilliant deduction," Catalina said with a smirk. She again pointed her pistol directly at Ralph. "I'm tired of answering questions."

"Were Donald Busby, Brian Glascock, or maybe Chuck Milton directly involved in eliminating Jack?" Matt asked, hoping Catalina would make another comment.

"I need to go now. I've answered enough questions, but it's been worth it. At least all of you should be fully aware of how stupid you've been." Catalina kept her pistol pointed at Ralph. "You were all easy to dupe. You'll die knowing that."

Ben suddenly turned his chair toward Catalina. His right hand somehow was filled with his Glock 22. He raised it to fire.

Catalina fired first. A muffled pop ensued.

Ben dropped his pistol before he could get off a shot and slumped to the floor.

Whirling and pointing her pistol in Ralph's direction, Catalina tightened her finger on the trigger.

A loud bang rang out.

Her Heckler & Koch USP bounced on the carpet. She twisted, staggered forward, and dropped to the floor.

Matt stood with his Glock 19 still pointed at her. He lowered his pistol and walked forward. He knew she was dead. The full metal jacket hollow point 9mm bullet had torn a hole in the left side of her chest, right where her heart was. He narrowed his eyes. "She had it coming."

"Good job," Ralph muttered as he looked toward Ben, who was groaning and stirring around on the floor. Everyone converged on him.

Ralph fished a handkerchief out of his pocket and put it inside Ben's shirt where blood was oozing out, just below his right shoulder.

Justine leaned forward and inspected the wound. "Not too bad, must have been a glancing blow."

"Yeah, I was moving fast." Ben put his hand on the handkerchief and held it in place. "Hurts like hell," he said, as he struggled to his feet.

Placing his Glock back in the holster, Matt stared at Ben. "We'll get you to a doctor."

"No big rush," Ben said. He pulled the handkerchief back. "The blood flow's not bad."

"Does your shoulder feel broken?" Justin asked.

Ben made a motion something like a shrug. "I think it's intact." He forced a small grin. "I lost my balance trying to get my shot off real fast. That saved my life. Catalina's shot was slightly off target."

"We need to check on Maria." Matt rushed to the door, Ralph on his heels.

They opened the supply closet behind Maria's desk. There she was, bound and gagged, but conscious.

"You okay?" Matt asked, as he removed the tape from her mouth.

"I'm not sure, but I think so," Maria said.

Matt and Ralph removed the tape from her wrists and ankles and helped her to her feet. She stood, rubbing the back of her head. "What happened?" she asked.

"You don't know?" Ralph stared at her.

"No," She muttered. "Everything was normal and then I woke up in the closet." She continued to rub the back of her head.

Ralph gestured toward his office.

Maria glanced through the open doorway. "Elsie!" She stared at Ralph.

"She clobbered you," Ralph said. "Probably best to refer to her as Catalina." He stared at Maria for a moment. "Guess it's obvious she won't do that again."

Maria looked at the blood on the carpet in Ralph's office and started to cry just as sirens pierced the air.

"No need to feel the least bit sorry for her. She's a bad person and she brought it on herself," Ralph said.

Matt nodded. "She got what she deserved."

Ralph glanced at the crowd of employees that had formed out of nowhere. "Best you all went back to work." He gave a dismissive wave. "I'll give everyone a full report later."

The crowd started slowly fading away.

"My men will be up here in a moment," Justin said. He glanced in turn at Maria and Ben. "I ordered an ambulance for each of you. You both should get some medical attention."

Seven police officers (one carrying a body bag) rushed into the area. Justin pointed toward the prone figure. Without a word, the officers went about their work.

Ralph glanced at Matt. "You apply any analysis this time?"

Matt nodded. "I don't think she knew you and I were packing heat all the time now, even in the office." He gestured toward the other three men. "Your actions gave me the opening I needed."

Ralph started to comment just as an ambulance crew rushed in. They stared at the body bag being carried out.

"That's not your concern," Ralph said to the ambulance crew. He gestured toward Ben and Maria. "These two are."

After things had settled down a bit, Ralph looked at Matt and Justin and said, "Let's go down to the conference room. We still have some things to talk about."

"Can you guys handle a discussion right now?" Justin asked. "Most people would need a little more time to catch their breath a bit and try to get back to normal."

Ralph gave a short laugh. "This has been our norm for a while now. I think we've adjusted to it."

Matt nodded.

"Shouldn't we check on Donald and Brian?" Justin asked. "They weren't in the crowd that showed up here to see what was going on and they might pose a danger."

"Maria had informed me earlier they had left on some kind of business trip and were scheduled to be back tomorrow," Ralph said, as they walked toward the conference room.

....

A few minutes later, Matt took a seat beside Ralph at the long table in the conference room. Justin sat across from them.

Justin stared at the two men in front of him. "Where do you want to start this discussion?"

"Let's start by trying to figure out who else is involved with Jack's murder and any of the related crimes," Ralph said. "I'm sure Donald and Brian are involved in some part of all this." Ralph looked at Justin and then turned toward Matt. "And don't forget, Brian was the last one to meet with Jack. Go ahead and get us started."

"We have a myriad of possibilities," Matt said.

Ralph narrowed his eyes. "What's your best guess?"

"I think Donald, Brian, Chuck, and the Fishers are all involved," Matt said.

Justin leaned toward Matt. "You've been telling us you didn't find any solid evidence against them."

"That doesn't mean they aren't guilty," Matt said. "I'm sure they've been involved for a long time."

"Amen to that. I'm convinced they're all involved in various parts of this." Ralph hesitated for a moment. "What do we do next?"

"We can start by having a meeting with Donald and Brian

tomorrow morning," Matt said.

"Am I invited?" Justin asked.

"Of course," Ralph said. "If Ben has recovered enough, we'll invite him too."

"What about Kevin and Butch?" Justin asked.

"I don't want to make the meeting too ominous," Ralph said. "Given the worst-case scenario, I think we can handle things. However, I'll call Kevin and Butch in a few minutes and let them know what we have in mind."

"Have you given any more thought to the possibility of Maria being involved?" Justin asked.

"I consider her very trustworthy," Ralph said, "however, I was wrong about Elsie, rather Catalina." He glanced at Matt.

"I have no reason to think otherwise." Matt glanced at Ralph and Justin. "But I think we've learned to keep all possibilities in mind."

Justin nodded. "This situation has taken more twists and turns than any other situation I've ever been involved with. It's been a surge of deception."

"I think we have a few twists and turns left," Matt said. "We should stay as prepared as we can."

Chapter 25

The next morning, Ralph sat with Matt, Ben, and Justin at the round conference table in his office.

Maria had offered to get coffee for everyone, but Ralph had told her they all were going over to Donald's office within a couple of minutes.

Ralph looked at Ben. "I'm glad you're okay?"

"No big injury, just a grazing wound as I thought," Ben said. "After getting the treatment at the hospital, I feel as good as new."

Ralph nodded slowly and then glanced at his watch. "Are you guys ready?"

Everyone stood just as Ralph's phone rang.

Ralph answered.

"Have you started your meeting yet?" Kevin asked.

"Getting ready to go over now, anything new?"

"I just got some information that should be very useful," Kevin said. "NSA intercepted a call that originated at Tustun five minutes ago and went to someone in Monterrey, Mexico. The call has been fully decrypted."

"I'm listening."

"Donald Busby assured the other party that he and the rest of his group would take the necessary steps to eliminate you and Matt."

"Any ID for the person in Monterrey?"

"No matches to any voice prints we have on record."

"Are you sure it was Busby on this end?"

"The voice print matches perfectly."

"Any other news?" Ralph asked.

"That's all for now," Kevin said. "We'll keep working on identifying the party in Monterrey and we'll keep in close touch."

"Thanks for the info." Ralph disconnected and gestured for everyone to retake their seats.

"It looks like Donald Busby and some others are going to try to eliminate us," Ralph said. "Donald made a phone call to Monterrey and assured someone that he would take the necessary action."

"Did Kevin know the identity of any others who would be involved?" Matt asked.

"No," Ralph said. "Donald was the only one from here who did any talking, and no other names were mentioned."

Matt leaned forward. "I think we can be positive Brian is involved."

"Don't forget Chuck Milton could be too, maybe even Maria," Justin said.

"I went back through a lot of information last night and I've found nothing suspicious about Maria." Matt looked at Ralph. "Of course, we found nothing about Elsie either until it was too late."

Ralph shook his head slowly, "Well, let's get ready to go take care of business. I think the four of us can handle it." He picked up his phone and called Donald's office.

When he heard Donald answer Ralph asked, "Do you have time for a short meeting right now?"

"That'll work okay," Donald said. "I have Brian and the Fishers here with me. We all need to talk about some things."

"Why didn't I know about the Fishers being here this morning?"

After a slight hesitation, Donald said, "I thought I informed Maria yesterday, but you know now, and we'll all be glad to meet with you."

"Any specific subject I should be prepared for?"

"Todd and Brenda have some security concerns as we move forward with our business plans. We're talking things over with Brian."

"I'll be over in a few minutes. I have a couple of things I need to wrap up first. Matt, Justin, and Ben are with me now. Based on what's been going on, I'd like them to join us."

"Yeah, that's okay and take your time," Donald said. "We'll all be here for several more hours."

"Okay." Ralph disconnected.

Ralph conveyed what Donald had told him and looked at Matt. "What's the latest on the Fishers?"

"If they're involved, they're superb at keeping everything secret."

"You haven't found anything suspicious?"

"I wouldn't say that, but I've found nothing conclusive."

Justin turned toward Matt. "Tell us some of the things you found suspicious."

"There were a lot of memos in the last week between the Fishers and Chuck Milton discussing various aspects of growing more cocoa plants in Mexico," Matt said. "Given that Chuck was replacing Jack, I didn't find that totally surprising."

"What was suspicious?" Ralph asked.

"There were several references to the best cocoa plants for producing an abundance of leaves," Matt said.

"Do you think they wanted an abundance of raw material for producing cocaine?" Ben asked.

"They never mentioned cocaine in the memos," Matt said. "But cocoa leaves are certainly the main raw material for producing it."

Ben grunted. "We know we've been dealing with a lot of people who're good at keeping secrets."

"Yeah," Ralph said. "Tustun isn't supposed to be in the drug business, especially the illegal part, but that apparently has been going on."

"We have a logical explanation for the large number by each of the circles on that map of Mexico." Matt scanned the faces around him. "Based on everything we've heard, Jack was obviously running a large illegal drug business."

"Brenda Fisher is Jack's daughter, right?" Justin asked.

"Yes," Ralph said, "but I don't think they got along well."

Justin leaned forward. "Think she could have been involved in Jack's murder?"

Ralph looked at Matt.

"The way things are shaping up, that's a distinct possibility," Matt said.

"Have you ever met Chuck Milton?" Ben asked.

"Ralph and I both met him several times when he came to visit," Matt said. "That was probably those times when he was preparing to go to Mexico with Jack. Maria always informed us when he was here."

"What about Maria?" Justin asked. "Think she could have had any involvement with what Chuck and Jack were doing?"

Ralph leaned forward. "You keep mentioning her. Is there anything that's makes you suspicious?"

"She's of Mexican heritage," Justin said, "and don't forget you trusted Elsie Farmer before you found out her true identity."

Ralph nodded slowly and again looked at Matt.

"Maria's family is originally from Monterrey, but she's never tried to hide that," Matt said. "Also, unlike Elsie, she kept her real name."

"You think she's okay?" Ben asked.

Matt shrugged. "If she's keeping a secret, she's very good at it."

"So were all the others," Justin said.

"That's why we'll use the backup plan Matt suggested." Ralph looked at Justin. "Do you have everything ready?"

"My SWAT team is close by. I'm wearing a tactical mike that I'll activate as soon as we start toward Donald's office," Justin said. "My mentioning 'danger' twice will activate the plan."

"What if you're unable to talk?" Matt asked.

"I'm prepared for that too," Justin said. "My not saying anything for two minutes will also activate things. The backup plan is solidly in place."

Ralph stood. "Well, let's go to Donald's office and see if we can untangle some more aspects of this surge of deception we've been dealing with."

••••

As they left Ralph's office and approached Maria sitting at her desk, Matt studied her closely. She had the normal expression. Her black hair flowed to her shoulders and her dark eyes were friendly. He figured if she had any bad intentions, she would at least show a little sign of nerves.

"We're going to a meeting in Donald's office," Ralph said.

Maria smiled and nodded.

While they walked toward Donald's office, Matt felt a wave of confidence surge through him.

Each man wore a sports coat which hid the pistol he carried.

As the four men walked through the doorway into Donald's office, Matt saw Donald, Brian, and the Fishers sitting at the large round conference table in a corner with seating for eight.

Donald stood and gestured toward the four empty chairs at the table. "I think this will work." He settled back into his chair while the four men occupied the previously empty ones.

Ralph leaned forward. "I don't think we need any introductions, so let's get straight to business."

"It's your meeting," Donald said.

Matt sat a little toward the front of his chair and kept his right arm inside the arm of the chair. He had made sure he didn't sit on the back of his coat so he would be free to draw his Glock 19 if necessary. He noted Ralph had done the same thing.

"When is Chuck Milton coming on board?" Ralph asked.

"Next week," Donald said. "I thought you already knew since you're the President." He gestured toward the Fishers. "We're preparing to have everything in order when he arrives."

Ralph narrowed his eyes. "It's a little early for that, isn't it?"

"There's a lot we need to cover," Donald said. "We wanted to make sure we had plenty of time. We don't want to get on the wrong side of our new chairman on his first day."

Todd and Brenda both nodded.

Matt noticed Brian eased a little forward in his chair. That could indicate a lot of things, but there was one thing that dominated Matt's thinking: Brian might think Ralph had everything figured out and he might be getting ready to draw his pistol.

"What legal stuff is so essential to have in order before the new chairman arrives?" Ralph asked. "Don't you think he'll give you a little time to address what he thinks is important?"

Brian pushed his chair back and a pistol appeared in his hand, but Matt had his Glock 19 pointed at Brian before Brian's Glock 22 could reach a firing position.

"Drop it," Matt said. He extended his pistol toward Brian.

Brian gasped and his pistol fell on the floor.

Ralph pushed his chair back and stood while pointing his pistol at Donald.

Justin and Ben covered Todd and Brenda.

"Anyone who makes any sudden movement will die," Matt said.

Ralph looked at Donald. "Okay, no more games. I want some answers. NSA intercepted your phone call this morning. We know about what you four are up to. He turned toward Brenda. "I know you didn't get along with your father, but I can't understand why you would allow someone to murder him."

"He wasn't a good man like you thought he was," Brenda said. Her eyes flashed. "You and Matt have been idiots. He had you completely duped." A look of defiance dominated her expression.

Todd leaned toward her. "That's enough."

She stopped talking and narrowed her eyes. After a couple of seconds, she frowned and glanced at Todd. Both remained silent.

"I simply made some necessary business calls this morning," Donald said.

"As I told you, the games are over. We know your exact words."

Ralph stared at Donald for a moment and then gestured to Ben.

"NSA verified it was your voice doing the talking from Tustun," Ben said as he looked directly at Donald.

Justin nodded. "We have all the solid evidence we need. We know all we need to know to make arrests."

After turning slightly toward Donald, Brian said, "I warned you about this. We should have left the country yesterday. That was a big mistake. They know all about us."

"Knowing all about us won't help them," Donald said as he looked past the four men pointing pistols in his direction.

Matt glanced toward the doorway. Chuck Milton and Maria Lopez each pointed a SIG 556 rifle pointed in their direction.

"I think each of you would be wise to drop your weapon on the floor," Chuck said, "Now!!"

With his finger tight on the trigger, Chuck pointed his rifle directly at Ralph.

Maria also extended her rifle toward the four men holding the pistols. A mix of anger and triumph blazed in her dark eyes.

Four pistols banged on the floor.

Chuck kept his rifle pointed forward as he reached back and closed the door behind him.

Matt looked at Maria. "How could you be part of this?"

"I have my reasons," Maria said. "There's a lot you don't know. I need revenge for my family."

Brian grabbed his pistol off the floor and pointed it at Ralph.

Donald, Todd, and Brenda also produced pistols and held them in firing position.

Brian looked at Chuck. "Let's take no chances and finish them off now."

Chuck laughed. "We have two rifles and four pistols pointed at them and their pistols are on the floor. I think we're safe. I want to see them squirm for a few minutes." He looked at Ralph. "You're going to die the horrible death you deserve and it's going to be slow, real slow."

Matt noted Chuck was confident he had the situation under his total control and obviously wanted to brag a little. He hoped they could learn a few things before resorting to the backup plan Justin had prepared.

Justin seemed to share Matt's thinking and remained silent. They still had over a minute before his silence would hit the two-minute mark.

Ralph kept his gaze on Maria. "What is it I don't know?"

Donald and the Fishers kept their pistols steady and in firing position but stayed seated. Brian stood and waved his pistol back and forth. Chuck and Maria kept their rifles pointed at Ben and Justin.

Maria glanced at Chuck.

"Go ahead and tell him. I want to see the look on his face." Chuck said.

Maria looked directly at Ralph. "Catalina was my half sister. We had the same father. I need some revenge for their deaths. All of you are going to pay a heavy price for that."

"Jack killed your father, we didn't," Ralph said.

"You and Matt both idolized Jack," Maria hissed. She looked at Justin and Ben. "You all deserve to die for your stupidity. None of you ever figured out he was a very bad man and mistreated a lot of people."

"How could you be part of this criminal activity and operate so calmly?" Matt asked.

"Catalina and I were born into a family of crime," Maria said. "While growing up, it was the only life we knew. We both developed the necessary talents at an early age."

Ralph nodded slowly. "You certainly perfected your acting. Even that bit about being knocked out, bound, and gagged before Catalina stormed into my office."

"You and Matt were easy to fool," Maria said. "I didn't have to try very hard."

Matt looked at Chuck. "Did you agree to killing Jack?"

Chuck laughed. "He had to be eliminated." He gestured toward Brian. "I'm glad he and Catalina took care of the details."

"Catalina put the poison in his coffee," Brian said. "I had a meeting with him while he drank it."

"Why did Catalina reveal you were the last person to see him alive?" Ralph asked.

"She knew law enforcement would discover that from looking at the footage from the security cameras," Brian said. "She needed to keep her credibility, and it worked."

"Why didn't the cameras pick up her putting the poison in the coffee?" Matt asked.

"You should have already figured that out," Brian said.

"Jack always wanted sugar and cream with his coffee." Matt gave a slight shrug. "I guess she had a good way to hide slipping the poison into the cup."

"Very good, but you're too late on figuring anything out. We've outsmarted you on everything," Chuck said.

"It seems you did." Matt looked at Donald. "So, you and Brian worked closely with Elsie and Maria the whole time?"

"All of us did," Donald said. "Like we've said, you were easy to fool."

Chuck looked at Ralph and asked, "Do you want to die first or watch your friends die before you start your agony?"

"I'd rather go first," Ralph said, "but there's one more thing I'd like to know before I die."

Chuck narrowed his eyes. "And what is that?"

Ralph looked directly at Chuck. "Jack was useful in helping you run a very successful drug trafficking operation. Why did you allow him to be killed?"

Chuck laughed and then gave a slight shrug. "Both Catalina and Maria insisted on it since he killed their father and then double-crossed them on a big payoff. Also, Jack wanted to expand the illegal drug business and everyone else wanted to play it safe."

"Apparently there were some strong feelings both ways," Matt said.

"Jack wouldn't listen to reason." Chuck glanced at Maria. "Her father and I tried hard to convince Jack to keep all the trafficking at the current level for a while, but he was stubborn. The discussion got more heated. Both Jack and her father drew guns, and you know the rest."

Maria narrowed her eyes. "Catalina and I decided we couldn't continue to work with a man who killed our father. Jack had to go."

Chuck looked at Ralph. "Yeah, Jack had to go as do all the rest of you." He continued to laugh.

Justin remained silent and turned his head to stare at the window at the back of Donald's office.

Knowing it was time for Justin's backup plan to be activated, Matt saw the door to Donald's office crack silently open. He was glad everyone in Chuck's crowd was looking curiously at the window while eight men in SWAT team gear eased into the room and spread along the wall by the door.

"Drop your weapons or die instantly," the SWAT team leader said, as he and the other seven members of his team targeted the six people with guns.

Matt saw everyone drop their weapons, except for Chuck.

Chuck swung his SIG 556 toward the SWAT team leader.

When several muffled pops ensued, Chuck and his rifle dropped to the floor.

"Everyone else put your hands in the air and don't move unless you want the same fate," the SWAT team leader said.

Matt, Ralph, Ben, and Justin retrieved their pistols as the SWAT team herded the remaining five members of Chuck's group into a tight huddle.

The SWAT team leader looked at Justin. "I left two men in the hallway as a safety valve."

"Great job," Justin said, "perfect execution." He looked at Ralph. "I have a medical crew standing by with body bags. They should be here within a few minutes. We'll take the rest to jail."

••••

A few hours later, after the local law enforcement crews had completed their work and the group in Washington DC had been given the latest news, Matt sat at the round conference table in Ralph's office with

Ralph, Justin, and Ben.

"Well, I think we've finally wrapped up the Tustun aspect of this long running secret operation," Ralph said. "I'm sure the Fishers were in a support role for many of the crimes. They'll get their just reward."

Justin nodded.

"Yeah, I think we've cleaned up this mess as it pertained to Tustun," Ben said. "We, of course, have more work to do on some related aspects of this."

Ralph turned toward Matt. "It's hard to believe so many people were so good at deceiving us for so long."

"They were all good at playing their roles," Matt said. "Catalina and Maria were great actresses in every way, and they were good at covering up any clues we might have noticed, even that bit about Catalina overpowering Maria and putting her in the closet."

"All that high-level math and chess logic didn't help you much in detecting what they were all up to." Ralph kept his gaze on Matt. "You should have at least gotten a few clues."

"Yeah, I could improve a bit," Matt said. "Sophisticated logical deduction can be very useful in business, but I'll admit it didn't help enough for this situation. A lot of things weren't logical and that added to the complexity. It's difficult to uncover dirty secrets from people who execute almost perfectly and who you don't suspect."

Justin narrowed his eyes. "The spat with Jack allowed us to uncover what had been a long-running conspiracy."

"Yeah, and I don't feel bad for Jack anymore," Ralph said.

Matt nodded.

"Catalina and Maria provided great cover by staying so cool," Justin said, "but crime was the only profession they had ever known throughout their lives. And they were experts at deception."

"Well, even with this surge of deception, at least we finally solved Jack's murder." Ben glanced at Matt and Ralph. "All of us in law enforcement are lucky you two business guys have the talents you do. I don't think we could have resolved this without your help." He smiled.

Justin also smiled. "Overall, our extended team uncovered a lot of well-kept dirty secrets from a lot of vicious and vindictive people."

Matt felt a surge of pride that he and Ralph were able to discuss things calmly immediately after the last skirmish where they again were almost killed. They indeed had a lot of grit.

"I think we all fought through the obstacles and rose to the occasion," Ralph said. "We got it done."

Each of the four men gave a thumbs-up.